live by
request

ROB PAYNE

live by request

HarperCollins*Publishers*Ltd

To contact the author,
email robbyrequest@hotmail.com

Be sure to visit
The Official Archangel Fansite
www.archangelband.com

Live by Request
Copyright © 2002 by Rob Payne.

www.harpercanada.com

HarperCollins books may be purchased
for educational, business, or sales promotional use.
For information please write: Special Markets Department,
HarperCollins Canada,
55 Avenue Road, Suite 2900,
Toronto, Ontario, Canada M5R 3L2

First edition

Canadian Cataloguing in Publication Data

Payne, Rob, 1973–
Live by request : a novel

I S B N 0-00-639174-5

I. Title.

PS8581.A867L48 2002   C813'.6   C2002-900526-4
PR9199.4.P39L48 2002

HC 9 8 7 6 5 4 3 2 1

Printed and bound in the United States
Set in Dante

For Lizzie, my rock star

1

"OK," Tyler begins, looking at us over the top of his orange-tinted Bono glasses, "if you were trapped in an elevator for an entire night with a famous person, who would it be?"

Janice glances up from her drink, a bottled beverage claiming to be a margarita (slogan: *twist off the cap of sophistication*). Her face expressionless, she leans back on two legs of her chair, balancing herself by hooking her right foot under the table. She wavers as she lifts her glass to her lips and takes a long swallow, staring at Tyler. With exaggerated care, she wipes the lipstick off the rim of her glass. I can see Tyler's impatience rising like mercury, which is exactly what Jan wants.

I sigh and stare at the ceiling. We're due to go on stage in less than half an hour, but the adrenaline isn't flowing.

"I don't remember signing up to play these games when I joined the band," Jan says finally. "I distinctly remember my audition and at no time did idiotic games of conjecture come up as a prerequisite."

Tyler stares at her blankly. I feel dryness in my mouth and a dull pain beginning in my temples. They do this sort of thing constantly.

"I thought you were an intellectual, Janice. I thought you of all of us would be eager to answer the question."

She lets out a short laugh and looks around the room. I follow her gaze, wondering if and how Tyler has just insulted me. There's a smattering of the usual crowd—thirty, maybe thirty-five people in total. Stu is obviously not overworked at the bar. He's hunched over reading a news-paper on one of the barstools. His long, curly brown hair falls over his face. I can see his lips moving as he reads. Stu studies business at a local college, not because of any great passion for commerce but because his father has agreed to pay all his expenses as long as he's enrolled. Unlike a lot of people I know, Stu doesn't feel any compulsion to pretend he's either industrious or ambitious. I admire his self-aware-ness and blunt honesty.

"Fine," Jan says, picking at her coaster. "Where am I? How did I get into this elevator? What's my motivation?"

Tyler exhales. He begins to speak, but Jan cuts him off. Her chair falls forward and she leans over the table.

"And why am I stuck in this elevator for an entire night? Realistically, there would be an alarm or one of those little emergency phones. I think they're probably mandatory. And if the person I'm with is so famous, why isn't anyone looking for him or her? An agent, paparazzi . . ."

Tyler slides his feet off the chair they've been propped up on and leans forward. They're face to face like two prize-fighters staring each other down. I can feel the warm mois-ture of breath intermingling and am astounded by the sheer pointlessness of this intensity. I'm the calm Zen of one hand clapping. If a tree falls in the forest, you can be sure that one or both of these two will be holding the axe.

"I no longer care who you'd spend the night with, because

you can't appreciate the spirit of this exercise. I'm trying to challenge you. I'm trying to keep your analytical skills honed."

"I just want to be true to my character."

Tyler ignores her and turns to me. "Jay, you're stuck in an elevator for the night—"

"I'm not in the mood, Tyler."

"What else is new," he says, raising his arms in exasperation and speaking toward the ceiling. "But say you were ever in the mood to be spontaneous and interesting, who's in the elevator with you?"

I shove a greasy fry into my mouth. "Anyone?"

"Anyone at all. Dazzle us."

I put my fork down and wipe an ultra-white paper napkin across my greasy lips. My plate is swimming with gravy and overcooked fries. A soggy leaf of lettuce is curled to one side. This could be the Rose and Crown's idea of either a garnish or a side salad. If it isn't deep-fried, it isn't a priority.

"How about Nelson Mandela?" I say.

Tyler frowns. "How about him, Jay?"

"Well, he's my choice."

"If you people aren't going to try, I'm not going to try," Tyler says, looking away. "I thought I could bring some interesting conversation to the table tonight, but neither of you is evocative enough to appreciate . . ." He searches for a word. "My evocativeness." He takes off his glasses and rubs his eyes dramatically.

"What's wrong with Nelson Mandela?" Jan asks. "He's a great choice. He's intelligent, well travelled, and he's been locked in small, confined spaces in the past, so he won't panic."

Tyler looks at her with smug disgust. He pulls off his light green fedora and runs a hand through his matted hair. Finally he turns to me.

"You're telling me that instead of twelve hours of solid talk time with Mick or Keith or Paul McCartney, you'd be chatting it up with Nelson Mandela about apartheid? Which, by the way, ended around the same time grunge ended. I don't believe it for a second. You're not political, Jay. You're a bartender."

Tyler is one of those dear friends close enough to know what really annoys me. I am a bartender. I am the static post and my friends are the spokes, spinning wildly around me, studying and working and moving toward careers and achievements. I want to throw Tyler's arrogance back in his face, but even Jan is silent, so that tells you where I fall in the food chain of respect. I'm stuck, rutted, chained to a beer fridge and a couple of taps serving domestic suds. I took this job as a stopgap after my aborted six months of university six years ago, as a way of compiling enough money to go back and get serious about my life, avoid the pub crawls and really hit the books. But a weekly paycheque and the advice of the bar's most unambitious clientele persuaded me that I was better off pouring pints than poring over essays on modern American literature or twentieth-century European history. After all, fascism and communism were things of the past, but people were still drinking.

Tyler shakes his head and looks into his glass. He snorts at its emptiness and waves impatiently at Stu, who is folding up his paper. A few more people have wandered in and there's hope yet that we'll have a decent crowd. Not that we ever get an overwhelming crush. It's Sunday night at a crappy English pub in a university town. People with real lives are ironing shirts, studying economic theorems, enjoying the

4

final free moments before Monday imposes itself on their weekend tranquillity.

"OK," Tyler starts again.

"What time is Noel showing up?" Jan interrupts.

"Seven," Tyler says, glaring at her. He turns back to me. "For argument's sake, say the other person wants to copulate all night long, just to relieve the boredom. Who do you pick?"

"Not Nelson Mandela."

Jan bursts into laughter.

I choke back the last of my now stiff fries. The pungent smell of vinegar and deep-fried potato fills my nostrils, and I feel too bloated to get up on stage. I see Stu coming toward our table with a tray of drinks. He puts a beer down on the table. Jan clears her throat.

"Stu, you're trapped in an elevator and the person you're stuck with wants to have sex all night long. Who do you choose to be that person?"

Stu slides a Canadian to me, picking up the empty. He pushes his long hair back behind his ear.

"Oh man," he says. "All night long. My knees would kill. That's heavy. But I'll say my girlfriend, 'cause she'd roast my ass otherwise."

He collects the empties and saunters back to the bar.

"Do you know who I'd choose?" Tyler says.

No one responds.

"Chelsea Clinton," he says. "She's educated, well bred, and if you watch her for long enough you'll notice that she has quite an intrinsic, smouldering sexuality."

Jan gets up from the table. We watch in silence as she wanders over to the small stage, which is really just a corner of the bar where the tables have been taken away and

5

replaced with a drum kit, some mikes and two large black speakers. She picks up her bass and brings it close to her ear, hitting strings and tuning. Her long fingers lilt across the neck of the guitar. Janice is not beautiful in that pure, generic magazine-cover way that we're all supposed to admire. But she's got character and attitude, which makes her compelling and immensely attractive to watch. Her hair is chestnut brown, shoulder length and very fine, falling around her face like silk threads to cover ears that otherwise would be a touch prominent. Her most striking feature is her posture. She has a certain adolescent awkwardness, as if she's never quite gotten used to being in her body. And she's got strong rock-and-roll chick energy, a Chrissie Hynde intensity that guys are attracted to. She dates many, loves none and eventually discards all. A part of me is hopelessly infatuated with her, but I find her intimidating. She has a strong sense of herself and what she wants. I feel like the opposite, muddled and befuddled, a shapeless mess of muted passions and underconstructed opinions who manages to just get by. But then, the best rule for any bartender is to avoid strong views on politics, religion or any other contentious issue. You never know who your next customer will be, and when it comes to tips, a conservative dollar is worth every bit as much as a liberal dime.

I am the Buddha meditating on nothingness.

"That girl needs to lighten up," Tyler says, sipping his beer. He puts his bowling-shoe-clad feet up on the chair again and leans back, surveying the room. "Sometimes I worry about her. I'm very sensitive in that way. People have told me."

The sound of sizzling grease echoes from the kitchen, barely audible above the drone of conversation. I peg the people who will leave as soon as the music starts. They're eating fish and chips and having intense conversations about whatever it is people who don't like live music feel intense about. Gardening, I suppose. I don't claim to understand them, but after performing live for the past year I can spot them. We call them aliens, because they're not like us. Even if a band is doing horrible Deep Purple covers, I still feel compelled to watch. There's an energy in music that I can't resist, in the pulse of a guitar plugged in and cranked up, that I've never been able to find anywhere else. This might sound corny, but I've always felt less *homesick* around music, even though I live in my hometown and have absolutely no desire to cohabitate with any of my family members ever again.

When I look around at these people I know they don't want to sit and listen to a ratty rock band playing R & B covers and early Police hits. But they're missing out, because as loose as we sometimes play, we can still drown out the mundane details of their lives for a few hours. Sting's music, combined with our riffs and tweaks, can pull anyone into the *fathomless ocean of sound*. That's the title of a song I've been working on.

"My mother always said I was the sensitive one in the family," Tyler continues.

"Tyler, you're an only child."

"So?"

I look at my watch. As if reading my mind, Noel slides through the doors in his navy blue sweater, guitar case in tow. He blows on his hand and gazes around the bar. The beer is racing to my head and I feel distant. I flex my hands and they feel cold. There's a tumbling tension in my stomach as the pre-set nerves finally begin to churn.

"It's about time," Tyler says.

Noel has stopped at the bar. He gives us a wave and turns back to Stu, who is popping the cap off a Sleeman's ale. Then he joins us.

"I see the aliens are out in strength tonight," he says, shaking Tyler's hand and sitting down. He appears flushed and winded. "This place looks like a Star Trek convention, not a pub on the verge of being *rocked out*. Obi-Wan might need to use the force to keep some asses in seats tonight. Are we all set?"

"We're set," Tyler says. "Where have you been?"

Noel looks sheepish. "I had some work to finish up before Monday. I should have done it Friday, but I've been really busy."

Noel is the only professional of the band. He's managed to finish university and make his way in the corporate world doing something vaguely important for an international food conglomerate. Currently, his job involves pricing and selling coffee to a major chain of cafés. He's the Gap addition to our thrift-store selves. And he plays his guitar like a shaman, his fingers floating above the frets, barely touching the strings before moving down the neck to whip up another prayer. Noel has a performance style all his own, one that I know he has honed on many nights in front of his full-length mirror. His mystical riffs and smooth liquid stylings are tainted only by his penchant for poorly executed scissor kicks.

"I was just talking about the book I'm writing," Tyler says, toying with the salt-and-pepper shakers.

"Oh yeah?" Noel says, looking genuinely impressed. "I didn't know you were writing a book. That's great."

"He's lying," I murmur.

"No, I'm not," Tyler says. "It's called *Jay Thompson: Not as Much Fun as He Used to Be.* It's a memoir." He gives a low shaking chuckle.

Noel is devoid of ego and always eager to have fun. He prevents Tyler and Jan from getting too nasty and keeps my confidence level at its peak, which, granted, is never terribly high. In fact, Noel's prodding is the reason I'm the lead singer of Archangel. Tyler and Janice are grad students at the university. He's in music and she's in English lit.

Tyler stands. We are due to start the set at quarter past seven, and it's time for the final sound check.

We open with a mondo-cool cover of "Building Bridges" by INXS. It begins slowly, snaking into a thick, liquid soul-funk groove. As it builds, bass strokes inflict a slightly dizzy sensation near the temples. We pull the main melody deep and let the supporting riffs take the listener in slow motion toward the bridge, which erupts like an earthquake just when you think you're safe.

At least that's how I would describe it.

I could see myself as a copywriter for a major record label, describing music on a visceral level. I mean, any marketing jockey can list a band's top ten hits and pigeonhole them into a category. But Smashing Pumpkins aren't the Foo Fighters, no matter how alternative both might be. I could market a band by grasping for the spiritual impulse that drives every riff, every note, every bass run. And that's the attitude we take into our own performance—a metaphysical sense of purpose and enlightenment. It's unfortunate, however, that we don't have louder speakers.

My greatest hope of all is to be a working songwriter and musician. And I do believe it's possible. I'm not saying I expect to achieve the level of success of Radiohead—that would be nice, though it isn't something I'm counting on—but I don't see why success on par with, say, Echobelly should be so elusive. They've managed to scrape together a few decent singles, find a small niche in the music scene and gather together a handful of loyal followers. That's all I really need.

The frustrating part of having a bit of talent and a quiet dream is the sacrifice. On paper, I appear to be a twenty-six-year-old single bartender with a high-school degree and no professional ambition. A few years ago my ability to avoid engaging with the world on realistic terms was viewed as rebellious and youthful. Everybody I knew wanted to play music or become an artist or find a place outside the *uncool* mainstream. But somewhere between Nirvana and Smash Mouth my pose has come to be regarded as tired, and most of my friends have moved out of town to bigger cities and more lucrative paycheques. Apparently the only thing less hip than the mainstream is poverty and sacrifice. I could have taken this hint and become a serious-minded, industrious drone; I could have sacrificed my creative freedom to train for a better, more secure job; I could have looked into RRSPs and no-load mutual funds, settled into a fulfilling relationship and allowed all of my rough edges to be worn away. I could have, but instead I did the sensible thing: jamming for bored bar patrons and a few free drinks.

After three covers, we play "Chill Out Chick," a song I wrote one rainy afternoon on a handful of cocktail napkins after Terry, a dark-haired waitress, reamed me out for making fun of boy bands. Little did I know that her spiky-haired misfit boyfriend was practising a series of well-choreographed moves and writing songs with such nauseatingly obvious metaphors as "our love is a bird that soars high in the sky." I saw his band practise once. Classic fromage.

"Chill Out Chick" isn't gold, but no one walks out while we play it. I think I've got a few songs in my catalogue that people will stop and pay attention to, but we know our audience mostly comes to hear songs they recognize, the background anthems of their lives: Van Morrison, the Beatles, Bob Seger. We keep a balance between decades. We tried an exclusively eighties night of classics, but the reaction was mixed, and Chad, the manager, suggested we get back to Chuck Berry's "Maybelline" or find a new place to haunt on Sunday nights. Just as well, really. Devo's "Whip It" doesn't sound right as an acoustic instrumental.

Do we wish we were more than a mediocre cover band? Sure. But as long as I know that we're moving forward and that the dream remains within reach, this gig is all right.

2

We've run through five standards and are taking requests from the audience. We play "Son of a Preacher Man," with Jan on vocals to give my throat a rest. Her voice is delicate and high, nice to listen to but generally limited in range and variation. I know she secretly wishes it was a low, mean feminine growl, like Stevie Nicks, but sometimes talent only stretches so far. It's moments like these that I feel like the Linda McCartney of the band. I stand back and strum a few chords, nothing more daring than an easy riff, a few slow-motion notes a couple frets apart that I can bend and hold.

I watch Jan as she closes her eyes and leans toward the

mike, her long, pale neck arching upward. I love the intensity she brings to her performance, the energy that radiates from her. I see the faint gleam of perspiration and wonder how warm her skin would feel to touch. I force myself to look at my foot pedals and concentrate on hitting the right notes. She finishes the song and smiles proudly.

A woman in the back shouts a request for Tina Turner, which brings a gentle chuckle from the crowd of semi-interested spectators. Most carry on conversations as we play, turning to watch from time to time, only peripherally aware of the music. A table of two couples in their late twenties calls out for Clapton, and we do a stunning version of "Cocaine." Noel and I congratulate ourselves with a high-five, having finally played the entire song without pausing once because of excessive feedback. These are the little signs of progress that really keep you motivated.

At the next break the woman in the back becomes even more adamant about hearing Tina Turner.

"We don't know any of her songs," I say into the mike. I glance around for more requests, but no one offers any. I lean over to Noel, who is drinking from his pint and wiping sweat from his forehead.

"Any ideas?" I ask.

Noel shrugs.

"Do you want to try—?"

"TINA TURNER!"

Others in the audience begin to clap. I hear Tyler snort derisively behind me. Noel leans toward my mike.

"Actually, we do know a rare Ike Turner song. He wrote it for Tina in the middle of a cocaine binge. Will that do?"

I feel a jerk of panic in my stomach.

"TINA TURNER!"

"What are you talking about?" Jan whispers, leaning in.

"We'll play 'Leave My Kitten Alone,'" Noel says.

"That wasn't Ike Turner," I say. "That was Little Willie John."

Noel shrugs and finds his place on guitar. "With Titus Turner. Do you think she's gonna know the difference?"

"TINA TURNER!"

We launch in and everything goes as planned until the second verse, when a large woman in a floral print dress bounds into the open area in front of the stage. She's at least fifty and clearly cut to the gills. She begins to flail her arms and legs in a painful sort of dance, as if someone is running a strong electric current through her ankles at irregular intervals. A large whoop rises from the crowd, and for the first time all evening everyone has stopped what they're doing to pay attention.

"Mom, get off the dance floor," Noel laughs.

Our new groupie turns away and shakes her posterior in our direction. I'm thrown off my rhythm, but quickly get it back. As Noel and I begin the next verse, she hits a patch of lucidity and tames a bit, looking around at the faces fixated on her. She steps up to the table with the two young couples and latches on to the closest male. He clamps a hand to his chair as she strains to pull him loose. Realizing he isn't coming, she lets go and approaches a table of forty-somethings. After several firm tugs, she manages to get one of the men up. He's dressed in a polo shirt and khakis, with wire glasses and deck shoes. They flail in unison for a few seconds, then begin to grind. I can't help but gawk, like a rubberneck at a traffic accident, compelled by both horror and amazement.

Then, finally, it's over. The audience offers a rousing round of applause.

"Ladies and gentlemen," Noel says, "I give you your private dancer and one unexpected backup."

They both wander to their seats. His table is laughing hysterically and offering him handshakes.

"Can the bar please bring this gentleman a drink and put it on our tab," I say over the mike.

"And more drinks for the band," Tyler says.

"Yeah," Jan says. "We're not going past the next song unless we get some fuel." She gives Stu a thumbs-up.

We do a mellow version of Elvis Costello's "American Without Tears," but it's an anticlimax. The audience has gone back to their conversations and we are once again peripheral entertainment. The rest of the set is standard: two originals mixed in with "Peggy Sue," "Johnny B. Goode," "Kansas City," et cetera.

We take an intermission after an hour or so and sit around enjoying the rush of an adrenaline buzz. A pale girl with freckles and curly red hair comes over, her full hips tight against the fabric of a sarong. She looks like she's just stepped off a speedboat.

"Tyler," she begins, ignoring the rest of us. "Remember me from the music mixer at the Den?"

He glances at her briefly. "Sure," he mumbles.

"I'm really having a great time tonight. You're a wonderful performer. And I love your outfit. Seventies kitsch is so you."

"It's poverty chic," he says. "And I don't mean to sound touchy, but I like to think of myself as an artist, not a performer."

I roll my eyes.

Red smiles and waits expectantly. Her eyes glow as she stares at Tyler, but he doesn't seem to notice.

"I hear you've been working on a really, really major composition in the lab at school," she continues. "My friend Amanda is a music major and she heard you working on it. She says it's compelling."

Tyler nods and checks his watch. Red grows visibly more uncomfortable. Tyler takes a sip of his beer and sighs. Finally, when I can no longer watch, Red takes her cue, murmurs an excuse and wanders off. Tyler takes a deep breath and lets it out slowly.

"Do you have any sexual impulses?" Jan asks, shaking her head. "That girl likes you."

Tyler glances at Jan, then looks back across the room.

"Too pedestrian," he says.

During the second half, we play two more of my songs and throw in a few modern favourites, including "Roxanne" and "Grace, Too." By the end of the night we've retained a third of the original crowd, which we interpret as success.

"I can't rehearse tomorrow night," Noel says, gently packing his guitar into its case. He begins to close the lid, then stops, picks up his beige chamois and gives the gleaming lacquer another wipe. "I'm way too busy at work."

"No problem," I say, sinking into a chair like gelatine and sucking on a much-deserved pint of Smithwicks.

"Yeah," Tyler says, "we wouldn't want to risk improving as a band."

"I thought we were pretty good tonight," Noel says. "And we've got a groupie. That's instant status."

Noel gives his guitar one final polish, then packs up his gear and slides away. Tyler and I sit in silence for a few minutes until he begins to tap his drumsticks against the corner of the table.

"You want to meet for breakfast tomorrow?" I ask.

"I can't. I'm working on the piano bridge for *Space Oddity #2* in the lab and it isn't going well. Where's Brian Eno when you need him?"

Space Oddity #2 is Tyler's great contribution to music, his opus. He looks at his watch and frowns.

"One more pint and I'm out of here. If I don't get at least eight hours sleep I can't perform creatively. I slept for five hours on Friday night and mid-afternoon Saturday caught myself humming a Phil Collins song."

"Frightening," I murmur.

He flashes a precocious grin at me and frisbees a coaster toward the stage area. Tyler has been my friend for seventeen years, ever since his family moved into our neighbourhood in elementary school. He was the strange kid with the green bell-bottoms and the long, straggly hair that covered his eyes. He was quiet, reclusive, shy. But then one morning we had presentations in which each of us had to get up in front of the class and talk about what we wanted to be when we grew up. There were doctors and dentists and nurses and teachers—the basic one-word occupations that kids are fed as they're growing up. But Tyler was a step better, even then. He had a long, black Halloween wig and wore a black *Rolling Stone* baseball cap. He put on a pair of sunglasses and described in great detail, with an intensity foreign to most fourth graders, his all-encompassing ambition to one day be a roadie for Wang Chung.

I liked Tyler because he was a music freak and because he didn't seem to care what anyone thought of him. I suppose he was the first person my age who was an independent thinker, who had his own opinions, likes and dislikes. But mavericks are never the most popular people, so he latched on to me as a steady friend and music cohort. We used to walk around with his boom box, sitting on the outskirts of the schoolyard with an assortment of part-time geeks and curiosity seekers. We'd talk and whittle branches with our pocketknives and listen to his ever-evolving library of recordings. Every week Tyler's mom would buy him a new tape, which allowed us to expand our tastes beyond the paltry offerings of mainstream radio.

We were tight in high school and into university, until I dropped out. He got involved with artists and musicians and actors. I learned to make Caesars and change kegs. He got inspired and more radical, and I got complacent and used to routine. But we'll always have music and a common history, and as far as I can tell those are enough for friendship after a certain age.

Janice returns and the three of us sit silently consuming free pints. When Jan and Tyler eventually leave, the bar is completely empty, and I'm left to drag the equipment into the storage room. I slide my guitar behind the cooler, in between a box of Cheezies and a case of Canadian Club. Tomorrow I'll be behind the bar and life will begin again, slow and constant.

3

Gary, a Don Johnson look-alike, lingers at the bar. He's wearing snakeskin cowboy boots and a cream-coloured T-shirt and for the last three beers has been telling me about his bitter divorce from Wanda. Wanda Osborne: waitress at Kelso's Sports Bar, thirty-five, red hair, hates dogs and pink roses, worked for a pizzeria when they first met, nauseatingly nicknamed Whippy, for a reason I have mercifully been spared. I want to sit down with a club sandwich and read the paper.

"You think you know someone," he repeats again. "She left me because of money. My brother told me it's better that she left me in the bad times, because it means she didn't really love me. What do you think?"

I think anyone who wears snakeskin cowboy boots and is slurring at ten in the morning will find himself on the rebound on a regular basis. I'm surprised he ever found a girlfriend in the first place.

"I don't know," I repeat. "You know what women are like."

He nods and we stand silently. I hate falling back on macho cop-outs and redneck speak, though sometimes I have to for the sake of peace, love and the rattle of coins in my tip jar. I pride myself on being able to adapt to any customer, to find the right kind of attitude to suck out the maximum gratuity possible. If you like hockey, I can talk about the Leafs' chances. If you like politics, I pick up *Time* on occasion. If you like wrestling, you probably have a pretty sad and pathetic life, but I do know a bit about Vince McMahon and Stone Cold Steve Austin and the rest of those Spandex-clad psychopaths. Please, drop a couple of quarters into my jar, have your say and then go sit at a table. You've bought my time at the going rate; you've earned your thirty seconds on the soapbox. Not that I'm a snob. I mean, sure, I went to university for a short while and most of my friends come from white-collar worlds, but I can relate to the average working man, because my family's roots are sunk firmly in the unionized grind and sweat of the blue collar.

At the other end of the bar is Len. He stocks vending machines for a living. He keeps looking at me, but I'm not going over until he needs another drink. He always initiates a conversation, then never keeps his end up, and it's stressful. Mondays are like this for some reason.

Gary becomes distracted by hockey highlights on TV, and I take the opportunity to duck out from behind the bar to the kitchen. Chad, the manager, is lingering near the door.

"They do get lonely, don't they?" he says, giving the general patronage a mocking glance. "Glad I'm not squirming behind that bar every day."

I shrug and pluck a crispy brown fry out of the deep-fryer basket.

"I don't mind," I say, chewing slowly. "I'm not flipping bottles and doing the 'Hippy Hippy Shake,' but it's OK on most days."

"Yeah, well, whatever you say. Personally I'd like to have half of them shot in the parking lot, but I like their money." He looks at me defiantly, determined not to be swayed.

Chad is new to the Rose and Crown. His uncle owns the bar, so Chad has hired his friends, most of whom are college party types and a few years younger than me. Fortunately he's carried on the live music program, which is why Archangel has a regular gig Sunday nights.

Later, as I'm wolfing down fish and chips, Chad wanders behind the bar. He pours himself a tonic water and sits on a large box of peanuts near the stainless steel dishwasher that looks like a Sputnik satellite.

"I figure I'll own this place one day," he says, indicating the dented beer fridge, the rusty taps and the smudged inverted glasses hanging over the oak bar, dripping onto the dirty tiled floor. "Education's great if it gets you somewhere—

don't get me wrong—but I hate how people push it as the only thing. Self-reliance. That's the best thing. Do you know who said that?"

"Sid Vicious?"

He squints at me. "No, Teddy Roosevelt. He was the president of the United States at the turn of the century. He did a bunch of stuff with trust companies and was a general in the war with the Spanish. They named the teddy bear after him. Did you know that?"

"I knew that," I say. "Some of it, anyway."

He fumbles for a cigarette in the front pocket of his plaid shirt. His hair is short, blond and spiky. He looks slightly uncomfortable.

"I read all sorts of biographies, you know. I'm quite well read." He looks at me for a reaction. "That's what I mean about school," he continues, lighting his cigarette and waving the match. "And I watch *Biography*, the TV show, because you can learn a lot. That's another thing. People say TV rots your brain, but I think it can be an effective learning tool."

I almost burst into laughter, but then realize he's serious.

"It's a good show," I say, shovelling the last piece of rubbery fish into my mouth. I put the plate on the counter and busy myself by straightening a row of glasses, then start wiping the counter behind the bar.

"Did you know that Jack Benny was dirt poor when he was little?"

"Really?" I say.

"Yeah, but he did burlesque. Worked his way up."

I get the feeling this is the groundwork for a motivational speech. I wonder if Chad's been reading a book on effective management, because he doesn't usually try this hard to engage me in conversation. I stop wiping and pour myself a glass of ginger ale.

"I need to talk to you about something later," he says.

"What about?"

He frowns and dabs his half-smoked cigarette into one of the ashtrays I cleaned a few minutes ago. I feel a chill of apprehension.

"Just come back to the beer fridge in a couple of minutes."

He slinks off to the kitchen, and a few seconds later I hear the heavy cooler door open with a metallic clunk. I serve a fidgety guy a couple of rums. After running scenarios through my mind and assessing how good business has been lately, I saunter back to the big walk-in beer fridge.

The door opens with a puff of bitter, acrid pot smoke and I'm quickly ushered inside, where Chad and John are sitting on stacks of beer cases, smiling flushed, contented smiles and passing a joint. John has recently been hired to work in the kitchen. He's a twenty-year-old stoner with a quiet, scraggly philosophical manner and eternally tangled bedhead hair.

"John just bought a new car," Chad says, his voice half-choked. He coughs, and John nods silently. Chad hands the joint to me.

"No thanks," I say, waving it away. "What kind of car?"

John's eyes light up.

"You want to see it? I'll cover," Chad says.

"No, really," I begin. "I can take a look at it after work. What did you want to tell me?"

Chad sucks on the joint, not looking my way.

"It can wait. Go see the car."

I'm about to protest further, but John is so enthusiastic that I feel compelled to go with him.

We step out the back door into the bright light of the dusty parking lot. Compared to the dank, pit-like aura of the pub, the outside world feels like the surface of the sun.

John leads me to a red Firebird with a dented hood and a lacy garter belt hanging off the rear-view mirror.

"Waddaya think?" he asks, looking at it with stoned admiration.

"I like the colour," I murmur, lightly kicking the front tire, which has tiny cracks in its side and appears to be a bit flat. "I don't really know anything about cars."

"Yeah, it'll take some fixing up, but I've got the time, and it was a good buy."

"How much?"

"Two thousand. And it was safetied," he adds quickly. He mumbles something about mileage, then opens the passenger door with a loud scrape of metal against metal.

"Wanna go for a spin?"

"Maybe next time," I say, motioning toward the bar. "I should be getting back."

"Ah, Chad won't care."

I look at his bloodshot, glazed eyes. He holds the door open for me, his head bobbing back and forth in slo-mo. I flash him a but-I-have-to shrug and back away from the car. As I make my way to the bar, he starts the engine and throats it several times. I pause at the door. He gives me a proud thumbs-up, puts the car into gear and does a loud and smoky brake stand.

"Piece of shit, eh?" Chad says as I step in beside him at the bar. He laughs. "He'll crash it within six months anyway, so it won't matter."

We stand silently for a few minutes. I'm waiting for him

to tell me whatever he has to tell me, but he's too stoned to sense my anticipation.

"You wanted to tell me something," I say.

"Oh yeah. I was going to mention that John's got a band, too. We were thinking of giving them a shot on Sunday nights. You know, we'll see how they do."

"Oh." I feel the blood drain from my face.

He shuffles his feet along the floor, looking around me at the shelves. "Yeah, well, you guys are great, but we want to see if we can attract a bigger crowd. Get a following together." He glances at me, only for a split second.

"Well . . ."

"Not that Archangel isn't good. But variety is the spice of life. Grass doesn't grow on a rolling stone. All that sort of shit." He takes a philosophical drag on his cigarette.

"Well . . ."

"You've got to understand," he says. "It's just business. Nothing personal."

4

The band has arrived at my apartment for a calm and reasoned discussion about our lost gig.

"This is totally bogus," Tyler shouts, pacing from my kitchen into my living room and then back again. "We had a verbal agreement. We've invested a lot of money in this deal. We had a verbal agreement!"

I look at Jan, who bites her lip. Noel is thumbing through the latest issue of *Guitar Magazine*. Twilight is lingering outside the window, punctuating my depressed, colourless mood.

"What money?" I ask.

"Clothes, shoes, equipment."

He's wearing a green Hawaiian shirt covered with large purple flowers and pink hula girls. I have no idea where he finds his clothes. It appears as if he's in the first stage of growing a goatee.

"We owned the equipment before we started this gig," I say. "The only new pieces are the mikes and one of the amps, and those belong to the bar."

"We had a verbal agreement. That's binding under North American law. It's civil law. We should sue."

"You can't sue someone for dropping your band," Noel says. "Except perhaps in California."

"Maybe it's common law," Tyler mumbles to himself. He looks at Janice. "Is it civil law or common law?"

"I think it's the law of physics. Or maybe the law of averages."

Tyler's eyes narrow, and I can tell he's straining hard for a retort.

"Maybe if we had a different name," Noel continues. "I never liked Archangel."

"Yeah, me neither," Tyler says, looking directly at me.

"It's not my fault," I say.

"We're not blaming you," Janice says unconvincingly.

"Trailer," Noel continues. "Now that's a name for a band."

"That's a dumb name," she says.

"It's a great name. Trailer. It's powerful."

"Pure Energy," Tyler says. "A band named Pure Energy

can't miss. We'll have herbalists and ravers checking us out, guaranteed."

"Hold on," I say, putting my hands up. "We don't know if we're losing our night entirely. Chad just wants to give this new band a shot. The name of the band has nothing to do with it. It's business. And Pure Energy is every bit as stupid as Trailer."

"It's a great name," Noel says under his breath.

"It's OK. But getting back to the real business, I say we let John's band play and see how they do. Who says they're going to have a big following? It's a small pub on a Sunday night. And this is not New York."

"That's not a bad name," Jan says.

"This is not New York. I like it," Tyler says. "Evocative, direct . . . But it's kind of long. It wouldn't fit well on a poster."

"Trailer would."

There's a quiet moment of reflection.

"Maybe we can sabotage their equipment."

Everyone glares at Tyler, but, as usual, he seems oblivious.

"At least Trailer sounds like a rock band," Noel says, staring at a centrefold picture of Radiohead. He tilts the magazine sideways in a manner that is borderline perverse. "A real rock band. Oasis. Trailer. Led Zeppelin."

"What do you think, Jan?" I say.

She bites her lip again and takes a deep breath. She exhales slowly. "Well," she begins, "I think maybe this situation is for the best."

Tyler groans. "Here it comes."

Jan looks back at Tyler, who has walked out of the room again. I get the sense that whatever she's about to say has been said before.

"I don't know how much I can give to the band right now," she continues. "I'm really busy at school and I'm not getting a lot out of it anymore."

"We had a verbal agreement!" Tyler screeches from the living room. "They have to give us at least a month's notice!"

"It was fun for a while," Jan continues, "but I've got to get serious about something that's going to take me somewhere, not a hobby."

My chest falls into my stomach. I hadn't realized my dream was a silly hobby. I want to tell Jan that I need this band for my sanity, for my self-esteem, so that I can convince myself that my life is moving forward. Tyler stomps around my living room and I cringe, hoping he won't break anything if he has a Tyler tantrum.

We all sit silently for a few minutes and listen to Tyler rant. Finally he calms down and comes back to the doorway. His Hawaiian shirt is thrown open for our benefit in a display of dramatic rage.

"I can understand what Jan's saying," Noel begins slowly.

Tyler hears this, grunts and walks out again with renewed steam.

I rub a hand across my temples.

"So you guys want to break up the band?"

Neither one of them says anything.

"We've got to be realistic," Jan says.

Tyler walks back into the room. "What if we change the style of the band," he says. "We'll get postmodern, innovative, nouveau riche."

"You're using nouveau riche incorrectly," Jan says.

Tyler looks at her blankly. "Language is always evolving," he says. "Which is why we don't speak in Shakespearean

English, Jan. You should know that. Deal with it. As for the band, we need to get students out."

"Even better," Noel murmurs, "we should go Christian rock. If you want to stir things up and get a following, we should rock for Jesus. Have you seen these bands on TV? Imagine forty thousand fans speaking in tongues and being moved by the power of the Lord."

"Archangel is a good religious name," Jan says.

Tyler shakes his head. "I'm going," he says. "I can't listen to this anymore. I haven't devoted my time to this band to lose our gig without a fight."

He jams his fedora on and storms out the door. His footfalls echo down the stairs. After the front door slams I go over and get the bottle of vodka from the freezer. I mix a can of concentrated orange juice and we toast Frank Zappa for good luck.

"We would probably stand a better shot of breaking through with Christian rock," Jan says. "Noel's right. There's a huge, specialized market and not a ton of bands competing for the spotlight."

"Yeah," I mumble, tasting the burning surge of vodka on my tongue. "We could just add Jesus to the end of every line. Or if it's a love song, like 'Alison,' we could change names."

"'Je-sus, I know this world is kil-ling you-u,'" Jan sings with a laugh.

"But it won't work when you get to the part about taking off her party dress," Noel says. "Bit of blasphemy to have the Chosen One in drag."

"So we'd change that line too," I say. "We could change 'I heard you let that little friend of mine take off your party dress' to 'I heard you let that little friend of mine take off your bloody shroud.'"

Jan stares at me for a few seconds with her mouth open.

"You are so going to burn, Jay Thompson," she says, smiling.

"As long as they have cigarettes in hell," I reply.

We laugh and drink. The warm trickle of vodka sinks into my shoulders and makes me slightly maudlin. I have the urge to put on BB King and listen to some good Mississippi Delta blues.

"There's the Virgin Mary, too," Jan says. "You can't forget about Christ's mom. Or Mary Magdalen. We could substitute Mary Magdalen for Roxanne. 'Ma-ry, you don't have to put on the red light.'"

She looks at me and then Noel, but the moment's passed and the realization that we're losing the only crappy gig we've got is beginning to sink in.

Noel looks at his watch, then downs his drink in three large swallows.

"I've gotta go, guys," he says apologetically. "I was in at seven-thirty this morning and I'm bagged. I wish we were rock stars so I could sleep all day."

Taking her cue, Janice finishes her drink and stands up too.

"Yeah, and stay up all night talking jive with Damon Albarn. God, he's cute."

"And Rick Dees and all the original Solid Gold Dancers," I mutter. "I'm sorry about this, guys. And if this Sunday is the end of our gigs for a while, I wouldn't mind doing more of our own songs. Or in case you guys do decide to leave."

"I'm not going anywhere yet," Jan says. "I'm just saying that I have a lot in my life at the moment. But if we're having fun, I'll stick around."

She looks at me with big green eyes. They're deep and

luminous and I always have trouble pulling my gaze away from them. I feel my stomach loop and endorphins leak from my brain. The chemicals in my body love her.

They leave and I'm left in my ratty apartment to drink vodka and orange juice while thinking about why I care so much about playing music. We don't make any money and we don't have fans. There's really more aggravation than rewards to putting on a gig. But then, on any given night, our luck could change and someone important could walk in and discover us. Even more important, a Sunday gig makes the other six days of my week a lot easier to bear.

I pull out Blur's *13* and start it on track twelve. The mood is deadly mournful and sincere.

5

To me, rhythms and riffs rank up on the survival list with nourishment and shelter. At least three times a week I faze out during a slow period behind the bar and lose myself in a world of adoring fans and glassed-in recording studios. I have imaginary conversations with David Bowie and interviews with the media about the rumoured project I'm doing with Fran Healy and Michael Stipe. My early influences include the Beatles, Culture Club, Duran Duran and Loverboy.

When I was twelve, I saved up to buy red leather hot pants because I thought they were the height of coolness. Of course, my father didn't share my fashion sense and went completely ballistic when I dragged him into the shop, a small hole in the wall covered with music posters and album sleeves. I remember they were playing the Clash. I also distinctly remember my face flushing as my father lectured me about *fag clothing* in front of all the sullen poseur ex-punk clerks. There I was on the peripheries of being hip and accepted and I was being cut down by an old man who listened to country music. No way could I go back to that shop, ever.

But my first public humiliation didn't kill my spirit. In a clandestine act of rebellion, I later used part of my savings to buy a very happening green Corey Hart T-shirt with white mesh sleeves and a jagged, cropped neckline. I wore it proudly, Corey's huge sunglasses-clad head snarling from my chest. I even wore it to little league soccer, a sport my father forced me to play in an attempt to make me more aggressive, more of a man.

Jay Thompson hit for early rebellion: "Rock the Casbah."

6

The next afternoon Chad is fluttering around the bar taping up posters for casino night, our semi-regular gambling event. He's doused them with wads of tacky silver-and-gold glitter. I feel a lump in my throat when I see the band name Stoned Quarry blazing across the bottom in big yellow letters. I turn back to the shelves and start restocking chips and peanuts.

Freido, our rotund cook, walks my plate of food out to the bar and drops it unceremoniously in front of me. Because it's Rose and Crown food I put liberal amounts of salt and ketchup on everything.

I take a bite of bland french fry and see Noel near the door, reading one of Chad's posters.

"You're going to be impressed with me," he says as he sits down and steals a fry. "Critical moments require critical action."

I'm not really in the mood for a success story. I'd rather commiserate with someone on his or her bad luck.

"It came to me as I was ironing my shirts last night," he continues, smiling and sitting back in his chair. "I always get my best thinking done when I'm ironing."

He almost leans back too far, catching the bar with his hand at the last second. Noel is the only person I know with an ironing ritual. He irons on Monday nights while listening to Paul Weller.

"Do you know what a band needs to do to be successful?"

"Sure," I say. "If we're talking unit success, they need to be a demographically positioned boy band that sings nauseating pop songs written from a tested template. That way they can capitalize on the lucrative eight- to eighteen-year-old girl fan market."

"But on a more local level . . ." Noel says, raising his eyebrows. He thrusts the newspaper at me. It's open to the entertainment section. Don Jenkins's Getting Out column is circled in red. It's about a local ska-punk band, Before After, who played the Staghead on Saturday.

"We need to play the Staghead? Good luck."

Every band in the province wants to play there and even the good bands will do it for a cut rate, because it's the only decent venue between here and Toronto.

Noel is shaking his head. "Granted, playing the Stag would be ideal, but look again."

I look again and shrug. If I knew what we needed to be

successful, I would have done it long ago. At least, I think I would have done it. In reality, I haven't been as aggressive with our musical direction as I could have been; I hate to harass people. I'm not good at sucking up and networking either. Sonny Bono used to drop off tapes to record companies every week, just hoping and believing that one song would catch someone's ear. And he was right. He became Phil Spector's assistant and opened up the avenues necessary to get his music to listeners. Where's my drive?

"Exposure," Noel says finally.

"Right."

"Hype and buzz are what drive those boy bands," he continues, tapping his finger on the paper. "The more you get talked about, the cooler you become. It's a fact. Every band needs positive press."

"That and money."

He makes a slightly obscene guffaw noise. "Guess who I called this morning and guess who's coming to see us play on Sunday?"

"Really?" I slap the bar with an open palm. My over-exuberance makes me realize my state of mind—an edginess that lingers like a mild, constant headache. Everything lately feels intense and I'm afraid I'm on the edge of cracking up. I'm more acutely aware than ever when Chad talks down to me, or when a customer is impatient and surly. If I was rich I could have a breakdown and go into hiding for a couple of weeks, chill out. I can't afford a breakdown.

"Yeah, really," Noel continues, eyeing me. "You OK?"

"Yeah," I say. "I'm just psyched that Before After is coming to see our gig. I love their music."

"No, not Before After, dude."

"Oh. Don Jenkins?"

"Yeah," Noel replies. "Don't sound so impressed. He usually does the bigger clubs, but I convinced him that we were worth it."

"How'd you do that?"

Noel grins and plucks another fry from my plate. He chews it slowly. "I told him Tyler was Neil Young's cousin and Neil would be at the show."

7

Tyler has heard the news and is determined to make a big impression on Don Jenkins. He has dropped by my apartment with a surprise: a manila envelope marked PRIVATE and an audiocassette. Right now, he's pacing in my kitchen and waving his arms anxiously.

"It's very compelling. You've got to trust my judgment, Thompson," he says. "Think Nick Cave meets Mark Knopfler, with a Boo Radleys undertone."

My TV dinner is rotating slowly in the humming microwave, and I've put on an early 10,000 Maniacs CD. After working with the public in the service industry all day I need to put my feet up and decompress. Tyler is infringing on my right to freedom of relaxation.

"I don't know if I can imagine that combination."

He stops pacing and looks at me. He stands bard-like, with one foot in front of the other, as if he's about to launch into a soliloquy—which in Tyler's case is always a possibility.

"That doesn't surprise me," he says gently, slowly nodding his head. "I'll be the first one to admit it's difficult to comprehend for most people. It's musical evolution—like the synergy of many parts creating a new, bold genre. The fact you're having trouble with the concept is good, because that means it's working. Luckily you're just the singer."

He puts a hand on my shoulder. He squints and stares at me intently. I think he's attempting a serious look of support, but compassion is not his strong suit. He looks like he's swallowed something bitter, his lips pursed, his eyebrows furrowed.

"And I know you'll be fine. If I didn't believe in your abilities, I wouldn't risk unveiling the opus."

"Did you do that yourself?" I ask, pointing to his hair. He steps back, smiles and runs a hand through his bright green locks.

"No, my cousin did it for me. She knows about these sorts of things. Do you want her to do yours too?"

"Not my style."

"No, you're right, of course. You have a Walt Whitman populist aura. It wouldn't suit your panache."

I drop the cassette on the table. "I don't know if we have time to rehearse new material and get it up to speed. And I was thinking we'd do some more of my songs."

"See, this is why we should work together," he says as he begins to pace again. "I could never comfortably use phrases like *up to speed*. I need your man-on-the-street grit. And as for rehearsing, we've got to risk it. My intuition is telling me this entertainment sectarian is our big break."

"His name is Don Jenkins," I say, taking a carton of orange juice from the fridge. "And I don't think you're using that word correctly."

Tyler regards me with an appraising eye. He runs his

hand across his shirtsleeve, drawing out the pointed silence.

"Trust me. We're professionals. I've cut the demo on the tape. Listen to it, read your chords and learn the lyrics. Think synergy."

I rip open the envelope and my suspicions are confirmed. There are several sheets clipped together under a cover page marked "Confidential. Under embargo until otherwise notified. *Space Oddity #2*, words and music by Tyler Dwyer. All Rights Reserved."

"How long is this song?" I ask, leafing through the pages. Up until now, Tyler has refrained from pushing his work on the band.

"It's a rock opera. The first two scenes run to approximately seventeen minutes, which is followed by a bridge leading us dramatically into scenes three and four, thus completing the first act."

He looks lovingly at the pages in my hands, the way people look at babies. I feel a shiver. The microwave timer goes off in a series of annoying beeps.

"I suppose you want to end the gig with this . . . thing," I say.

He snatches the papers off the table and puts them back together with the paperclip.

"This *thing* is a complex exploration into the very essence of modern composition. It's intelligent and thought-provoking, and every note contributes to the synergy of the whole. And, no, I believe it should be played first, because I don't expect any reputable critic to stay for the entire night. That would be absurd."

The smell of my nuked dinner makes me feel slightly nauseated and my mouth fills with the taste of copper. I think the notion of a rock opera is absurd. But I suppose the line between inspiration and silliness is a thin one when you're breaking new ground. People ridiculed Darwin. Einstein was initially dismissed as an eccentric little patent clerk with a bag full of strange ideas. For all I know Tyler might be a genius.

"Tell me again why I'm like Walt Whitman," I say.

Tyler stands in quiet contemplation as I root around the nearly empty shelves. I notice him leafing through a pile of bills on the table. I close my eyes and wonder how I can get him to leave so that I can deal with his ambition later. I think of the midafternoon crowd at the bar, think of the beer delivery guy with the crippling B.O. who took forever to bring in the new kegs.

I feel a hand on my shoulder.

"We can do this, Jay," Tyler says. "This would mean a lot to me."

As far as I can tell he's being sincere. It's almost unnerving. I take a slow drink from the orange juice container, willing the vitamin C to rejuvenate me.

"OK, but I want to play a couple of my songs in the first set, too."

"That's a bit risky, isn't it?"

"What do you mean?"

"I mean no disrespect, but I am a trained composer and, well, there are going to be comparisons. It's your decision."

"I'll take my chances."

My headache comes back with a well-centred throb. I butter my TV dinner mashed potatoes. He looks at the plate and grimaces.

"That's truly horrible."

"Point conceded," I say, biting into the leathery steak.

"But my mother doesn't make me prosciutto and pickle sandwiches."

"She doesn't make me prosciutto and pickle sandwiches. Those two foods don't even complement one another."

Tyler still lives at home. I remind him of that fact whenever I want to prick his pride. Not that much upsets Tyler's strong sense of self. The best I can do is pick at his minute insecurities and hope that has a cumulative effect in undermining his occasionally over-inflated ego. Lately he has been referring to his parents as his patrons and making speeches about their enlightened sponsorship of the arts.

"I'll leave you to your feast. If you have any problems— any problems at all with the opus—please call me. You've got my pager number."

He slips on his Starsky and Hutch sunglasses and flashes me the patented Dwyer grin. "Destiny is calling us, Jay," he says, clicking his heels together like Dorothy. "The phoenix from the flame."

He descends the stairs buoyantly, his feet barely touching the steps. I continue to stand in the doorway as he disappears into the night, wondering if destiny could suddenly pick up a lowly bartender and his Sunday-night garage band.

I finish my meal and push the flimsy plastic tray away. I look around the apartment at the fading yellow walls and the clock ticking above me. The upper corner of my Suede poster has begun to pull away from the wall, and I realize that I put that poster up six years ago.

Six years of my life have passed by without much change or growth or personal insight. I moved here when I dropped out of university. The place was a bit expensive for me at the time, but I didn't want to live with anyone and I had enough student loan money to carry me for a while. I've had the same furniture since the day I moved in and have never once rearranged the place. Tyler might still live at home, but I might as well be living on a seventies sitcom set. I'm in a time capsule. At least he's been going to school, working for something tangible, a degree that will prove he has been productive and industrious. Anything I've earned, I've spent. Though obviously not at Ikea.

After I wash my fork and bread plate, I retreat to the living room, shut off the CD player and plug in my guitar.

I look over Tyler's notes and then put on his tape. In my heart I'm truly hoping that it will be brilliant, as new and innovative as *Pet Sounds*, or *Sergeant Pepper*, or *OK Computer*. After a few moments of silence as the tape spins and hums, an eerie synthesizer begins to pulse, building slowly to a crash of breaking glass. The strumming from Bowie's "Space Oddity" begins, followed by more breaking glass and finally the first movement. I walk to the fridge and get a beer.

This is going to be a long night.

8

"Well maybe you can mumble the lyrics?"

Janice is standing in my kitchen. She's wearing a light blue, slightly cropped tank top and her new yellow vanity glasses. I'm not sure the glasses match the top, but being no fashion expert I keep my opinion to myself. The cropped tank top is a definite distraction. I've caught myself glancing at her navel seven times in the last forty-seven minutes.

Once you lust after your friends, the friendship is doomed. Sometimes I wish I were one of those guys who can seduce women. I wouldn't do it all the time, because then you become sad and sleazy, but I'd like to have the power for these situations. Jan is a bit of an enigma, close enough to be my friend, but aloof enough to keep me from trying to be anything more. I can't figure out what she needs, which is the first step in making someone want you. Half the time I don't even think she wants a man. I think she just likes toying with them out of a jaded sense of amusement. Maybe she's wearing the crop top to tease me. I like Jan so much that she has unleashed a well of insecurities I wasn't aware I had within me.

"Tyler would kill me if I mumbled," I say. "And besides, he had a sincere moment and said it was really important to him."

"Tyler had a sincere moment? Are you sure it wasn't gas?"

"He calls it his opus."

"Yeah, he dropped the sheet music off at my house. He compared the bass line to childbirth, asking if I could play the notes like a child's heartbeat in my uterus. He said something about my maternal energy and the fertility rites of rebirth."

We look at one another and laugh.

She wanders out of the room and changes the CD. As usual, Jan has tampered with my levels and the bass is so deep the pictures on my walls vibrate. I feel cardiorhythmic irregularities in my chest.

Jan and I have recently started eating dinner together every Wednesday night. I made the mistake of trying to make coq au vin the first time she came over and added way too much wine, undercooked the chicken and over-steamed the broccoli. I'm not great at multitasking and keeping track of cooking times. I've been cautious and kept the menu pretty simple ever since.

Before she comes over I'm always nervous—about cooking and about being alone with her. Once we're together I'm fine. But the buildup is nerve-racking. I feel like a teenager. She's probably not interested enough to fall for me. I'm a bartender. I'm average-looking. And if I tried to initiate a relationship and she gave me a sympathetic look and said something about us being really good friends, I'd want to hang myself.

She really can carry off a cropped tank top.

Glance number eight. Fifty-six minutes.

"Mind if I take a look at Tyler's lyric sheet?" she asks. "He wouldn't give me one. He said it was on a need-to-know basis, and I didn't."

"Tyler gave me strict instructions not to show it to anyone. It's on the bookshelf."

Janice fishes a piece of spaghetti out of the pot. She cuts it with a fork and throws one half up onto my ceiling. It sticks and she laughs freakishly.

"I love that," she says.

I try to picture us as a couple, making meals together every night and talking about our days. She sits down at the table and looks through Tyler's notes. After a few seconds she whimpers.

"'Brown bag lunch of despair, don't make me sit at the table alone,'" she reads. "'Talk to me like Kissinger, I'll bend to you like the cosmos.'"

I look over her shoulder at the lyric sheet, bleeding red from last-minute notes and additions etched down the margins. I breathe in her warm smell, feel the perfume-tinged air tumbling down into my lungs, making me dizzy.

"He said he wanted a wide range of references for didactic purposes. He said pop culture is the only way to indoctrinate the masses."

She flips the page and scans the rest of the lyrics, then shoves the sheets haphazardly back into the envelope.

"The music isn't bad," she says. "But you'll never hear Thom Yorke spouting off about 'a May Day deception in the airport of lost-luggage dreams.'"

"You might . . ."

"Good point."

"And I kind of like that line."

I scald my hand as I drain the noodles, a direct result of accidental glance number nine. I pour the sauce into the noodles and stir it around, noting that I haven't drained the pasta sufficiently. The sauce is diluted and runny and looks awful.

Janice gets up and stands next to me at the stove. She's in my personal sphere—that area where your body heat finds resistance and radiates back to you. I feel a bit flushed and slightly giddy, like I could flake out at any second and grab her . . . I casually slide to my left.

She splits a white dinner roll and begins to butter it, spreading the butter thinly and evenly across the entire surface. I can't think of anything to say. My mind is blank. I glance toward her.

"What?" she asks, looking at me and chewing vigorously, her mouth moving up and down like a turbine.

I force a smile.

"Dinner's almost ready."

She takes another healthy bite and dips a corner of her bun into the pot and tastes.

"Hmm," she says. "Needs something."

"Like spices?" I look around the kitchen, knowing I don't own anything more daring than salt and pepper. I really do have to buy a cookbook.

"No, just something."

"More clams? Mushrooms? Wine?"

"You put wine in spaghetti?"

She thinks for a few seconds, pushing the last buttered corner of gummy bun into her mouth.

"I'm sure it's fine," she says.

"But you said it needed something."

She walks over to the table. I've folded the napkins to look like miniature swans—my specialty when I was a waiter. I spent my evenings during the last years of high school working at a Greek restaurant for a man who insisted we call him Aristotle, even though his name was Nick. I think he thought the allusion to Onassis brought a sense of refinement to his establishment, but he was wrong. The place was a dive, full of tacky, faded pictures of the Acropolis and the tinny buzz of bazooki music. From waiter to bartender: how many people can say their career has been stalled since high school?

"Most things in life need something, Jay. That's the point: to keep moving, to always be looking for the missing intangibles that will make us complete. Take love, for instance. Love is a desperate attempt to fill the gaps in our lives."

For a split second I wonder if she's subtly hinting that I can save her from her loneliness. But I know she's just talking. I feel my cheeks begin to blush.

"That's original. Tyler should use it in act three. See, I thought the point of life was to be completely self-absorbed for twenty-odd years until you get married, lose all capacity for spontaneity, have kids and watch them be completely self-absorbed for twenty-odd years. Then you play golf, complain about the decline of society and spoil your self-absorbed grandchildren. Do you want to add something to the sauce?"

She shakes her head and picks up the fork, scraping her nail in between two tines with a look of concern on her face. I nearly choke, thinking I've given her a utensil encrusted with congealed macaroni and cheese or TV-dinner burrito.

"No, it's fine."

She puts the fork down. I don't see any large bits of guck. I stir the sauce, trying to gauge the clam-to-mushroom ratio and wondering if I should add more tomato paste. But this is the way I always make it and I've never noticed anything missing.

Janice is staring aimlessly at the cupboards over the sink. I plop two heavy tongfuls of spaghetti onto the plates, trying to keep them even. I have two nice plates that I bought at a garage sale. They have gold around the edges and floral designs that you can see only when you finish everything you've been given to eat—like a reward.

"Do you know the band Rabid Angels?" she asks.

"They're terrible. Tyler and I saw them at the Platform a few months ago. We were tempted to walk out, but drinks were cheap."

Rabid Angels is a local band with a small, loyal following and a huge identity problem. As a band they are so eager to please that they suppress all of their own original ideas and become totally mundane and generic. On the night Tyler and I saw them they covered both an Alice Cooper and a Lyle Lovett song. That should be musically illegal. Of course, I also dislike them because they get more attention than us, despite sucking so badly.

"Well, I went out with the drummer on Friday."

I feel like I've been punched hard in the trachea.

"They do have a few good songs," I say. "In their own way, they're all right, I suppose."

"Their music sucks, but I'm trying to illustrate my point."

"Fair enough. And thank God."

Their ballads sound like they're inspired by Air Supply. They have mullet haircuts. The lead singer has a guitar shaped like an axe, for crissake! I want to shake her and tell her she should go out with a good, decent, caring guy—one who may or may not always be a bartender.

"Yeah. See, the drummer is somewhat cute and smart and I thought we had a lot in common, because we both love music. Sure, his taste is a bit suspect, but I was thinking that with a bit of coaching he would come around. But by the end of the date we were hard-pressed to make small talk about the weather. He looked good on paper, but he was missing the intangibles I need to feel complete. I have to keep moving, keep looking for the next guy."

I put the plate down in front of her and she smiles up at me.

"It looks great, Jay."

I point to the green, glittering container of Parmesan cheese. "There's also old cheddar."

She makes a face and prods the spaghetti with her fork, as if she expects it to jump back at her. "No, this is fine."

I wish I had one of those long, fancy pepper grinders like restaurants have. I could stand over her and twist the little head.

"Do you want wine?"

"There's already some in the sauce, isn't there," she smirks. "I don't want to get loaded."

I pluck a corked bottle of red from the top of the fridge and pour a couple of glasses. She's digging in, twisting the spaghetti around her fork. The intense look of concentration on her face is endearing.

"So you won't date him again," I say, trying to sound casual.

She shakes her head and reaches for another bun. "No, but I'm going out with the lead singer this Saturday. And we have nothing in common. He's an arrogant jerk. But you never know who is going to fill the gap in your life. That's why opposites sometimes attract. I'm flowing with whatever comes my way, looking at every possibility."

My momentary surge of optimism does an Olympic tuck, flip and no-splash entry into the pool of reality. The Russian judge gives it a 9.5. Despite being outwardly cool, I sometimes think Jan is as messed up as me. She has strong, firm opinions on music and society and puts on a good show of being in control of her life, but occasionally I glimpse a fissure in her persona.

"You'll never be happy with a jerk," I say. "You've got too much self-respect."

"You never know. That's all I'm saying. People are pretty complex."

There is no way any fan of Rabid Angels, much less a member, should be allowed to go out with Jan.

"I'm being totally cool," she continues. "I've decided that from now on I'm not going to try to find fulfillment. I'm going to put all prejudgments aside and let love come to me."

"That's what you've decided?"

"The way I see it, real love should happen. You should feel love on a chemical level and not be swayed by misguided notions. Sometimes jerks are really nice once you get to know them. Sometimes you have to take a chance and see what happens."

Jan looks at me, then into her bowl of salad. She picks a few pieces of lettuce with her fork, one after the other, from various regions of the dish.

"Of course, with that said, I'm not very good at these things. I could be completely wrong. I don't always know what I'm doing."

Neither do I.

Someone must know what they're doing. How hard can finding a good relationship be? And why does it seem harder for my generation? My grandparents were married for forty-one years and they didn't impress me as being particularly enlightened. My grandfather used to sit in his armchair cracking peanuts with a tack hammer while my grandmother fed pigeons on their back steps. They worked hard and were proud people. My grandfather was the breadwinner, working for forty-five years in a series of sales jobs, mostly for appliance dealerships. My grandmother was the mother. They were civil to one another, tolerated each other's quirks and raised their children according to their narrow view of the world. They knew something about making a relationship work.

Of course, on the flip side, there are my parents, who confirm that two people can be completely wrong in a relationship. My father has never seemed entirely comfortable with the notion of sacrificing for his family. Maybe he always dreamed of doing something else and we got in his way. He moved between plateaus of contentment to lows of discontent and detachment, sometimes swinging quite suddenly. I remember he bought me Michael Jackson's *Thriller* for no reason other than I really wanted it. He was the coolest dad on the planet, hands down, no competition. The next day he fell into a funk and wouldn't let me play the record for weeks.

As for Mom, I love her, but she can be just as selfish. I don't mean that she's been particularly horrible, but she has rarely asked questions about my life, has never known my friends' names and has paid only scant attention to my comings and goings. Her one astounding positive, however, is that she loves music and doesn't think my dream to be a professional musician is silly.

As a couple, however, my parents are poorly matched. They've always bickered and looked out for themselves. Given their rocky relationship as a guide, no wonder I don't know anything about love.

"Do you ever have those Saturdays," I say, "when you want to go downtown, wander around looking in windows, browse in bookstores, maybe stop for lunch—but you don't want to do it by yourself?"

Jan looks at me for a few seconds, then nods. "Sure."

"Well, at this point in my life, that's all I want. Someone to go with me."

She soaks up the last dregs of tomato sauce with a bun and pushes her plate away, as if she can't stand the sight of it anymore and is expecting a waiter to come by and pick it up. She looks at me and smiles.

"God save the hopelessly romantic."

9

Thursday night. I'm sitting in Tyler's basement drinking a bottle of homebrew that his mother made. She hovers above me as I take the first swallow. It's yeasty and dark with a nutty aftertaste.

"You like?" she asks, her eyebrows arching. She's a small Romanian woman with large, uncertain eyes. Even when you have her undivided attention her eyes tend to be scanning behind you. Despite the air of paranoia, she's pleasant and talkative and fond of breaking into impromptu Rod Stewart songs.

Tyler's parents are opposites who have attracted. His father is an austere professor of history who is usually locked in his study whenever I come over to the house. Maybe they know what they're doing. They're still in love. Mrs. Dwyer always makes moony eyes when she talks about meeting Tyler's dad while he was doing research in Bucharest.

"The best yet, Trish," I say, holding the bottle to her in toast.

She beams. "I knew you'd like that one, Jason. It's Hungarian. The girls made a batch of Hungarian and a German lager. Der Muncheneisen, I think it's called."

"Very nice," I say.

Tyler's mother works for the university, in the admissions department. She has a club of neighbourhood women who get together every month and make beer. Trish has a great sense of wonder and joy that Tyler tends to suppress in himself. In fact, he seems to do everything he can to distance himself from his mother's spirit, as if he's a bit ashamed of her. If you want to annoy Tyler, call him a peasant. If you want to really annoy Tyler, call him a Romanian peasant.

"This is the second time we made this one, but the first time I added extra sugar as it was cooling. Never do that. We had to throw the entire batch away. I poured it into the garden, next to the carrots." She shakes her head tragically.

"Have the rabbits been weaving around the house since then?" I ask, smiling.

She smiles politely and pats me on the cheek. "Well, I'll leave you kids to your practice," she says. "I know you don't need an old person interfering with your aura." She takes her litre bottle of ale and ascends the stairs.

Tyler has been fiddling with his synthesizer since I arrived and only now wanders back to the paisley couch. He brushes some dog hair off the cushion and sits down.

"It's just like those two to be late," he says. "They do it as a means of asserting power, you know. They make us wait for them."

"Chill, Tyler, they'll be here. It isn't even six-thirty."

He looks at his plastic McDonald's watch. Grimace's hands are on the five and the six. He gets up and paces to the stereo and begins flipping through his hundreds of CDs. His collection is indexed according to Tyler logic—that is, according to his estimation of their worth to humanity.

First CD: Captain Beefheart, *Trout Mask Replica*. When I told Tyler how much I disliked it, he nodded sagely and said he understood, because the Captain's music was made for those on a higher plane of appreciation.

Last CD: Andrew Lloyd Webber, *The Music of Andrew Lloyd Webber*. Tyler insists the CD was a gift from a demented aunt, but I once caught him humming "Magical Mister Mistoffelees" while we were setting up for a gig.

I'll give Tyler credit, though. He has a very impressive and diverse collection. The only genres he won't touch are hip-hop and soft pop, because he says they're too homogeneous and bland. He says that when the measure of success is sounding identical to everyone else in the genre there is clearly a need for change. I have to agree, though I generally try not to agree with Tyler.

He flips on a CD as Noel comes down the stairs. Tyler glares at him.

"Traffic," Noel says, cutting him off.

"You look tired," I say.

He gently lays his guitar case across the table and rubs his eyes. They're red and rimmed with dark circles.

"My schedule is killer right now." He tosses me a cassette tape. "I know you're a bit down, so I made you a mix tape from my U2 bootlegs. Listen to 'The Fly'—I swear there's a sitar in the background."

I smile. "You do sleep, don't you?" I say.

Leave it to Noel to sense my need for comfort music. He's got a sixth sense for cheering people up, whether through a laugh, commiseration over a couple of beers or a small gesture like this one. He goes to the fridge.

"What's on tap tonight?" he asks, peering into a forest of bottles. He picks up a bottle of the German.

"Thank God for beer. Beer and ginkgo biloba."

"Song title," I say.

Tyler has wandered back to the couch and is hovering above me. "Did you have any trouble with the tablature, Noel?"

"I had a look at it, but haven't had time to really run

through it. Sorry about that, Ty. I've got it at the top of my day planner for tomorrow night."

Tyler slumps into an armchair. On the stereo, the singer yowls like a heat-stricken cat. I'm not in the mood.

Tyler clears his throat. "OK, say you're shipwrecked on a desert island and you have to choose one band to be stranded with. Who would it be?"

"CDs or the actual band?" I ask.

"Oh, the band, for sure."

No one shifts gears like Tyler.

"Do they have to be together or can they be split, like the Police or the original Beach Boys?"

He considers this for a few seconds. "I'll say they can be split, but all of the members still have to be alive."

"Joan Jett and the Blackhearts," Noel says almost instantly. "No question. They rock hard, and I'm pretty certain she'd know how to build a grass hut."

Tyler turns to me. "Thompson? And don't say anything weak like Crosby, Stills and Nash or Simon and Garfunkel or I'll have to kill you."

I run through a plethora of possibilities, imagine cavorting on a sun-drenched beach with Courtney Love or fishing using primitive methods with Billy Corgan or Neil Finn. Then I wonder if I've gone off my nut, because I'm twenty-six and seriously wondering who would be on a desert island with me.

"I have to put my vote in for Hole, because I want to rub coconut oil on Courtney's sinewy back while the sun bakes us golden brown."

Tyler looks surprisingly impressed. "Very nice, Jay. Good choice. If I didn't know better, I'd say you've thought about this before. Now ask me."

"OK, Tyler, give us the right answer."

He smiles proudly and is about to enlighten us when Jan's slender legs appear on the steps. She is wearing jeans and white socks, but unfortunately no cropped top. When her face finally appears she looks flushed. I feel the usual tumble of chemicals.

"Lost track of time," she says.

She snaps the latches of her guitar case open with her long, gentle fingers. Her nail polish is sparkly silver.

"I trust you were practising," Tyler says.

"I brought you some discount coffee from work," Noel says, taking a swallow of his beer.

"How do you people live such banal lives?" Tyler asks.

"We get by," Noel replies.

"OK, let's get started," I say, getting up and strapping my guitar on. I plug into my amp and play a couple of quick chords. Jan hurries to the fridge, grabs a beer and hurries back. Her sock feet slide across the tiles. Noel plugs in and plays the first progression of "New Orleans Is Sinking." Jan takes a swallow of her beer.

"Hey, is this Hungarian?"

Tyler looks shocked and Jan smiles slyly.

"Your mom told me," she says, strapping on her bass.

"So I thought," I say, "before we dive into *Space Oddity* maybe we should play a couple of up-tempo songs to get everyone in the mood. Maybe start with 'She Falls for Haircuts.'"

Tyler glares at me. "We start with *Space Oddity #2*," he says. "I don't want the mood tainted by your mock-rock sensibility. We have one opportunity to impress this newspaper scribe and have to utilize our best material."

"Yeah, but—"

"Don't worry, we'll split the night, Thompson. But I've already called dibs on the first set. After a year playing your songs, I think my request is quite reasonable. Next time you can open. I promise."

I want to argue, because in all fairness my songs are the impetus for the band, but in a way he has a point. I don't want to be petty. And from the look on his face, I can tell he won't easily be swayed. Assertiveness isn't my strength. I turn the volume up on my guitar.

"Fine. Let's just start."

Tyler has the synthesizer programmed with effects and wired to a foot pedal. He dims the lights slightly and then sits quietly behind his drums as we begin our long day's journey into night.

Bowie.

Drumming.

Breaking glass.

We play a shaky first run through the material without vocals. The second run is interrupted several times with Tyler's advice and admonishments. By the third run our shaky vibe is getting even worse.

"Emotion, Noel!" he shouts as the bridge comes crashing down.

Noel stands clenching his teeth, clearly using all of his strength to keep his composure.

"This isn't paint by numbers," Tyler continues as the vibrations fade out of the amps. Jan's hands creep into tiny fists. "You can't just play the notes. You've got to feel the momentum growing. This is a vital part of the progression. Major Tom is lost in space and his wife is emotionally adrift. Listen to the lyrics."

"OK," Noel says diplomatically. "OK, I hear what you're

saying. I can see where you're coming from. I'll add a bit of anguish to the riff."

Tyler nods and looks at Jan and me.

"OK, let's take it from verse three, 'My soul isn't ironed and my dinner's cold . . .'"

We rise again and run through verse three to the bridge. Noel is intensely focused, staring at the neck of his guitar as he runs through the solo. He's drawn it out a bit and has varied the tempo. The drums cut out and we collapse again.

"Hold it, hold it," Tyler shouts, putting his hand on his cymbals to silence their clatter. "What are you doing?"

Noel looks tired.

"I was being anguished," he says, looking down at his guitar. "It wasn't a stretch."

"But you weren't playing the progression in situ. You got way off the mark."

"I added a bit. I improvised. I was thinking that—"

"No, no," Tyler says, shaking his head. "This isn't one of Jay's pop songs. We don't improvise. Every note has been painstakingly examined and weighed."

"Oh come on, Tyler!" Jan blurts, staring at him.

"You come on," he retorts, pointing a drumstick at her. "You're playing like you haven't even listened to the tape. Do you realize how much work I've put into this?"

The four of us have an Abbey Road moment, thick with simmering tension.

"OK," Noel says calmly. "There's no use ripping one another apart over this. I say we run through it again. I'll play it your way for Don Jenkins on Sunday. I think it can be improved, but you've got your own strictly defined ideas and I can respect them."

"That's a shot at me, isn't it?"

"Tyler!" Jan puts her bass down and strides stiffly up the stairs. I close my eyes and feel a certain kind of pain, a wish that everything good and worthy didn't always get derailed by trivialities and ego. We should be compromising now, working slowly toward our long-term goals, learning as we go. I pinch my brow and take my guitar off my shoulder.

"It's late," I say, looking at the clock over the mini-bar in the corner. "Why don't we each mull this rehearsal over and come back fresh tomorrow night."

Tyler throws his drumsticks into the corner and marches out without a word.

10

With the biggest gig of our lives coming up, I've been thinking about the first time I performed.

My first gig happened in grade six, a few years after I met Tyler, when I convinced our music teacher—an emaciated fifty-year-old nun—to let me perform for the class. By this point I had become aware of social conventions. The school had cliques and cool kids and geeks and losers. I certainly didn't want to be a geek or a loser, because they were always getting shit on, getting tackled hard in soccer, getting told that they were worthless by the cool kids. I wasn't particularly smart in school and didn't enjoy sports, but I wanted to be liked, noticed, not just that kid in the brown corduroy shirt on the end of the first row in the class picture.

So I practised. I spent the days leading up to my first performance honing my skills on a song carefully selected for its power and emotion. Also, it was the easiest piece to play.

Jay Thompson hit for elementary school: Bette Midler, "The Rose."

The first few minutes of my performance went amazingly well. The class was silent, everyone's eyes were on me, and the room echoed with the constant and soulful transition from G to C to E.

Sister Myrtle told me to sing.

I didn't want to sing. I suddenly realized that if I sang badly the whole plan would be for nothing. If I sang really badly after begging to get up and play, I would cement my place alongside Steven Lawley, the nose picker, and Cheryl-Ann, the rotund girl who had never been allowed to forget breaking her small plastic chair in class. Kids don't know about gland problems. They only know about weakness.

I asked if everyone could sing.

I was told that no one else knew the words.

I said that I didn't know the words.

Sister Myrtle pointed out that they were on the page in front of me.

The sound that came out of my eleven-year-old throat can't be classified as singing. I started off in a mumble, unable to get on key, my breathing shallow and strained. As I became more conscious of my lack of oxygen, my voice got weaker, and by the second verse barely rose above a whisper. I felt near tears, desperate to get away from the sea of elementary eyes fixed on me. By the end I was only strumming, unable to make a sound. Afterwards one solitary girl approached me and told me she liked it. She wore a polyester jumpsuit and smelled like cheese. As for Tyler, he shrugged and told me I was doomed from the start, because

Bette Midler was so uncool. Such was my start in the high-pressure world of rock and roll.

From that moment onwards I stayed behind closed doors, refining my style, imitating the intonations of John Lennon and Little Richard, Ric Ocasek and Simon LeBon.

Looking back now, I don't know why I didn't try again to play publicly in high school. Tyler and I jammed occasionally, an erratic noisefest featuring his still-rudimentary drumming and my amped-up electric guitar. I suppose I was scared to take the big step of forming a band, because, though I didn't ever fall to the echelon of the hardcore geeks, I never quite rose to the heights of true and sustainable popularity. The cool guys started bands, because they could deal with the scrutiny. For me, the prospect of humiliation was too great, so I watched and listened and collected Cult posters for my room.

And then, after graduation and a few years of bartending boredom, came Archangel. One night about a year and a half ago, Tyler invited me to a university Battle of the Bands competition at the Den, a student bar on campus. The lineup wasn't stellar, a mishmash of hard-rock types and pop duos playing the same predictable tunes with badly clichéd lyrics. I sat near the stage, feeling almost angry that these people were masquerading as serious musicians. I was also keenly aware of the reams of enthusiastic young and nubile female fans who seemed enraptured by their presence. Obviously I hadn't fully comprehended the fringe benefits to being in a band. Not having had a steady girlfriend in well over a year, this weighed on my mind more than I care to admit. So, I debated for a couple of months, polished some tunes and finally penned an ad for the local paper after a night of intense, highly satisfactory solo jamming. *Musicians wanted: Archangel, a progressive rock band with Brit pop leanings. Some covers. No weepy love songs!*

I secured a tentative Sunday-night gig at the Rose and Crown, and immediately had Tyler's interest. At the time, he was in a university band, Radical Juice, a rock-funk collective that played sporadically on campus, but he was eager to jump ship for a regular gig and more creative control. I was a bit hesitant, for a few reasons. First of all because he's headstrong Tyler, and I wanted to keep control of the band. I had written the songs and done the groundwork, so there had to be a reasonable payoff. Secondly, I hated Radical Juice and their pretentious, self-indulgent music. But the more we talked, the more I saw that Tyler's enthusiasm for music would be good for the band.

We needed lead and bass guitarists and a singer. I intended to be the rhythm guitar player and prime songwriter, nothing else. I felt my voice was best suited to background vocals, occasional harmonizing and in-depth, exclusive interviews with music journalists. For lead, Tyler recommended Noel, who had never played a live gig in his life but who occasionally took part in informal jam sessions at O'Reilly's music store downtown. I liked Noel immediately, mostly because he took a genuine interest in my music and asked loads of pertinent questions. And he knew the sound I wanted. I played him a couple of my songs and he improvised a few great riffs. Also, he really encouraged me to sing lead, assuring me my voice was solid and my songs would get priority if I were the frontman.

So then came Jan, from an open audition on campus. We had six people show up, including two who didn't want the band to interfere with their studies and two who made a lot of horrible, rhythmless noise, then confessed they didn't know how to play but were eager to learn. Jan was the obvious choice. She played well, handled Tyler with cool sarcasm, and was wearing jeans and a pink T-shirt with "Superstar" across the front that made her look really sexy.

I suppose if I had had more guts in high school, if I had formed a band and been focused, maybe I'd be earning a living as a musician instead of sacrificing for a chance in a ratty pub.

On quiet days when the bar is empty, the stereo is on and I'm thinking back to other days, I always imagine the sun shining through the window, falling on the sheet music and a younger me with my guitar. Usually I'm playing "Please Please Me" or "Don't Be Cruel." But sometimes I'm singing "The Rose." And it's dead-on perfect.

11

A few days before the big gig my father asks me to drop by and help him move a cabinet. My family home is a small, two-storey structure in a neighbourhood of houses built just after World War Two. The interior is cozy and still features the tasteful brown, orange and avocado colour scheme my mother chose in the mid-1970s. There are pastoral prints on the wall, a fair smattering of dead relatives in dusty frames and the ever-present smell of creeping mildew. Everything in the place feels a bit worn out, my father included.

"It's upstairs," he mumbles as he pushes open the door. He walks back to a plate of eggs and bacon steaming on his cheap, plastic-coated table. My father always sits at the table to eat, never in front of the television. It's a source of pride to him for some strange reason, as if it demonstrates his discipline and etiquette.

"I don't suppose you made enough for me, did you?" I ask, my stomach growling and my mind flashing white hot for a fix of coffee.

"No. I didn't know if you were coming. Don't answer the phone anymore?"

He's eating in blue sweatpants and a sleeveless undershirt that reveals the flabby curve of his breasts and stomach. His face is haggard and rough and his hands are chapped. My father looks old.

"Dad, you called at what time? I was asleep, like most normal people."

He mashes his egg yolk and swirls it into ketchup, stabs a piece of fatty bacon and shovels it and a corner of heavily buttered bread into his mouth. It's an automatic motion, like a machine. I think of all the years he's done this, every morning with the same breakfast.

"If you had a normal job, you'd be up. It's not healthy to stay in bed as late as you do. You'll get bedsores. You have to take care of yourself."

He drinks his coffee with a brutal slurp.

"Well, maybe I will get a real job," I say quietly, taking a cup from the cupboard.

He glances up at me, and I know he thinks I'm mocking him. He rattles the morning paper.

"What's the matter with your brother?"

I pour myself a coffee, dump in three spoonfuls of sugar and a spoonful of chalky powdered milk substitute and sit down. My father resents foods that have expiry dates, viewing them as some sort of ploy to make him throw out his purchases before he's completely used them. He continues to read his paper, then looks up impatiently.

"Shel?" I say.

"You got another brother?"

Sheldon, my younger sibling, is fifteen and has lived with my father since my parents' divorce. I know teens are supposed to be awkward and confused, but Sheldon really breaks the mould. In the past two years his body has exploded from short and lumpy to big and really lumpy, and now he's at least six inches taller than me. His running shoes look like something trappers would portage when travelling the Northwest Passage.

My father forks another mound of dripping yolk and a white sliver of bacon fat into his mouth.

"What do you mean, the matter with him?" I ask.

"I think you know, Jason."

"Nothing's the matter with him."

He glares and points a thick, callused finger at my face. "You're supposed to watch out for him."

I eye his plate. What am I supposed to be, omniscient? As revolting as his breakfast seems, the whole mess is appetizing and the smell is making my stomach anxious.

"Mind if I make myself a plate?"

He looks at me reluctantly. I know he's calculated the exact number of eggs and servings of bacon he needs for the week and has shopped accordingly. The man is obsessed with preventing food wastage.

"You don't have time."

"But you're eating."

"But by the time you make anything," he begins slowly, "I'll be done and it'll be time to get this cabinet out of the attic and onto the street. I've got a guy from that Jewish store downtown coming for it."

I take a deep drink of coffee and feel the warm liquid surge to every cold place inside me. My eyes and forehead de-clench. I get up. "I'll make toast."

As I'm dropping two slices of white into the machine, he clears his plate and runs water over it in the sink. He's barely cleaned the yellow and red from the surface when he wipes it with a towel and puts it in the cupboard. I want to mention bacteria and the need to wash in hot water, even soap, but it's no use. I'll put the toast on a paper towel.

"He's masturbating in the shower, you know."

I laugh, but realize he doesn't mean it as a joke.

"I nearly killed myself this morning, and it's not the first time. Gets goddamned slippery."

I can't stop smiling, despite the look on his face. I don't need to hear this dilemma. I'd like to laugh and say Sheldon has made one of the great discoveries of teenage life, one that will leave video games in the dust. I'd like to look my father straight in the eye, nod philosophically and say, "Our boy's really blossomed." But I won't. Depending on his mood, my father would either laugh or get angry, and today he doesn't seem particularly lighthearted.

"What do you want me to do about it?" I ask.

"I don't know. Talk to him."

"Why can't you talk to him?"

This is the wrong thing to say. My father drops a pile of envelopes onto the table.

"I work hard. I can't always be the one to fix every problem. You should understand and respect that. You both should. We all have responsibilities in this family. Do you know how many years I've been getting up at five in the morning to go to work? Do you know? Twenty-eight fuckin' years. You haven't been alive that long."

"Fine, I'll tell Shel: don't whack off in Dad's shower because it brings down the value of the house. Better yet, why not a sign. For everyone, in case you have sexually frustrated houseguests."

I have the feeling that he's taken my comment as a poke at his current run of celibacy, because he's staring at me, clenching and unclenching his jaw. In the early 1980s his union sent him away for a week-long course on anger management—except they called it something else, like channelling your energy in productive ways.

"A little respect would be nice," he says.

"Dad, you're blaming me for—"

He walks out of the room. I sit down and chomp hard on my toast. There's no taste now. I suppose I should just agree with him, tell him I'll broach the subject with Shel and make life a bit easier. But sexual issues aren't my sphere. I wish my father would relax and not treat every situation as a crisis or burden. The man is way too intense for his own good.

"He's not normal," my father says, reappearing at the door with a toothbrush. "At least with you, you were normal. Except for the poetry."

"Those were song lyrics. And I wouldn't worry about Sheldon. He's fine."

"Well, maybe he'll be fine, but I tell you . . ." He leans in close. "It's pretty damned embarrassing. The lads at work are always talking about their fucking kids getting jobs and making money. What can I say? Sheldon's just repolished the bathtub for me. I've got the slacker and the masturbator."

"So you sold the cabinet," I say.

"I'm getting rid of all the crap." He motions to indicate the house.

"You buying new stuff?"

He shakes his head. He walks to the sink, spits and turns to me, licking his lips. From the look on his face I know what's coming. I've kicked the soapbox under his feet. My concentration wavers in and out through his speech.

"In life, you can't be afraid of making a few changes. Weak people never change . . . It's not much of a life, you know. You can't believe that crap about fulfillment and things always working out. You have to get a good job, benefits, not this music thing you've been doing . . . It's not real life, Jason. Real life is tough and it's hard work." He looks at me earnestly.

"Let's move the cabinet," I say, getting up and walking out of the room.

12

Over the course of the past few days, I've felt the band momentum wavering. No one seems eager to be critiqued by Tyler. My suggestion of another practice has been ignored. No one has contacted me and I haven't contacted them. I know they're all being stubborn because of the blowout the other night, but they're also all busy with other pursuits, meaningful pursuits that require real effort and attention, unlike anything in my life. I don't belong to any clubs, don't visit sick kids in the hospital and don't take courses. Lately, my greatest sense of accomplishment has come from cleaning all the mouldy green things out of my fridge and doing my laundry. I actually stood and admired my basket of clean, fresh-smelling clothes.

Chad and I have been avoiding each other at the bar. I get the sense he blames me for making him feel guilty, like I forced him to derail my band instead of volunteering to step aside. Yesterday, near the end of my shift, I refused to change the box of concentrated fountain Coke even though I knew it was nearly empty—my own personal work-to-rule campaign. Let him get his hands sticky for a change.

Now it's my day off and I'm lying in bed looking at the cream-coloured ceiling above me, wondering when it was last painted and when I might find enough motivation to paint it again. I never intended to end up mediocre, but when I look at the credit and debit columns of my life my net worth comes up a bust. I finished high school. I'd hate to think that's my high watermark, but with the band on the outs and my prospects remarkably limited, that fear has begun to creep in. What can I do? It's too late in my life to become a doctor or a lawyer or a teacher. I'm really not qualified to do anything.

The clock blinks 10:32 as I get up and wander into the kitchen, forgoing another cup of English Breakfast tea in favour of beer. As I feel the first rumbling splash of carbonation on my tongue, I wonder if I'm poor white trash. What are the criteria? If it's a subsistence wage, degradation and subservience on the lower rungs of survival, I think I qualify. If it involves a genuine fascination with wrestling and monster truck rallies, I'm safe.

What about genetics? I suppose my father earns enough money to be classified as lower middle class, but his attitude clearly dips into the generally less-revered echelons of society. He has no respect for education or government. He believes in vigilante justice and drinking beer from a can. He doesn't see anything wrong with using a flag as a bedroom curtain, doesn't believe in international travel and has no interest in expanding his knowledge of other cultures, traditions or philosophies.

Strike one against me.

As for my mother, though she enjoys dipping into dart leagues, she clearly strives for greater status. Sure, she's a bartender and uneducated, but she works in a nice hotel with professional clientele, and she's proud of that. She dresses decently for a woman on a low income and she tries to project an air of moderate refinement.

Strike two?

I'm not like my parents. I'm not like my parents. I'm not.

I'm going to have to give this more thought.

I flip through my CDs searching for understanding. Today's mood might entail Kurt Cobain or the Birthday Party or even the late bloated Elvis—*Aloha from Hawaii*—some true distress from the edge of self-destruction, sweaty and erratic. Or maybe just the deep and serrated anger of a sexually confused Sinéad O'Connor or the Sex Pistols. Or the sarcastic, nihilistic melancholy of Morrissey. I can't decide, so I slump on the couch and listen to cars rumble past the window. I take another swallow of beer, but it's starting to taste bad and I push it away.

This is why I've always wanted to make music—for people like me at times like these, times when you can't think straight for fear of falling to pieces on the living-room floor. My identity is swirling around me like a funnel cloud, threatening to tear up my self-esteem and reduce me to my base parts.

I flip Shane MacGowan, circa the Popes, into the CD

changer. As I sit back and listen to his inebriated voice slurring through the pain of being alive, I think of how music has always been intertwined with the events of my life. All of my most vivid memories have a soundtrack: my first sweaty summer job as a dishwasher is eternally set to George Harrison's "All Those Years Ago"; my first fistfight to Van Halen's "Jump"; and my first sexual encounter, unfortunately, will always be re-enacted to Bryan Adams's "Everything I Do, I Do It for You" (or at least the first thirty seconds of that song). And I remember that my mother left to Bowie's "China Girl" when I was eleven. Maybe that's why I've always had a distanced appreciation for him, but no great love. I sat under my covers the night she left with my small radio tuned in to the Top Five at Ten. Bowie was still number one. His voice was like glass. I don't remember the other four songs. They don't matter.

This was not long after my father almost lost his maintenance job at the university, the event that precipitated my parents' divorce. Apparently he and a couple of guys had a few drinks over lunch one afternoon and he returned to work drunk and flipped a riding lawn mower while cutting a grassy slope by the football field. The only reason he didn't get fired was because he was in the union and they threatened to sue the university for improper safety precautions. The whole mess was in the papers for weeks. My father was suspended with pay for a couple of months and when he went back to work he was pushing a broom around the psychology building.

My father spent his suspension time with my mother at a euchre club making friends who liked to drink deep into the night. After he was reinstated he kept the friends but quit the card club. My mother joined darts, they barely saw each other, and the tension grew. Despite what people think, kids notice when their parents become angrier and more abrupt with one another. Most of the conflict was verbal, biting remarks disguised as jokes, but not always.

Skin hitting skin sounds different than on television. There's a hollowness that television never quite manages to replicate. And they miss those little, shallow exhalations that the recipient makes when the blows are really solid. My dad hit my mom on one occasion only, but that was enough. I remember sitting mutely on the couch a few days later while she cut the sheets and pillowcases of her marriage bed with a long Ginsu knife. I sat and listened as the fabric hiss filtered down the stairs. And then she was gone, her voice missing from the house and replaced by the radio.

Having a part-time relationship with a parent is never fulfilling, but I do have a few good memories. I remember after the split she would take me to darts night every Wednesday at the Unicorn and Firkin, and I would cheer her on as she and her teammates smoked a copious number of cigarettes and gradually got more and more pissed. She would let me drink sips of beer and would high-five me when she made a really good shot. She was a star. I was happy because my mom was happy and because her friends were nice to me and because I'd usually be a bit drunk.

I flip through my CDs once again and feel helpless. I want the problems in my life to be easily fixed by a song.

13

"We can't do this. We can't do this. We're not ready."

Tyler is pacing double-time tonight. He's wearing red leather pants, a tuxedo shirt, his bowling shoes and a bright yellow bandana around his green hair. We're tucked in a corner table, watching the room slowly fill up. The crowd is twice the usual size.

Butterflies circle like punch-drunk fighters in my stomach. Noel and Janice look completely unfazed and are eating tonight's special, curried chicken on rice. Even the smell nauseates me.

Jan and Noel haven't yet spoken to Tyler, but I don't think he's noticed.

"What was I thinking?" he says, glaring across the bar. "This composition represents years of my life and I'm unveiling it in a pub." He turns to us. "I'm doing this for the band. You guys know that, don't you?"

Jan is about to shovel a forkful of curry into her mouth. She stops and glances at Noel. Neither says a word. Tyler looks at the door and exhales deeply.

"Five minutes," I say, getting out of my chair. I don't see our friendly neighbourhood entertainment critic anywhere.

"You're sure he's going to show, aren't you?" Janice asks.

"I didn't say I was sure," Noel says a bit desperately.

Chad wanders over to our table. He points to his watch. I nod.

"Well . . . ," I say.

Tyler clutches my arm. "We'll start with your songs," he says. "We'll buy time until Jenkins shows up."

"Won't that taint the audience's sensibility?" I ask.

"We've got to risk it."

We take our positions. I feel a touch of sentimentality as I pause to stare into the crowd, just in case this is the last time I get to stand here with this band. I recognize the regular faces, with a few notable absences, and wonder how many will last the entire night and how many will wander off.

"Hello," I say into the mike, letting my voice echo and fade into the lacquered wood and matted vinyl of the corner booths. "Tonight we'd like to do something special—"

"So stay for more than two pints," Noel interrupts, "in case you never see us again."

Jan claps her hands above her head. I glance back at Tyler, but he seems utterly distracted and not just a little pale.

"So we're going to play a few new songs tonight," I continue.

"We're taking you on a Magical Mystery Tour," Noel says, looking at me. "We're going to rock down Penny Lane with the mondo sophisticated stylings of our lead singer, our driving force, our Billy Shears—the Walrus himself, Jason Thompson."

Sporadic applause greets the announcement, and I feel the butterflies take another tumble.

"Yeah, thanks," I mumble into the mike. "Our first number is called 'Away Game Afternoon.'"

We launch into the song, a rollicking guitar-driven number.

Take me away
where the games are being played
Sit me on that wooden bench
and speak to me in fluent French . . .

My voice is wavering slightly, but after a couple of verses I begin to settle into a zone, relieved that no one has walked out at the thought of sitting through an extended playlist of my music. As we're into the third verse a man who could be Don Jenkins wanders through the front door. I try to match his face with the grainy column photo I remember from the newspaper. He's wearing a dark trench coat and crooked fedora. He scans the crowd and then settles his Jerry-Garcia-sized body into a small table in a dark corner. As I belt out the chorus with Jan, I see him pull a small notebook out of his jacket pocket.

> Yeah, just for today
> I'll be who I wanna be
> They'll say what they're gonna say
> But you can run to first with me . . .

> And we'll slide, slide away together

As we wrap up the song I wonder if Tyler has seen him. As the thought forms in my brain, and before the last chord fades from the amp, the lights above the stage dim and a slow, deep synthesizer hum begins to pulse around us. I hear David Bowie softly filtering from a speaker and glass begins to break. I look at Noel, who has his eyes closed in pain, and we begin act one. As we build up the introduction I feel angry, not just because Tyler has automatically side-swiped the set after one song but because everyone in the audience is going to think I wrote this under-rehearsed, experimental, self-indulgent mess.

"'In her eyes I see his stiff corpse, in her hands I feel my inner child . . .'" I begin.

Tyler's mother is now standing and clapping at a table near the middle of the bar. She's brought the brewing ladies out tonight.

We feel our way through the song, but I can tell by the faces staring back that we're not pulling this off. There's no movement to get caught up in. There's nothing to make anyone's foot tap. Every time I look in Don Jenkins's direction my heart falls. He looks mystified and unimpressed. I fight the urge to leap off the stage and wrestle the pen out of his hand every time I see him begin to write in his tiny notebook. As the song progresses, my throat constricts and I begin to force the words out, pushing hard to sound like I've got any feeling for these lyrics.

Twenty-seven minutes later we're met with a moment of smoky silence, followed by tepid applause—except from Tyler's mother's table. They're going wild. Don Jenkins has finished his pint and is writing feverishly, looking up every few seconds toward the stage.

"We're doomed," Noel whispers. "We're doomed, doomed, doomed . . ."

As I see Don Jenkins with his head down, still writing frantically, I have to agree. We were bad. I feel every hope I've ever had drain out of my body all at once and the only emotion left to complement my exhaustion is anger. Anger at Tyler for bullying us, anger at Chad for taking our night away, anger at Jan and Noel for wanting to break up the band, anger at my stunted life.

We play a couple of covers to try to recapture the room, but somehow we can't regain an edge. We've clearly lost the audience; most are distracted, deeper into their conversations than usual. I keep looking over and praying that Don Jenkins will have a second pint, maybe some food, but as we wrap up the first set I see him scanning the meagre crowd and putting away his notebook.

Doomed.

Doomed like Disco.

Doomed to an unfulfilling life pouring suds into an infinite number of streaky pint glasses.

Tyler disappears after the second set, not even bothering to take apart his drum kit. Stu drags a tray of drinks over to our corner table without being asked—never a good sign. He shrugs as he places them in front of us and says nothing.

We sit in silence and suck on our pints. The sense of anticlimax is palpable, like slimy condensation on the walls of a heaving club. For a second I wonder what it would be like to play for a packed crowd, bodies crushed together, pushing toward the stage. You can play to 90,000 in Rio, 70,000 at Wembley.

Finally Noel hauls himself out of his chair and runs a hand over his sweater to iron out any wrinkles.

"Everybody has a bad night, right?" he says.

Famous last words of a thousand calamities, I think. Noel leaves, and Jan offers to share a cab, but I'm feeling so Paranoid Android that I decide to walk and clear my head. I know that I won't be able to fall asleep when I get home. I'll end up lying on the couch watching MuchMusic videos and drinking. I'll replay tonight's performance in my head and second-guess every decision I've ever made. And tomorrow I'll wake up with the same crappy life but without the one sliver of hope that has sustained me this long.

This is what I'm thinking as I open the door to my decrepit apartment building and force my weary legs to mount the stairs. But even these paltry plans are thrown into orbit by a lump lying outside my door—a lump with big white high-tops. He's crumpled sideways in the small landing with his feet arched against the wall.

"What's going on?" I ask as Sheldon hears me coming and sits up. He nods, and I instantly feel ten times worse. Not only does he look exhausted and pale but he isn't even attempting to hide the sadness in his face. He starts to cry, shaking violently. I put my arm around him.

"It's OK, Shel," I say. "What's up?"

But Sheldon seems incapable of speech, so I unlock the door and help him up off the floor. He's a heavy kid and, as he rises, he pitches against me, lunging us both backwards, heaving my spine painfully into the wall. I get pinned between teen bulk and crumbling cement, suddenly trapped in a ridiculous slapstick routine.

I deposit him on the couch and get a blanket from the linen closet. I return to find him tucked into the fetal position. He looks like the world's biggest infant. Or a beached baby whale. I throw him the blanket.

"What happened?"

He shrugs.

"How long have you been out there?"

He shrugs again. Given appearances, I'm forced to conclude he's been lying outside my door like a dog for most of the night. His eyes are rimmed from fatigue and his clothes are even more wrinkled than usual. ·

"Want something to eat?" I ask.

He nods.

"I have Pop-Tarts, soup. Nothing much else. I've been eating most of my meals at the bar."

He looks at me but doesn't say a word. Poor kid. He's shown up here before, but never this late or this upset. I walk to the kitchen and put my head against the cool hum of the refrigerator door. My own teenage years in the Thompson home weren't easy. My father didn't like closed doors or long phone calls to friends or potential girlfriends in his house. He liked order. If I wasn't eating my dinner fast enough, my father would flick cigarette ash near my plate as a form of motivation. I can only imagine how hard life must be for Sheldon.

Before I raid the cupboards I take a look at the answering machine. The light isn't blinking. My brother has gone missing for most of the night and there are no messages.

"I'm making Pop-Tarts," I say quietly as I plop down on the couch. I give him a playful punch on the leg. It's the best I can do. I know brotherly affection is supposed to go something like this.

"Wanna watch TV?" I ask, handing him the remote. He shakes his head. "There might be a movie on. Movies make everyone feel better."

"Movies after midnight are crappy," he says, rubbing his eyes. "Everyone knows that. If they weren't, they'd be on during prime time."

"So what happened?"

Shel sits up. I hear the toaster and smell Pop-Tarts, but don't move.

"Nothing," he says, looking toward the kitchen with interest. "Grub's up."

"What do you mean, nothing?"

He looks at me anxiously. "Nothing."

"Did Dad hit you or yell at you or accuse you of masturbating in the shower again?"

He blushes and looks at the TV, but shakes his head. "Nothing happened," he says. "I just had enough."

"Enough what?"

"Dad teasing, other stuff. Who cares? We're moving anyway. He's selling the house."

This is news to me. My father has lived there since the year he got married. When he talked about making a few changes, I thought he meant ridding the place of its claustrophobic clutter and maybe slapping a new coat of paint on the bathroom. The place is a dumpy, worn-out sty, which is a perfect fit for my dumpy, worn-out father. I never thought he'd bother with the hassle of moving. I thought the place would collapse on itself in a supernatural maelstrom after he died, like the house in *Carrie*.

"Where are you moving?"

"He won't tell me."

14

My father is indeed selling our family home, and apparently he's been making a number of comments about Sheldon being *the final obligation*. The next afternoon when I get home from work, Sheldon is sprawled on the couch playing my Sony PlayStation. There's a pizza box full of crusts on the coffee table, next to his huge socked feet. He's wearing a wrestling T-shirt and, for some inexplicable reason, a pair of my silk boxer shorts, which look like Spandex on his thighs.

"Hey, Shel," I murmur. "How was school today?"

He keeps playing, but his shoulders tense. He immediately crashes his video motorcycle into a digital retaining wall. His eyes flicker in my direction and he makes a very faint grunting noise.

I wait for more of a response, but he continues to stare at the screen. A new motorcycle appears and revs its engine. I sigh, hang my jacket up in the hall closet and root around in the nearly barren fridge for something edible. I find an apple in the crisper and check the freezer. My stomach turns as I mull over four varieties of TV dinners and an almost empty carton of chocolate mint ice cream. I put a hand on my soft, pudgy stomach and feel a definite need to make a change. From the kitchen I can see the digital motorcycle shooting around the bends of the track, spinning and revving and racing against imaginary adversaries without a hint of fear or trepidation.

Sheldon's red motorcycle hits the straightaway and speeds past a blue bike. Above the track there are video clouds and an electronic blue sky. I think of Bowie singing "Blue, blue, electric blue . . ." At the opening turn there is a pixelated patch of green grass and palm trees. I consider the consequences of having Sheldon living with me, consider my personal limitations, both financial and emotional. I'm willing to help support him, but I've got my own priorities and needs. I pick up the phone and reluctantly dial.

"Hello, Jason," my mother says coolly. "I hope you haven't spoken to your father."

For a few seconds I can't speak. For a few seconds I'm caught between wanting to cry, wanting to scream and wanting to hang up. I feel childish and weak and petty. I see Sheldon's motorcycle burst into flames on an oil slick.

"No," I say slowly, clearing my throat. "I haven't talked to anyone."

"Good." She sounds relieved. "I knew you were on my side. If he thinks he can sell that house without compensating me for my years of devotion, he is sorely mistaken. This is just like on Oprah. She had a show about women who were mentally and financially abused. No, it's not like physical abuse, but it's just as traumatic. I realize I'm a victim. I can admit it. I'm not afraid."

I see Sheldon's hand reach into the pizza box and re-emerge with a crust.

"Listen, Mom," I begin, whispering, "I'm not really concerned about the house or the money or what happens between you two."

"Jason! You're on his side!"

"Mom—"

"I'm your only mother!"

I close my eyes. "Mother," I begin again, "I'm not taking sides. I love you both."

The words linger in my head for a few seconds as I try to equate love with the way I feel about my family. I feel rage, contempt, sadness, embarrassment—and I do have to admit that love is in the mix somewhere. But it's a convoluted emotion, a swirling confusing love mixed with impediments.

"Jason, your mother loves you too. But she has to eat. You don't want me going to a soup kitchen with all those filthy bums and heroin addicts, do you? I see it all the time. You don't want that, do you?"

"Oh, for crissake," I blurt.

"Jason!"

I thumb the black lever on my toaster as I take a few seconds to compose myself.

"Are you calling to help me?" she says finally.

"Sheldon can't live at my apartment. I'd like to help you

and Dad torment one another over a stupid house, but I'm afraid I've had other things on my mind. I have a very small place and my own life. Someone else has to take care of him."

The line is silent. I look back toward the living room. The game has been paused. Motorcycles are suspended in mid-motion, the riders bending awkwardly at a corner, leaning against gravity. I'm clenching my fist so hard that my knuckles are white and taut.

"That's a pretty selfish attitude, now, isn't it?" my mother says evenly. "If we all had that attitude, where would we be? Wouldn't life be grand if everyone looked after me? Sheldon is old enough to stay with you for a while."

She gives a bitter laugh. I hold the phone away from my ear and grind my teeth. When I put the receiver to my ear again there is only deep silence.

"So your father isn't taking care of Sheldon?"

"No, I guess not. He hasn't called or shown up."

I'm startled when she lets out a quiet yelp.

"We've got him," she says. "Do you realize what this means?"

Sheldon is now standing in the kitchen doorway, watching me.

"We've got him."

"What do you mean?"

"He isn't the guardian. If Sheldon isn't living with your father, then we're taking care of him. Any lawyer can see that. And if we're taking care of him, your father has to pay support."

She laughs on the other end. My mouth is dry and my head feels light. The fluorescent bulb above me seems to weigh on my shoulders, pushing my lungs into my stomach.

"What do you mean?" I ask again.

"Jason, I'll speak to my lawyer today. He'll nail your father for support and we'll split the payments. I knew you were on my side."

And then she hangs up. She doesn't say goodbye. She doesn't ask to speak to Sheldon. She doesn't ask how we are.

For a second I feel what my father must have felt the night he hit her, the night their marriage ended. They had been out with their friends Dan and Linda, playing euchre and drinking and being the asses they always were with their friends. I don't know what set the argument off, but it was worse than usual, bad enough for them to move behind their bedroom door. My father never hit her except this one time, one series of punches that split her lip.

I can barely breathe.

I remember my father crying and apologizing, banging on the closed door of the bathroom, asking to be let in. My mother stormed out and my father tried to stop the car from leaving the driveway by gripping the driver's side mirror, his feet sliding beneath him. I remember hiding in my room, trying to make everything disappear.

Sheldon stares at me in silence, then lifts a pizza crust to his mouth. He takes a bite, chews it methodically. I look at the clock above the table and imagine for a second that I am wearing surgical scrubs, that a flat line is droning in my ears.

Sheldon wanders back toward the couch.

"I could've told you so," he says.

15

On Wednesday at noon Noel strolls into the bar and hops on a stool.

"Sarsaparilla, barkeep," he says in his best Wild West voice, tapping his knuckles against the bar. "And don't give me no fuss."

"Didn't I used to be in a band with you?" I say.

He forces a smile. "That's what I'm here about." He pushes a magazine clipping toward me.

"Another brilliant idea?"

I read the clipping twice before I respond. I have this urge to break into frenetic laughter. Noel is watching me with a smile on his face.

"First of all, dude," I say, handing back the slip of paper, "I'm having way too bad a week to dive into anything so potentially humiliating. Second of all, you can't be serious."

"What's with you and the word *dude*? That's my word. And yes, I'm totally serious. I see this as an excellent opportunity to advance our careers in one quick and painless thrust. You've got to trust me."

"The five most dangerous words in the English language."

"Sorry about your bad week. Jan's filled me in on recent events. How's Sheldon holding up?"

"He's OK. And I don't mind having him around for a bit. He's a quiet enough kid, doesn't complain, but he does eat a lot of Pop-Tarts. Of course, he can't stay. Who's going to buy him clothes and shoes and make sure he eats vegetables? As my father is fond of pointing out, I can't even afford to take care of myself."

My throat feels dry as I think about all the things

necessary to support a kid, especially a teenager. Besides food and clothing, there are expenses like driver's education classes and spending money, and he'll need to be driven places and picked up, and he needs a room of his own, and someone has to check his homework and listen to stories about his *totally bogus* math teacher. These are the same thoughts that have sprung up the last two nights after I've turned off the light. I've barely slept.

"It's strange how quickly things can fall apart," I say.

Noel pushes the clipping back toward me. "Not everything. Maybe this is our wonderwall. Five thousand dollars prize money, record contract . . . I've got a really good feeling about this deal, which is why I've already signed us up."

"We are not entering a fundamentalist Christian talent search," I say.

"Come on."

"None of us even belongs to a church."

"Exactly. There's nothing they can hold against us."

"I used to be an altar boy," I murmur.

"You were until you saw the light and became a fundamentalist Christian. Converts are always the most devoted. Everyone knows that."

I pinch the bridge of my nose.

"Come on," Noel continues, adjusting himself on the stool. "Things at work are slowing down a bit, and I need a break, even if it's just a short road trip over the border. It'll be a blast and we'll have a laugh. And who knows, maybe we'll win."

"Border?"

"American contests always pay the big bucks. The real action is in the States. And Detroit is an amazing rock-and-roll city."

I watch Julia, another recent staff addition, walk from the kitchen with a heaping plate of fries. She strides across the room to where Chad is sitting hunched over an invoice book. She stops and talks to him for a few minutes, both of them laughing. She recently dropped out of college, so we've had a few good conversations about our mutual hatred for school. She's no Jan, but I have mentioned her to Noel a few times.

"She's one hot chick," Noel muses, watching them. "Imagine how much she'll want you when we win this talent search and get a record contract."

I push the magazine clipping back.

"There's a whole subculture, Jay. I looked it up on the Internet. If we put on a good show, we stand to be the next Anointed, or Bloodgod, or Rock of Ages, or even X-Sinner. There's Christian punk and soul and rock-and-roll. And there's a big controversy about whether Christian rock is the music of the Lord or the music of Satan. I can see both points of view, of course. Tyler will be happy. He's always wanted to be controversial."

"Listen, Noel, I've spent most of my life trying not to be engaged in anything remotely controversial, and I don't plan to end that streak now."

"Then I fear you'll never taste the Lord's fruits. Or see yourself on a CD cover. Think of it, we change a few lyrics, rock hard, and see if we're blessed."

Leave it to Noel to see the positive potential in the utterly absurd. I watch Julia walk back across the room toward the kitchen. Noel dumps a bag of pretzels into a wicker basket.

"And who knows, if Julia heard you singing 'No, Not the Highway' for God, she might fall for you."

"That song is about the dog I had when I was ten," I say.

"That song is about losing your relationship with the Lord, only to find it when you contemplate resurrection."

I groan.

"You've got to trust me."

I wave my dishtowel at him as a burly guy in a Montreal Canadiens jacket comes to the bar. "No, I don't."

I serve hockey jacket a tall rye and Coke and he leaves me a nickel tip. I burn the back of his head with my atomic laser eyes. Usually hockey jackets are good for a couple of quarters, because they've been in my position and know how much a bartender depends on tips. Doctors and professionals are the ones you have to be wary of. I had a doctor tip me seven pennies once, meticulously picking through a handful of change to extract all the insulting copper bits.

"Do I look like an indentured servant?" I ask Noel. "A five-cent tip! What am I supposed to do with five cents?"

I say the words a bit too loudly. When hockey jacket glances back at the bar, I hurl the coin into the garbage bin with a ringing clatter.

"You know what you need," Noel says.

"What?"

"The healing power of our Lord and saviour Jesus Christ."

16

Entering a Christian rock competition is clearly silly, but at the moment it seems to be the only way to get the band to reunite. If nothing else, I suppose we can use the practice and experience to build momentum toward more legitimate opportunities. I agree to Noel's scheme, and a week later we're in my rusty, cramped Hyundai on our way to Detroit to pick up our registration package and assorted fundamentalist propaganda. A tape of eighties classics is playing on the stereo. New Order is pumping out "Bizarre Love Triangle."

When we pick up Tyler, he's on his front step, shivering and looking irritable. Tyler is not a morning person. Today his hair is blond with purple tips. He's wearing a lumberjack jacket, brown cords and yellow shoes.

"Been waiting long, Ty?" I ask.

"Long enough," he mumbles. "I don't see why we have to take this car."

He glares at Noel, who recently bought a brand-new cherry red Saturn, fully equipped with a five-CD changer and Dolby speakers.

"I'm protecting my investment," Noel says.

"You're insured."

"I'm protecting it against wear and tear. Do you know how damaging highway travel can be on a car?"

"Isn't that why you buy a car?"

Noel fumbles for a justification.

"I'm a city driver. And besides, I'm pretty sure Detroit is the stolen car capital of the United States. Dude, why risk it?"

I accelerate sharply in the hopes of cutting off the conversation. We will never win a contest for the world's most mature band. Jan fiddles with the stereo. I've been meaning to get a new one, but my list of items to buy is long and a sound system is not as big a priority as an iron that doesn't leave rust stains.

"Ideally, Tyler," Noel says, "you could have driven us all in your mother's minivan. Right now we could be cruising on those quilted seatcovers and ergonomically correct hemorrhoid pillows."

Jan and I burst into laughter. Tyler's mom has added a few home-craft touches to the family van that embarrass him to no end.

"Those are ordinary seat cushions," Tyler says. "And the van is being used today. Her club is entered in a homebrew competition and she's in charge of transporting a couple hundred litres of beer."

Sheldon, as usual, is caught in the middle of the argument. He's hunched between Noel and Tyler with his hands squished penguin-like on his lap. He's been spending too much time alone in the apartment lately and I thought the trip would do him good. Jan flips out the cassette and takes advantage of the collective captivity of the car to expose us to her latest musical find.

"I'm not listening to this," Tyler grunts.

"You are unless you want to crawl up here with your puny body and change the tape," Jan says.

"What is this horrible mess?"

"They're called Lund. They're Scandinavian."

"Since when have you jumped on that bandwagon?"

Jan ignores Tyler, who sulks in the back seat. I'm not completely hot on Jan's music either, but I pretend to like it as a sort of bonding exercise. If you want someone to fall for you, you definitely have to like the same music.

"Someone should tell the lead singer she's not Björk—"

"Is anyone else nervous about today?" I ask, cutting Tyler off.

No one responds.

"What if they ask us skill-testing questions about the Ten Commandments or about who begot who after David offed the big guy with the slingshot. What was his name?"

"Hercules," Jan says.

"And Noah built the ark, right?"

"Uh-huh," Jan murmurs. "Because there was no room at the inn." She cackles quietly.

"You're hilarious, Jan. Aren't you even a bit nervous?"

"Well, if it's a scam to recruit us or convert us or do whatever, I'm gone. If anyone asks if I'm saved, I'm out the door and into the nearest pub."

"If anyone offers me grape Kool-Aid, I'll be right behind you," Noel adds.

"Very tasteful," I say. "I'm sure these people take their beliefs very seriously. I know I would if I believed in anything. And I'd probably have a belief system if I had caring, compassionate, sensitive friends."

"Caring, compassionate friends," Jan says, "wouldn't know the words to any Smiths songs. And that's borderline criminal."

"Shoplifters of the world unite."

"And compassionate people would never listen to the Ramones, or get excited about a remastered Pixies CD. They might get weepy to hear the Eagles are doing another tour. Are those the sort of people you want to cavort with?"

"Sensitive people don't cavort," I say.

"Sorry, are those the sort of people you want to spend quality time with?"

"It might be an interesting change."

"Well, then, this is perfect," Noel says. "Jesus freaks are always looking to be caring and compassionate, even if they have to firebomb an abortion clinic to do it."

Tyler is staring out the window, refusing to take part in our conversation except to tell us from time to time that the music is atrocious.

Maybe I need to feed my spiritual side. I've been to church a couple times, for weddings and funerals and one rather disturbing baptism. Apparently no one told the baby what a sacred moment his baptism was, because as we all stood around pretending to be sombre he filled his diaper with an atomic poo. I'm talking mustard gas spreading through the tiny, stuffy chapel. His parents were visibly horrified, but I figure if God has any sense of humour whatsoever, He probably had a good chuckle.

From my experience people go to church for one of four reasons: they're old and the pressure is on to hedge their bets for the afterlife; they were raised in the church and going is a habit; they want a traditional wedding and one of the accessories is a church; or they're really unsure about their lives and are desperate for a higher power to sort out problems they can't control.

As for me, I haven't reached the desperation stage yet. I doubt any dogma is going to settle my nerves. But I *am* looking for some answers.

"Last night I fought a very strong urge to call the Psychic Friends 1-900 hotline," I say.

Jan raises her eyebrows. "So what stopped you? Fear of the unknown? Or was it some semblance of pride?"

"Neither. They're just really expensive, and I'd rather spend my money on CDs."

"Ah," she says. "Now you have attained true wisdom. The CD litmus test is never wrong."

Noel unveils four Cuban cigars he has purchased to celebrate our foray into competitive music. He passes a chocolate cigar to Sheldon, who unwraps the silver foil and eats the bar in two bites. Jan and Tyler tuck their gifts away for later, but Noel and I light up even though it's nine-thirty in the morning.

"So, Sheldon," Noel begins, "how's school going?"

"He doesn't go to school," I say.

Shel glares at me in the rear-view mirror.

"So what do you want to be when you grow up?" Tyler asks. "One of those street people?"

"Tyler . . ."

"I'm not going to end up like a street person," Sheldon mumbles.

"Well, do you have another plan? Lotto tickets? Maybe you can become one of those lowlifes at red lights who runs a greasy squeegee across my perfectly clean windshield. They're a great contribution to society."

"*Tyler* . . ."

He looks at me defiantly. "What? I'm taking an interest in the kid's life, which is more than your parents have ever done. Isn't that right, Sheldon?"

Sheldon shrugs. I rub my temple and rotate my neck. True, Tyler knows more about my family life than anyone, but I don't comment on his workaholic father, because I can respect certain boundaries. I roll down the window to let out some of the cigar smoke.

"You hoping to live in a men's shelter or are you more interested in a tent city?"

"Tyler!"

"What? I'm trying to rescue your brother from a life of searching for the perfect grate on a cold autumn night. At least I'm part of the solution. Do you not even try to get the kid to go to school? Sheldon, you really should be thinking about university by now, or at least college."

I accelerate and pull into the passing lane. I'm not Sheldon's father. I'm not even his legal guardian. I can't make him do anything he doesn't want to do.

"Dad does this," Sheldon mutters in the background.

"Does what?"

"Drives really fast when he's pissed off."

"Shut up, Sheldon."

"He does that too."

We arrive at the border in aggrieved silence, pay our toll at an automated booth and pull up to a customs window. I roll down the window, releasing a great cloud of sickly sweet smoke.

"Ask for two Big Macs and a large Coke," Jan says. "I dare you."

A woman in a cap and faux cop uniform punches our licence number into the computer and leans out her little window. I wave smoke away from my face as she makes chitchat, asks where we're going and why. She looks a bit skeptical when I tell her we're on our way to register with a religious organization. She leans down to my window and glances into the car.

"Are you all Canadian?"

We respond yes, except for Tyler, who is huddled unhappily against the window, staring aimlessly at the way station. The customs agent stares at him through the grey-purple haze.

"How about you, sir?"

"Yes, I'm Canadian," he says tersely. "But I think the guy in the trunk is from Haiti."

I feel the blood drain from my face. The customs agent is not impressed. Although Tyler is clearly only being an ass, we have to pull up to the main hut for a vehicle search.

"I'm voting for a body cavity search for some people," Jan says. She pokes Tyler in the chest.

"This is ridiculous. I made a harmless joke."

"The world has changed, Tyler," Noel says. "You know that for a fact. Nothing is taken lightly anymore, dude."

"But the customs service should still recognize humour. You'd think they'd want a bit of stimulation sitting in those ice boxes all day watching senior citizens trying to smuggle polyester pants and Metamucil into the country."

I remember as kids, when the American and Canadian dollars were closer to equal, we used to go shopping across the border. My parents would buy cheap American gas, watery beer and groceries. They'd buy me clothes from a big factory-seconds store, and I'd be in the back of the car wearing three T-shirts, a sweater and two pairs of pants. I'd wear old shoes across the border and new ones back. My father would buy a glut of snack food and we'd always open a tin of Pringles in the car, passing them back and forth until they were gone and our mouths were parched from excess sodium. He'd get so excited when we got across the border without paying duty, a supreme achievement. He would gently poke my mother's leg and say, "What do you think of that? I should have been in the CIA." My mother would giggle and act impressed and proud of him. One time he bought firecrackers, and before we got back to the border we parked in an empty lot by the lake and set them off. I remember the acrid smell and the plumes of smoke cascading over the water.

A serious-looking man our age comes to the car with a clipboard. Because I own the car, I have to stand next to him as he searches. He pats down the seats, runs his hand under the dash and points to a pile of envelopes and wrappers on the floor.

"Sorry, I haven't had a chance to clean lately," I say. "I've been pretty busy."

"Open that," he says.

I open an envelope; he glances inside, then moves on. He searches the trunk, looks under the car and then instructs me to open the hood.

"So, what's the worst thing you've ever found?" I ask.

He unscrews my windshield wiper fluid and smells.

"The usual," he says. "An hour ago we caught a car with several kilos of marijuana. Their back seat was very hard and when we pulled back the fabric all the stuffing had been replaced with drugs wrapped in cellophane."

He writes something on his clipboard.

"That's impressive."

"And every now and again we'll get a biker carrying a gun. These things happen."

He hands me a sheet of paper.

"OK, you're clear. But you've been issued with a warning. If you imply you have contraband in the future, you can be fined up to five thousand dollars and face a prison sentence."

"You're kidding."

He shakes his head.

"God forbid anyone make a joke around here," Tyler mutters.

I drive very slowly and carefully the rest of the way through the no man's land between Canada and the U.S. Traffic is thick and the duty-free shops are teeming with people carrying out bags of booze and boxes of cigarettes.

You always know when you've entered the United States.

The signs change from metric to miles and there are flags on every second home. A part of me envies Americans their patriotism and pride. We pass by a trailer park.

"Hey, Sheldon, do you remember going camping at Uncle Gary's cottage?"

"No."

My father's brother has a cottage not far from Windsor. We used to go there every summer until he and my father had a falling-out. They're similar men in terms of attitudes and prejudices, but Gary did all right for a few years selling real estate. I think his success was part of the problem, as it tends to be within families for some reason. The schism between Dad and Gary was long in coming and eventually blew up when my father drunkenly hooked Gary's wife with a misguided cast while they were fishing for trout. I don't know all the details, I just remember the shouting. We never went to the cottage again, and I felt like a big piece of my summer had been obliterated. I know my father missed going too, because he would mope around the house on hot weekends and debate calling Gary to sort out the mess. But he never did pick up the phone.

"My family never went camping or to a cottage," Jan says. "Our idea of roughing it was a roadside Howard Johnson's without a swimming pool."

"What about you, Noel?"

"My parents like their amenities," he says. "My mother needs a plug for her hair drier."

"I'd rather be shot than camp," Tyler says. "We vacationed in Europe."

Noel, Tyler and Jan have an animated conversation about well-heeled family vacations in warm climes, to which my brother and I don't contribute. I don't even know if Sheldon has ever been on vacation. He was only one or two when my parents split, and my father was never much for leaving his own neighbourhood. I'm a bit depressed that no one else is able to join in my memories of campfires and swimming with leeches.

We hit traffic on the outskirts of Detroit and are soon lurching in the middle of a metal line-up of Chryslers and Fords. My unpatriotic Hyundai stands out, and I'm sure we're a prime target for a random act of violence. But then, my car is so battered and rust-eaten that abusing it would be pointless.

We creep through an area with which I'm not familiar. The houses are small and homey, and there is a car in every driveway and a flag on every pole. I think we're in blue-collar territory, where families who work the production lines gather in solidarity. This is union country. My father would thrive here. I look at the other faces in the silent car and see that everyone is staring at our surroundings. Jan's father is an agriculture official in Ottawa, Tyler's father is a university professor, and Noel's father is a dentist. This is another world to them.

We check the address and pull up in front of a non-descript community centre.

"OK, everybody, get out and act saved."

We're met near the door by a woman with short, limp hair whose face conveys an eerie calm that does nothing to help us feel at ease. She looks like a Dali rendition of a suburban housewife—far away, unfettered by time. She is holding a 1950s-style TV dinner tray topped with small orange mounds.

"Sweet potato?" she offers.

"Sorry?" Jan says.

The woman's eyes drift to the corner of the room before coming back into focus. I get the feeling that greeting people at the front door is not her task of choice.

"It's a dessert," she says.

"You're joking."

"Moses ate them in the desert. He ate them for many years while leading his people, then as he stood on the outskirts of the Promised Land he died."

"Poor bastard," Tyler murmurs. "But I suppose there isn't much to eat in a desert."

We decline the sweet potato and head into the main hall, which is bustling with people, most of whom are teenagers standing together in the far corner. I expect them to be vibrant and gleeful and perceptibly full of God's love, but quite frankly they look like normal kids—bored and self-conscious. A large woman in a floral dress is darting around like a hummingbird issuing instructions and suggestions.

A cardboard sign reads in Magic-Marker bubble letters: REGISTRATION PACKS. Two hippie-like people are lingering in front of the main desk.

"And the Fergus Family were wonderful last year. Those girls!" the woman is saying joyously. She is wearing a flowing robe and her long, straggly hair looks like it gets washed in the river every other week using natural oat and honey shampoo made in a barn. She has a strange vibe, all peace and love, but with over-dilated pupils suggesting either too much speed or slight dementia.

"God love them," the man says.

They notice us. The woman smiles gently and steps forward, corralling Tyler in a hug.

"God bless you," she says, kissing his cheek.

"Thanks," Tyler says, visibly stunned. He looks cautiously at Noel and me.

"Our Father who art in heaven," Jan says as the woman grabs hold of her and pulls her into a hug.

The woman proceeds to hug each of us in turn, while the man stands back and smiles peacefully. I imagine some sort of swapping-for-Jesus communal key-party deal happening with these two, but quickly put it out of my mind.

"We're Ann and Roger. The Mowatts. We love God. Roger's an engineer."

I'm disappointed that their names aren't something more fitting, like Peace Mother Flower and David Jeremiah Moses.

"We're Trailer," Noel says, sweeping his hand to indicate the band collective. "We rock for Jesus."

"So are you here for the blessed competition?" the woman behind the desk asks, shuffling papers.

"Oh, yeah, that's us," Noel says. "I'm *Noah* Michaels."

"Of course," the woman behind the table says joyously. "I'm Beatrice."

Beatrice shuffles through a box beside her chair, then passes Noel a manila envelope.

"So do we fill something out?" Noel says, looking sideways at the papers in front of Beatrice.

"Oh yes," she says. "You need to fill out this form. Just basic information. Have you done missionary work abroad, that sort of thing." She shuffles her papers together and licks the end of her pen. "So your name is Trainer?"

"Trailer," Noel corrects.

Beatrice wrinkles her nose.

"We're not married to the name," I say.

"That might be a good thing," she says. "But you never know. Denomination?"

Noel looks confused. "Sorry?"

"Your denomination? What is it?"

"Oh, right," he says, nodding. "We paid in Canadian dollars."

Beatrice laughs uproariously, so much that the floral woman and the group of morose teenagers all stop to look our way. I notice that several more people have entered the hall and are milling around behind us. A few have long, stringy Foo Fighters hair and are wearing leather pants and black shirts with the words "Jesus Loves You."

Twenty minutes and three coffees later we're ushered downstairs into a sparse room.

"Hey, Noah," I say. "All these years I've been calling you by the wrong name and you never once corrected me."

"Just chill," he says. "I'm looking for any advantage we can get. Besides, Noah was a dude. He saved your ass from the flood."

A stern man in an orange sweater is standing in front of a blackboard. He glares at his notes.

"OK, everyone, quiet, please," he says to the silent room. "It's time to get started. For those of you who don't know me, I'm Pastor Peterson. You can call me Pastor if you like."

He sweeps his hand across the green blackboard and steps back. There are three points written on the board in yellow chalk.

1. Lyrics must contain correct doctrine
2. The Word is more important than the music
3. No special effects

"Now, most importantly, the lyrics for all songs entered in this year's competition must be expressed clearly. You and I both know how misleading some metaphors can be. There must be no room for question, doubt or misinterpretation. For example—I love Jesus, Jesus is good, Jesus will save us, all praise to Him. This is very clear and edifying."

Tyler is fidgeting. This is clearly strike one. All of our lyrics will have to be changed, especially anything he's penned.

"Last year we had a bit of trouble with the band Heaven's Kitchen, who entered a song comparing God's love with a volcano. Well, I don't have to tell some of you the uproar that song caused. We had a lot of anti–Christian-rock groups arguing that a volcano is a symbol much closer to Satan. In retrospect I think we can all see their point."

"The dirty blasphemers," Jan whispers.

I look around the room and see that everyone is listening intently.

"Second, the rhythm and the beat of your music cannot overpower the words. Your melody must be simple and must only serve to support the words that you are using to praise the saviour. Your songs should be strictly Christian, with no heavy guitars, extended solos or musical tricks."

Tyler raises his hand. "Sorry, sir?"

"Pastor."

"Right. How about some breaking glass?"

The pastor looks confused. I close my eyes and wonder how fast I'll be able to get up the stairs and to the car should the congregation decide to stone us.

"What do you mean?"

"What if the sound of breaking glass was used as part of the song?"

The pastor shakes his head. He taps point number three on the board with his stick of chalk. "There should be no special effects. And the rhythm of your songs shouldn't compel anyone to gyrate or boogie. People may choose to sway, perhaps even to dance quietly and respectfully, but there should at no time be an urge to twist about the waist or make any sort of thrusting motion. Is that clear?"

"Sir, trust me, I would never try to compel anyone to gyrate. But what if the glass was symbolic of an individual's fragile and multifaceted nature?"

The pastor shakes his head. "There's no need for symbols. You can simply state, 'I am weak.' That's simple and no one will be confused."

"But say, just for example, we wanted to be nouveau riche?"

"I don't understand."

"Well, say we want to get post-Revelations with the revival crowd—you know, challenge and stimulate our audience."

The room stirs restlessly. I feel the faint sensation of adrenaline being released as my body prepares itself for fight or flight. I want to reach out and physically shut Tyler up.

"There is to be no stimulation whatsoever," the pastor continues. "Perhaps you don't understand that when we deviate from our set standards we are opening the door for Satan to slip in and betray our intentions. You don't want Satan to play your music, do you?"

"It's only a few seconds."

"That's all Satan needs. Eve only needed a few seconds to betray mankind."

Jan raises her hand. "I object to that."

"We all do, of course. She got man cast out of the garden and condemned us all to original sin. She ruined mankind."

For a second I think Jan is going to choke. She's about to

protest when Noel places his hand on her arm. She frowns and sits back.

"Obviously we don't have time to review everyone's material, but please keep these rules in mind and read the literature I'm handing out. Should you fail to follow these instructions, we will not hesitate to cast you out of the competition."

We're each given small packages. I pull out a wristband with WWJD stencilled on it. I show it to Noel.

"Any clue?"

He shrugs. "OK, kids," Noel says, getting up from his chair. "Time to get back to the pagan world before my ass bursts into flames."

I trudge behind the group, once again thinking there must be another way to get a break in the music world.

"Excuse me?"

A cute blonde is smiling at me. She's standing by the door holding a black suede bag that is embroidered with a cross and the word "Love."

"Oh, hi," I say.

"So you guys are from Windsor, too? I've never seen you around the church before. What's your band's name?"

"Well, we might be Trailer, but who knows."

She looks puzzled.

"They said something about us changing our name," I explain.

"Oh yeah, they do that. All you have to do is explain why it's biblical—like, you trail behind Christ on his pilgrimages."

"Right."

"What *does* it mean?"

"I have no idea."

"That could be a problem. I'm Natasha."

"Jay," I say, thrusting my hand out from under my package.

"I see you've got your info pack. Jeez, every year they give the same stuff. I mean, how many What Would Jesus Do wristbands does a person need?"

She tugs up her black sleeve to reveal a W W J D wristband made with crushed fine diamonds.

"Nice," I say. "The church gave that to you?"

She laughs. "No, of course not. It's a present from my ex-boyfriend. For Christmas. He's training to be a pastor."

"Really? That's great."

She looks at her watch and sighs. She has a certain young impatience. She's definitely in her early twenties.

"I've got to go now, but maybe you'd like to get together some time and talk about music? I'm always interested in hearing about new bands."

I feel my face flush and my body tense. I have no intention of interacting with real believers and exposing myself as the pariah I am. Of course, I also tend to accommodate assertive people.

"Yeah. Maybe."

"I think bands should support one another, because we're such a small community. My band is Upon This Rock. We're Christian reggae, which is pretty controversial. Have you heard of us?"

I shake my head.

"Oh well, maybe someday we'll be famous. Give me your number and we'll get together."

Her eagerness is overwhelming. I give her my number. I hope she won't call.

"I'll definitely call you," she says, winking as she slips away.

17

Janice and Tyler are hanging out near the bar, nursing a couple of drinks and waiting to see the band that has replaced us. Casino Night has arrived and soon our stage will be usurped by Stoned Quarry.

"This crowd is nothing like our crowd," Tyler says. "From an evolutionary standpoint, I'd be curious to see how many of these people still have tail stumps."

"It's not that bad," I say, wiping the bar with a white towel. "Although I will say that gambling has attracted a new clientele. I haven't seen a lot of these faces."

"Is it true the bar is giving free tetanus shots in the bathrooms?" Janice asks with a smile.

"Zip it, doll," Chad hisses, striding by the bar.

"Great way to get our gig back," Tyler mutters, sipping his beer.

The brief lull ends when a porky, greasy little guy waddles up and orders two bottles of Labatt Maximum Ice, a disgustingly sludgy brew that boasts the highest alcohol percentage of any North American beer. Chad has ordered it especially for tonight. He tips me two quarters and smiles widely.

"If only I'd brought my mace," Jan says as the man walks away.

"It's not that bad," I say again. "Everybody's entitled to a bit of fun."

"Populist," Tyler mutters.

Tyler is annoyed at having to interact with the proletariat. I wish Noel were here to balance the discussion and bring a bit of levity, but he's working late. Janice helps me by picking up glasses and chitchatting whenever someone looks like they're on the verge of becoming overly impatient at the bar. The tip jar is swimming. I go to the beer fridge to get another case of Export. When I open the big steel door, I'm met by a waft of cold air and thick smog of pot smoke.

"Don't let it out!"

I step inside and see John sitting on a keg with a large homemade bong in his hand. The rest of his band is sitting on stacked cases. John smiles at me.

"We're warming up," he says.

Everyone laughs.

"We rock."

Back at the bar I think that if I had to go on stage after a session like that I'd be dead. My hands would never find the right frets.

"The big tacky sign says karaoke," Janice says, sucking on a wedge of lime and running glasses through the dishwasher.

"You shouldn't do that. Lime juice will ruin your teeth."

She clenches the lime between her teeth and flashes me a bright green wedge smile.

"Who's Lady Astor?" she asks, indicating Julia, running around the bar.

"One of Chad's waitresses," I say. "And don't encourage them to start karaoke. Someone in this crowd is bound to like Dwight Yoakam."

"You like her?"

"Who?"

Jan motions toward Julia, who is serving a basket of battered vegetables to a group of scruffy-looking guys. I feel a nervous flutter in my chest. I wonder if she's been talking to Noel.

"Lady Astor," she says.

Janice's hair is pulled into pigtails and her cheeks are a crimson hue. She looks Alpine, like I imagine Heidi would look if she grew up and worked in a bar. Very sexy.

"She's nice."

"She's cute," Jan emphasizes. "You do think she's cute, don't you?"

"Yeah," I say, ripping open the beer case. "She's cute."

Jan turns back to the dishwasher and feeds it another couple of glasses. I wonder if Noel has told her about my good conversations with Julia and that I think she's attractive.

"Why don't you go for her?" she asks casually.

"I don't want to go for her."

Jan's face is illuminated by the glare of the three hundred-watt bulbs that hang above us. The bulbs used to be covered, but the shade got broken a few years ago and has never been replaced. Now the bar glows like a lighthouse. She smirks.

"Why not?"

We're interrupted by Chad's voice booming over the PA system and by a guy in a wrestling T-shirt who steps to the bar and orders tequila—straight, no ice, because he's not a pussy.

"I've had the privilege of seeing this band develop and jell over the past six months," Chad announces.

John sniffles loudly into the microphone. He appears to be having some trouble getting his guitar plugged in. The tall bass player with Slash hair leans over and helps.

"Jean jacket," Tyler says, shaking his head. "I can't believe we've been replaced with a band that wears denim. How humiliating."

"I know that years from now everyone here tonight will

be telling their kids that they saw their first performance," Chad is saying. "This band is hot and cutting edge. They are Stoned Quarry!"

He steps off stage and a tepid round of applause trickles from the crowd. The gambling tables near the stage are closed, but the back of the bar is still hopping.

John leans toward the mike.

"Um, hey. Thanks for showing up tonight. We're really geared to get in your heads and mess you up. We're going to start with a number we call 'Death Tiger.'"

They play loudly. I don't know how else to describe the spectacle unfolding under the nervous white lights. I don't want to be overly critical, because this is their first performance, but they play like they've never picked up instruments before. Their bass player constantly stops, grimaces and then gets back into the rhythm. Their tempo is erratic, they miss their marks, and on at least two songs I'm sure they're playing in different keys. John's fingers fumble over the chords, and when he sings his voice is almost inaudible. He mumbles the down-tempo lyrics and then howls through everything else. Even I feel insulted that we've been replaced by these guys.

At the end of "Death Tiger," Tyler is on his feet clapping wildly.

"They're horrible," he says. "They're absolutely horrible."

John nods at the crowd, obviously pleased with the debut. His eyes are barely open. "The next song," he mumbles, "is our tribute to Santana."

The drummer, a large guy with a bird's-nest tangle of hair, holds up a maraca. Tyler takes a bitter swallow from his beer.

"Why not replace us with a big-screen TV showing a

monster truck rally. Isn't this typical of society. Well, this dump will be sorry when we win the competition."

"If I don't slug that pastor guy," Jan says, swirling her beer. "I thought religion would have evolved by now. Eve ruined mankind . . ."

"No hitting," I say.

"What about biting?"

We laugh and make eye contact and for a few long, conscious seconds neither of us pulls away. I wipe my dishtowel across the bar and feel something buzzing in my chest.

By the end of the first set, my relief bartender arrives and I'm free. The room is half empty as the night falls to hardcore drinkers and hangers-on. It's like we're on the *Titanic* and all of the first-class passengers have sailed off in the lifeboats, leaving the riffraff to linger in the smoky air as the bow descends inch by inch. Jan and I stand near the bar with a collection of drinks we've commandeered for ourselves. John shuffles over.

"What'd you think? Pretty good, eh?"

I shake his hand. My ears are still ringing and I feel worn out from the constant bombardment of sound waves. I feel like I have a chunk of ice lodged in my sinus cavity.

"Yeah," I say. "You rocked."

I look to Jan for support. She smiles at John.

"Really, really . . . OK," she says.

John puts his hand between Jan and me and leans against the bar, facing her and blocking me out.

"So what songs did you dig?"

Jan's eyes flit to me nervously. I slide her drink along the bar and John steps back, letting me into the dyad.

"Um . . ."

"I liked the one about the submarine," I say.

"'Love Under Water?'"

"Oh yeah."

"Same here," Jan says, sipping her drink. "Very touching."

John snaps his fingers quickly and launches into a high-powered rendition of the chorus. As we step back he performs an impromptu drum solo on the countertop with his fingers, closes his eyes and slowly spreads his arms apart like a symphony conductor.

"They both drown when the torpedoes hit," he says.

"See, I didn't get that part," Jan says.

"It's right at the end. Just before Leo launches into his massive killer solo. Except he sort of missed his mark, but we got it sorted out. You guys didn't notice, did you?"

Jan shakes her head.

Chad steams over. He puts his hand on John's shoulder. "That blew chunks. We're going for karaoke instead of a second set. It sounded like you were torturing farm animals up there."

He walks behind the bar and pours himself a glass of tonic, squeezing in a quarter lime. He puts one foot on a chair and surveys the room, still shaking his head.

"It wasn't that bad," John says, pulling a cigarette out of his pocket. "You've got to remember it's the first show. There were bound to be a few minor glitches."

"Don't talk to me. I'm thinking about all the revenue I've lost by letting you get on that stage. That's the end of live music at the Rose and Crown."

John takes a long suck on his cigarette. He doesn't appear fazed. Jan and I exchange looks, and she turns and walks away. I wonder if she wants me to follow her or if she wants to be alone. I decide I'll let her be. John and I stand in silence by the bar. After a few minutes Chad exhales loudly and steams off.

"Ah, well," John says, staring into the crowd. "Fuck him. So, is your friend single?"

"You like her?" I ask.

"She's pretty hot," he says, nodding. "I wouldn't kick her out of bed." He fidgets with his cigarette. He taps it and puts it to his lips. "If you guys aren't . . ."

"No, we're just friends," I say.

"'Cause I kind of sensed something."

I smile despite myself. If other people sense it, maybe there *is* something. Maybe she digs underachievers. He inhales carcinogens deep into his lungs, pauses, then blows a stream of white through his nostrils.

"Trina in the kitchen said she's got it for you," he says, winking at me.

I laugh and then cough from a sudden inhalation of his smoke.

"Why'd she say that?" I manage to say in a weak, wheezy voice as I try to regulate my breathing.

"The way she was looking at you one day. I told Trina she was crazy. No offence, but that chick is way out of our league."

I don't say anything at first. I want to laugh at the fact that John thinks we're so similar. He's a nice guy, but we're from different planets. His idea of a cultural pursuit is Ozzfest. I can identify with his working-class-hero perspective, but we're clearly not brethren.

"Why's she out of my league?"

John takes a long haul on his cigarette and shrugs. "Oh, you know. Girls like that always want looks and money. Regular, hard-working guys like me and you don't cut it."

"Maybe she's not like that."

"Whatever you want to think. But in my experience a girl like that is a cat. She might play with you for a bit—bat your sorry, no-gold-card mouse ass around for a while—but sooner or later she's gonna find a more interesting toy."

He slaps my shoulder. "But fuck her. We don't need her. There's enough hotties in the bar tonight for both of us. I say we pour booze down some throats and see what happens."

He goes back to the table where his band is sitting with some girls in acid-wash jeans. The entire table looks like they've been frozen since 1987. I watch John chat up a girl with a high, hair-sprayed do. She's wearing white leather boots.

I take a sip of my drink and feel a continental drift between my brain and body. My nose and hands are cadaverously cold.

Tyler sits down beside me.

"I'm going," he says. "Tonight has really opened my eyes. I've seen the true depth and breadth of the world's ugliness."

"I know what you mean."

18

Natasha calls me for five consecutive nights. I'm not used to such attention from the opposite sex.

"Why don't you pick me up and we can go to the youth group coffeehouse?"

My throat feels dry. I'm running out of excuses for why I can't see her.

"I'm steam-cleaning my rugs tonight. I rented a machine from the supermarket. Have you ever rented one? They're really complicated."

She doesn't respond.

"I was taking care of my friend's dog last week and there's hair everywhere. But maybe we can get together one day this weekend. You know, have a coffee and talk music."

"They have coffee at the coffeehouse," Natasha says in a voice that is mocking, but not too mocking.

"Yeah . . . But . . ."

"But nothing. It'll be fun. And don't worry, it's not full-on evangelical ranting like some youth groups, if that's what you're worried about."

It is.

"We get together, read a few Bible passages and eat yummy food. It's fun."

"Well, I've got a bit of a confession to make, actually . . ."

"Great, we'll meet at six and you can confess all you want."

She gives me her address and I hang up the phone. I run a hand through my hair, wondering what would be the best drug to cope with a night of fundamentalist love and wisdom. Oh well, how bad can it be? I scan my wardrobe for something pious and am almost set to go when the doorbell rings.

"What are you wearing?" Tyler says, his face crumpling up.

"What's wrong with it?"

"What's right with it? You look obscenely Italian. No one wears silk shirts anymore. And certainly not with the top two buttons undone."

He shields his eyes from me. As much as I resent Tyler, I wonder if Italian is a good image to project. I don't want to appear papal. Tyler, meanwhile, is wearing a paisley bowling shirt, purple jeans and a purple beret. He looks like a squashed grape.

"I've been doing some research," he begins. "Did you know that Mormons don't drink, dance or take blood transfusions? At least I think it was the Mormons . . . Maybe it was the Jehovah's Witnesses . . . And there's a group in the American South who commune with God by handling poisonous snakes. Every year at least a couple of them die, but they still keep doing it."

"All very helpful, Ty, but I've got to go."

"Where are you going?"

"I have a date. Well, sort of a date."

Tyler arches his eyebrows.

"It's no big deal," I continue. "Remember how I mentioned that I met a girl who's entered the competition? Well, we're going to some sort of youth group meeting."

Tyler claps his hands and springs up. "Excellent. A chance to check out the competition."

"It might be a date, Tyler."

"It's an opportunity, Thompson," he says, smiling coyly. "Besides, if it's a prayer circle you won't get any tête-à-tête time with this girl anyway. And there's a good possibility that her sect doesn't even allow her to be alone with a non-member. Some sects are like that, you know. It's safer if I go with you. And more to the point, I'm feeling bored tonight. What say we two swinging bachelors stir the fundamentalist pot a little."

Part of me wants to argue, but part of me is relieved not to have to go by myself—the whole strength-in-numbers scenario. I agree to let Tyler come along, as long as he behaves, and we part company on the street. I pop *Odelay* into the cassette deck of the bomber and speed off to pick up Natasha.

Tyler is waiting for us when we get to the meeting place, a student home on campus. He is leaning impatiently on his father's Volkswagen. Apparently he has brought a notebook to record any juicy bits for later recounting to Noel and Jan. Religiously sensitive we are not. I can hear their peals of laughter already. I introduce him to Natasha, and he gives her a nod.

"So do you let many *outsiders* into these gatherings?" he asks.

"Sorry?"

"You know, pagans."

Natasha looks toward me tentatively. There's a slight smirk on Tyler's face.

"Of course," she says slowly. "Anyone can drop by. We're always looking to educate people about Christ's love."

The youth group is hopping when we get inside. A girl with long brown hair hurries toward us with a plate of cookies.

"They're homemade apple cinnamon and chocolate chip," she squeaks. "My name is Emily. I'm in poli-sci!"

She smiles perkily and bobs her head back and forth. I take an apple cinnamon from the plate and feel like I've stepped through the looking glass.

"This is Jason," Natasha says, putting her hand on my shoulder. "The one I told you about."

Emily's mouth forms an excited O.

"And this is Trevor."

"Tyler," he says.

"Do you boys want a drink?" Natasha asks. "Coffee, tea, juice . . ."

"I'd love a glass of wine," Tyler says, gazing around the room.

"Oh, we don't drink here."

I notice the sly smile creeping into the corner of his mouth again.

"Our church doesn't promote drinking," Natasha says. "We don't condemn people for doing it, but it causes so many problems that we don't want to support the industry. And let's face a fact, kids these days don't need the peer pressure that comes with the image of drinking. All the advertising is aimed at children."

"I couldn't agree more," he says, biting into his cookie and flipping his notebook open to a blank page. He takes a pen from his chest pocket.

"How about coffee?" Natasha asks.

"I'd love one," Tyler says. "Though I've got some reservations about the exploitation of Brazilian coffee pickers. Do you buy unionized beans?"

My windpipe constricts.

"Tyler," I say gently, "I don't think this is the place to debate consumer politics."

"He has a point," Natasha says. "We build churches in South America and send missions to help dig wells and set up schools. We pray that someday soon South Americans will be able to grow useful crops instead of cash crops bound for selfish Western nations. We only buy fair trade coffee."

I'm surprised. I usually associate churches with persecutions, rules and condemnations, not actual good deeds. I feel vaguely ashamed, but not enough to feel guilty about bringing Tyler and his sarcasm along.

"Do you take cream? Sugar?" she asks.

"Both are fine."

Natasha excuses herself and scampers off to get us some caffeinated cash crop. Emily floats away with her cookies.

"Enjoying yourself?" I ask.

Tyler flashes his pearly whites at me and shrugs. He seems almost giddy with amusement. "Research. If we want to win this competition we must become one with our . . ." He searches for a word. "These people," he says, sweeping his hand to indicate the entire room.

He wanders over to the coffee table and browses through some magazines. The room is filled with university students looking eager and happy. I sense a distinct lack of the cynicism found in most of my friends.

"Disappointing," Tyler murmurs when he comes back. "They're normal magazines—*Tennis World*, *Time*—and an envelope with Ed McMahon's giant head on it."

Natasha is taking her time with the coffees, chatting happily with a group of earnest-looking friends. Her blond hair sweeps around her face as she laughs.

"So, you and Natasha," a voice behind me says. I turn to see a short, stocky girl with blond hair. Why is every fundamentalist female blond?

"I'm Vicky," she says, smiling flirtatiously. "I'm a friend of Natasha's. So what's going on between you two?"

I take a bite of cookie. "Not much. We've just met, really."

"Uh-huh. That's not the story I've heard. Be careful. I know what she's like. She's a friend and all, and a good Christian, no doubt, but the flesh is sometimes weak . . . if you know what I mean?"

"I'm Jay, by the way," I say, thinking how easy it is to dislike someone on a deep, almost molecular level based on only a few sentences.

She winks at me. "I know who you are."

"And this is Tyler."

Tyler nods absently. He is scanning the room and has begun to scribble something into his notebook. Vicky continues to stare at me, holding her cup to her mouth and swaying softly from one foot to the other.

"So, you and Natasha know each other through the youth group?" I venture.

"That is correct," she says. "I can tell you things about dear, sweet, innocent Natasha. I'm a good person to know. I can tell you a lot of things."

"There's nothing going on between us," I say.

"So what do you think of her mother? There's no need for me to mention the alcohol problem, is there? Sad, really. The whole congregation is praying for her."

Suddenly she takes a step away from me, putting her hands out in hug anticipation. "Natasha!" she screams. She steps forward and gathers Natasha into a hug. "I feel like I haven't seen you in ages. Has God been good to you?"

"He has."

Natasha hands me a steaming coffee. "Have you met Jay?"

Vicky beams at me. "I certainly have," she says. "He's wonderful. Really wonderful. You two look really great together."

Natasha nods. I seem to have missed a step in this relationship and don't know whether to feel angry or flattered. The person I'm desperately interested in, Jan, has given me nothing but mixed or unclear signals, and the person I have no interest in, Natasha, has made her intentions unequivocally clear. It would be an amusing irony, if it weren't quite so agonizing.

We're interrupted when an athletic guy begins waving his

hands in the centre of the room. Apparently this is the signal to begin, as everyone finds a chair and settles in expectantly. Dan introduces himself and thanks us all for coming, and we do a grade-school round of the room where we have to stand up and say our names and why we're here.

"My name's Amanda. I've been coming to coffee night for four years. I'm here because I love Jesus Christ."

"My name's Mark. I study engineering and enjoy racquet-ball. Jesus Christ is my mentor and coach. He pushes me hard to be the best I can be."

Tyler licks his lips and stands up. "My name's Tyler. I've never been here before, but I'm overwhelmed by your spirit. You are some of the most staunchly faithful and pleasantly sedate people I have ever met. Thanks for letting me share in your lives. And I thank Jesus for making this coffee taste great."

I expect instant hostility, but the room is awash with smiling, receptive faces. As I look around a thought slowly dawns on me—this is another world, different from mine. This is a world in which it's OK to drive with a Jesus of the highway crucifix hanging from the rear-view mirror, where a "Jesus Loves Me" T-shirt is cooler than Tommy Hilfiger, and where John 3:16 isn't just a silly sign held up by nuts at televised sporting events. This is the real deal, low on cynicism, high on Christ.

"I'm Jay," I say, my chest constricted. "I'm here with Natasha. This is my first time . . ."

I realize I should say more, say something about God and how the spirit has moved me, but I can't formulate the words. We really are interlopers. After a few seconds of awkward silence I look to Natasha. I see Tyler staring at me.

"I believe that there is a God who created all of this. And I believe in goodness."

From the crowd's reaction I have not said enough. I feel awkward stares burning my skin.

The rest of the meeting is a washout. Dan reads a couple of Bible passages and we all sit in silence and look thoughtful for an extended period of time. Some people make some deep and meaningful comments about the text, we all nod, someone asks a probing question, but the whole scene floats over my head.

I drift off into a daydream in which I'm interviewing Sting for Q magazine. We're sitting in the living room of his estate in Bath, surrounded by tasteful art and memorabilia from his years of touring. There's an autographed photo of him and Iggy Pop on a gondola in Venice. *With appreciation, Ig.* I tap the strings of a guitar given to him by George Harrison, and he says later we can plug it in and jam in his studio downstairs. He's wearing a terry-cloth robe and has just finished his daily yoga routine. He asks if I'd like a high-protein yogurt shake and I follow him into the kitchen, where he drops bananas, lemongrass and ginger root into a blender while giving me exclusive details about his next project and the real dirt on the Police years. I ask him where he finds his motivation as we drink our thick shakes. He looks away thoughtfully and tells me about the spirituality of music. After the interview he says I really know my stuff. Maybe I should hang out at his house for the weekend, because he needs help with the lyrics to a few new songs. And maybe I could play on his next album. And there's a tour . . .

Dan turns on a cassette and everyone listens silently to a wistful and folksy song.

When I'm lying in my room
And I think no one can love me
He does
Oh, He does

A few people begin to sway, linking hands and closing
their eyes. It would be quite a Woodstock moment, except
everyone is completely straight. I look over at Tyler, who
moves a Bic lighter back and forth above his head. He winks
at me.

"So what did you think?" Natasha asks me as we're leaving at the end of the night. "Weren't you moved?"

"I was touched," Tyler says. "There's lots of love in that
room. I'll definitely be back."

He flashes the peace sign and climbs into his car. I watch
him dart off, and then I stand in the silence of the street for
several minutes. I feel an overwhelming sense of relief to be
outside again, to be free. The sky is dark and the stars
sparkle with a clear, clean gleam. They seem close enough
to catch, like fireflies you can put in a jar.

"My birthday is coming up and my parents are taking me
out for dinner. Would you like to come?"

I'd rather have my eyeballs sucked out by a vacuum
cleaner.

"Yeah . . . sure. I guess so . . ."

19

"Rock is a sacrifice to the demon god Moloch."

Jan is also doing some research on the new world we've

entered. She's reading a magazine that is opposed to Christian rock as I drink my coffee, watching the usual shopping mall crowd shuffle back and forth along the gleaming tiles, under the dull ache of fluorescent bulbs. You can go to any mall in the world and find the same stores, atmosphere and people. You can breathe the same recycled air. I have a theory that there's a secret factory in Nevada that makes nerve gas and mall people all out of the same chemical compounds. They're mass-producing the pudgy security guards, the elderly speed walkers and the teenagers wearing headbands with wallet chains hanging from their baggy blue jeans.

"Oh, this is good," Jan coos. "The beat of rock-and-roll causes muscles of the female body to contract into orgasm."

She sweeps hair away from her pale, freckled face. I watch her as she reads. Unless you're in love with a person you never stare this hard. And unless you're spying or in a relationship you never get a chance to really look at someone's face, because the intimacy is too telling.

"I might have to stand closer to Tyler's drum set at the next gig," she adds. She catches me looking at her. "What? Do I have ketchup on my face?"

She wipes around her mouth. She probably knows that I'm in love with her. I think I'm pretty obvious, without coming right out and saying anything. I've decided to try a bit of Dwyer-style manipulation to get at her feelings for me.

"So you think I should date Julia from the bar," I say.

"Lady Astor? I didn't say her particularly. I was just wondering why you don't date more."

"Who am I going to date?"

"There's lots of girls. I never see you flirting with anyone."

I laugh. Some people walk past us with plastic trays and wax-coated Pepsi cups sprouting straws.

"I don't think I remember how to flirt," I say. "If I met the right girl I'd probably ask her out. If she wasn't seeing anyone else or dating a whole bunch of different guys."

"Why should that matter?"

"For obvious reasons."

She flips the lid of her latte up and down. The foam has congealed into a thick white paste. This is getting me nowhere. WWTD: *What would Tyler do?* Jan points her cup at me philosophically.

"Unless someone is married, I say go for it. A lot of people are scared to be alone, even girls who appear to be really confident, so they date losers. I'm sure they'd jump ship in a minute for a nice guy who took a chance on asking them out."

"A nice guy. Am I that generic?"

"There's nothing wrong with being a nice guy."

I'm not sure what she's telling me. I want to interpret her words as some sort of cryptic code meaning I should jump over the table and sweep her into my arms, but she's probably just talking. If she were interested, she'd follow her own advice and make a move. Wouldn't she?

A weedy man with a plate of french fries sits down across from us. His hair is receding, his skin sallow. His thin black moustache looks like it's made of felt. I wonder if he's sick. I wonder if I'm seeing a prophecy of what I stand to be if I don't pull myself together. I don't want to be alone anymore, like this poor sap. There's desperation in the way he digs into his junk food, garbage food, poison. I wonder why he's been drawn to the mall. They used to build churches in every community to bring people together. Now they build malls.

"Wanna check out some CDs?" Jan asks, getting up.

"Sure," I say, gathering up the tray.

When I look over, thin man's mouth is full of white potato. He rips open a package of ketchup and sucks directly from the tear.

20

I'm the last to arrive at Tyler's house for the next practice. Jan and Noel are drinking beers downstairs and tuning their guitars. In the corner I see a redhead who looks vaguely familiar. Then I remember her from the intermission of one of our last shows at the Rose and Crown. Nicole.

Tyler walks out of the laundry room wearing a white fleece suit, complemented by a thick ugly yellow tie and his bowling shoes. His hair is now orange.

"Mon dieu," he says. "Nice of you to grace us with your presence."

"Sorry I'm late." I put my case down, throw my jacket haphazardly onto the back of the couch and head to the refrigerator. "What's Mom brewed up for us this week?"

"Scotch ale," Tyler replies, leaning against Nicole's shoulder. She puts her arm around him and looks up with rapture. I'm completely shocked by this new development. "They brew it with peat moss."

I take a bottle of the dark ale, screw off the top and cautiously sniff the contents. It smells smoky. I take a taste.

"Lovely," I say.

I want to ask Tyler about Nicole, but obviously can't.

Practice begins, and Noel and I introduce a new song we've put together, entitled "Have Mercy." So far, writing religious rock hasn't proven terribly different from normal songs. The melody is rock-and-roll with a funk backbeat—a James Brown meets Paul Weller sort of rhythm.

> You think those lips are going to save your soul
> You think heaven's like a cheap road toll
> Don't serve me french fries on those fallen arches
> Or you'll be lost where Satan marches . . .

At this point Noel breaks into a really intense solo, pulling the notes low and holding them long. You can really feel the agony in your chest, as if the strings are screaming to be released.

A string breaks on my guitar and I run out to the car to get a replacement. When I return Nicole is whispering something to Tyler. He whispers back. I look to Jan and Noel, who both shrug.

"We've decided to take a vote on songs for the play list," Noel says, handing me a sheet of paper with potential songs. Most are typed, but there are several additions written in Tyler's scrawl.

"New songs, Ty?" I ask.

He confers with Nicole.

"We think we've struck a nice balance between secular and religious tones."

I read his song titles. "Mona's Moaning," "From Here to My Mind's Eye," "Nero's Dream."

"They're part of an interactive art and music exhibition Nicole and I are arranging. When she heard we were delving into Christian rock she showed me her paintings. She uses a lot of religious symbolism."

"We've already arranged for display space at the library

gallery," Nicole says quietly. "I realize these songs are technically parts of a solo project, but we're willing to lend them to the band as long as our copyrights are protected."

Though I should have expected some bizarre new development from Tyler, this catches me off guard. Nicole smiles at me pleasantly. This is exactly what we don't need, someone else to further complicate the inner workings of the band. I hand the sheet back to Noel, who exhales slowly.

"Band majority dictates what we play," Jan says, reading my mind. "And I'm certainly not going to be a part of another fiasco."

Nicole tugs at Tyler's sleeve and he leans down. She whispers in his ear. Tyler nods and looks at us.

"Given the inherent limitations of democracy," he begins, "we suggest that only qualified writers should be given a vote on the play list."

"Four feet good, two feet bad," Noel says.

"No way, Tyler," I add.

"Fine," he says, putting his arm around Nicole. "We expected a proletariat reaction. We'll decide by secret ballot."

Obviously Tyler has given this matter a great deal of thought, because he walks over to the stereo and comes back with a handful of envelopes. He hands one each to Noel, Jan and me. He walks back to the corner and hands one of the remaining two to Nicole.

"Whoa, flyboy!" Jan says, getting off her chair and stomping over to Tyler. "The only people who vote are the people in the band. These aren't the People's Choice Awards."

Tyler and Jan face off and glare at one another. After a few seconds, Tyler takes a step backwards and puts his arm around Nicole.

"She's a cowriter, therefore she's in the band."

"No," Jan says, taking a step forward. "She isn't. When we play songs by the Cure, it doesn't mean Robert Smith is in the band. Get it? And besides, you've been together for what, like, five minutes?"

"We've been together for nearly two weeks."

"People," Noel says, putting his hands up to regain the peace. "Let's settle down. This is totally bad karma."

Jan walks back to her guitar. She straps it on and takes a sulking swallow of her beer.

"This is totally the wrong attitude to take into a religious competition," Noel continues. "Shame on you sinners. We've got to have the spirit in our hearts, the spirit of grace and forgiveness. Think of this competition as Live Aid or the Rainbow Concert or the Tibetan Freedom Concert—as much as we might hate one another, we're gonna feel love."

"Why don't we pick three songs, one of which can be a new Tyler song?" I say grudgingly.

"A Tyler and Nicole song," Tyler says. "The copyright is Tycole Inc."

21

The next morning, I make Sheldon and myself a large breakfast of eggs, half a pound of bacon and hot buttered toast and vow not to dwell on the band's latest schism. I feel the need to revitalize my life, to start fresh, and the best way is to force positive thoughts through my synapses, no matter how difficult. I sing a medley of my favourite Beatles songs in the shower in operatic voice and then shine my worn Doc Martens. I avoid television news programs, contemplate the beauty of green grass for several enlightening minutes, and eat a ripe, firm apple. Then, as if determined to undermine my karma, my car wheezes to a dead stop at a red light a block from my apartment. I swear long and hard and pound the crap out of the steering wheel.

A large man in overalls comes and hooks my car up to his tow truck, and we drive in slow silence along the quiet streets. He has one tanned arm resting on the window base and is humming to Willie Nelson playing on the cassette deck.

"You a big Willie fan?" I ask.

"Willie was country before country was good," he says.

"Did you know he wrote 'Crazy' for Patsy Cline?" I say. "He was a poor songwriter living over a laundromat in Nashville. And he had a different name. He changed his name to Willie Nelson to sound more country."

He looks at me approvingly. "Ain't that something," he says. "Poor Patsy. She was a good one."

He starts to sing "Crazy," his voice crackling with enthusiasm.

"I want to be a songwriter," I say. I don't know why I tell him this. Maybe I just need to vocalize my ambition to keep myself from losing all hope and falling into real depression. My driver slips his right hand out of his glove and offers it to me. We shake. His hand is large and warm and swallows mine.

"I'm Roy—Roy's Tow Truck Service. That's me."

He's my father's age, greying around the temples and a bit soft around the middle. His skin is glistened with sweat and grease.

"So did you always want to be a tow-truck driver?"

"Oh, I suppose. I do what comes natural to me and towing is natural. Pays the bills."

My father has a couple of Willie Nelson cassettes. What was my father's dream?

"Did you ever want to be something else?" I ask.

He shakes his head. "People are always wanting to be what they're not, and that's stupid. That thinking gets in your head, then you don't like nothing."

"Yeah, I suppose," I say. "But it's OK to have dreams."

"As long as you're happy with who you are now."

He launches into an enthusiastic duet with Willie.

The garage smells intoxicatingly of lubricant and oil. I thank Roy for his help, settle my bill with cash and wait in a small room that looks very similar to a doctor's waiting room—coffee table covered in magazines, uncomfortable chairs, framed diplomas on the walls and an unfriendly receptionist behind a high counter staring at a computer.

"How long do you think it'll be?" I ask again.

She looks at me blankly. "Difficult to say."

I phone the bar and tell them I won't be in today. Chad seems perfectly indifferent. I don't want to lose the wages, but somehow it feels necessary—like a gift to cheer myself up. And in the grand scheme, a few bucks either way isn't going to solve my problems. I might as well feel good now and buy lottery tickets for the future.

Finally a burly mechanic with receding hair comes through the door of the main garage.

"How is it?" I ask.

He takes a deep breath and wipes his hands on a cloth. "Your carbo accelerator module gave out, so we replaced the hub gasket."

Or something like that. The problem will cost me five hundred dollars to fix, which leaves me broke.

With the smell of gas and carburetor fluid in my nostrils

comes a moment of clarity. I am poor and my life is slowly slipping away. I have nothing tangible to show for my last six years except some ratty furniture, a decent CD collection and some moderately good quality amplifiers. People I went to school with own houses, they're married, they have careers. I have a dead-end job. I have a dead life. I have a dream that is ridiculous.

22

That night, Pisa's, my favourite greasy diner, is quiet, and I take a booth by the Pac-Man machine. I have come to be amongst my people, the underclass and doomed. The light seeps into the bone of the evening and I can't shake the slow touch of a looming Monday night. The Formica feels cool under my palms. I scrape some crud off the cutlery and order a gin and tonic, because I haven't had one in at least two years and somehow it feels like a change.

My waitress is young and pretty in an ugly sort of way. She's awkward and has a thin, crooked nose, but her body seems vibrant under the pink uniform and she moves with a certain instinctive sexuality. I'm lusting for a waitress and haven't showered in at least twenty-four hours. I feel coated, deep-fried in the Colonel's secret recipe and aching for someone to recognize me and sit down, explain the point of being here, in this world, in this city, in this place and time in a seedy diner looking for inspiration in the gutter wail and turbulent light of passing taxis and police cars.

"Slow night, eh," I say, smiling at my waitress, wondering if I can still flirt.

"You ready to order?" she asks, pad in hand.

"What's the specialty of the house?"

She looks nervous.

"What's the best thing on the menu?" I ask.

"I . . . I'll have to check with the cook."

I put my hands up to stop her from going and to calm her down. I smile. "I'm just wondering what most people order."

Her eyes are large and brown and the hair falls down in wisps across her freckled face. She might be my age or a few years older. She hesitates.

"I don't know. I can ask. I don't know if we keep track of that . . ."

"But—" I stop. "Just a burger," I say with a polite smile, handing her the menu.

She seems relieved as she writes it on the pad. Without another word she scampers off, her thin ankles flopping in heavy-soled black shoes.

And suddenly I'm alone again. There are two guys in jeans playing pool on the other side of the room. One guy wears a Harley-Davidson hat and is as long and skinny as the $6.99 all-you-can-eat spaghetti special. The other has a beard and thick, muscular arms littered with dark splotches of tattoo ink. My food arrives and I dig in.

"Mind if we join you?"

I look up to see two shadows framed against the phosphorous burn of the fluorescent lights. For an instant they appear as photo negative outlines. Jan punches me on the arm lightly, the act punctuated by the clear, crisp clattering of billiard balls colliding.

Noel and Jan sit down, and my eyes readjust to the waves and spectrums and shadows of the restaurant.

"Hey, what's going on?" I say.

Noel pushes a paper across the table.

"So you got my e-mail," I say.

Noel frowns. "I'm assuming it's a joke. If you think we're letting you quit now, you're dead wrong."

"I just think it's better to leave as friends rather than repeating what happened last night. And I've moved on. And as for the competition, we're not religious."

"Oh, come on, Thompson," Jan says, nudging me playfully. "Last night was fine. Tyler's excited because a female of the species is oddly attracted to him. He'll settle down. And as for the competition, this is going to be great. Rock-and-roll, visions, partings of the Red Sea, smiting the demons . . ."

"And it might knock a few years off our purgatory," Noel adds.

I look at him.

"I can't."

"Listen, bonehead, you're our cornerstone. If you leave, we have no band. And I might kneecap Tyler."

I take a bite of burger. "There comes a time when everyone has to grow up," I say. "I need a real job—one with benefits. Life isn't easy. You've got to accept who you are."

Jan's amusement wells up from within—first she shakes, then her face flushes, then she erupts in a series of spastic giggles.

"What?" I ask.

"You have no sense of who you are," Jan says.

"Of course I do." But my resolve is already fading. "I have to become responsible at some point in my life," I murmur, unsure that I ever will. What I want is to be irresponsible but financially secure, like every true rock star.

Noel steals a fry. "We promise to help you get a job in a factory right after the contest," he says.

I sit back against the vinyl booth cover. "I hate you people," I say.

"So you're still in the band?"

"All right. But on one condition."

My throat tightens as I look at Jan's smiling face. I don't know why I'm asking her.

"My mother's family is getting together on the weekend and I need a date."

She looks at me cautiously. "Go on . . ."

"I'm going to confront my mother face to face about Sheldon and I need some moral support. I can't afford to have him living with me anymore."

Jan exhales slowly and licks her lips. After a few seconds, she speaks.

"And I always thought our first date would be romantic."

23

Sheldon goes into our uncle Art's house first. I introduce Janice to my aunt at the front door, then head to the kitchen and fix myself a rye and cola while she gets grilled. I drink it quickly and take a deep breath. Then I make two more drinks.

From the doorway of the living room I watch Jan squirm between two aunts. She shifts from one foot to another, nodding politely and smiling. Her brown hair is glistening in the sunlight beaming through the large living-room window. For a split second I imagine her in a white wedding dress, lace and small pale flowers. The whole room is flooded in light. I shiver at the thought of her family mingling with my Scotch-soaked clan. We would have to elope. I rescue her and we escape into the dining room.

"I'm going to exact revenge for this, Thompson," she says, staring out the window.

"Isn't everyone's family like this?"

"Honey!"

My mother, a fifty-year-old woman with dyed black hair, wearing a tight black dress that doesn't really flatter her decent though no longer young and lean figure, has arrived. Her bracelets clatter as she hurries over to us on high heels.

"Hi, Mom," I say.

"You've put on weight, Jason," she says, slightly winded, giving me a hug.

"No, I haven't."

She smiles and pokes my stomach. I'd rather she didn't treat me like a child in front of Jan.

"It's a loose shirt," I say.

She looks happily at Janice for a second. "Hello, Becky," she says.

I begin to rub my temples.

"This is Janice, Mom. She's a friend of mine. Becky was three years ago."

My mother laughs and covers her mouth in mock embarrassment. "It's tough for your mother to keep up with all these girls, Jason. Maybe if you called more."

I feel my face redden and I glance at Janice, who is smiling politely. My mother continues to stand with an expectant smile on her face.

"How's Russ?" I begin.

"Russell," she says.

"Russell."

"He's good. Very busy, already gearing up for the Christmas season. Can you believe that? He'll be playing at all sorts of functions. He even has a bar mitzvah. He's extremely talented. I guess you could say he's nothing like your father."

Her voice has a singsong quality whenever she talks about my dad. Russell plays piano in the hotel bar where my mother works. I took Becky, my last girlfriend, there—a mistake—and he did this cheesy lounge-lizard flirt-thing, playing her favourite mellow seventies songs.

"Russell is a pianist," my mother says to Janice. "He's a genius, but he doesn't believe in his talent. I have to be so supportive."

"The next Jerry Lee Lewis," I say.

"No, show tunes mostly," my mother says. "He does a wonderful Elton John. You'd love it. The bar goes dead quiet when he plays 'Candle in the Wind.' The Lady Di version."

"So have you and Dad decided anything about Sheldon?" I ask.

She looks as if she's waiting for me to clarify the meaning of my question.

"Your son," I add.

"Thank you, I'm quite aware that Sheldon is my son. I talked to *my son* a few days ago and he seemed perfectly content at your place. He sounds happier than he's been in a long time."

"I doubt he's enjoying his life as much as you think."

"Oh, please, I know the situation isn't the best, but it's good for brothers to spend time together. And there's a time and place for this conversation, Jason."

She takes me by the shoulder and points toward the buffet. There's a long table set with a white paper cloth, on which is arranged an assortment of mini sausages on toothpicks, white-bread sandwiches, bowls of olives and bags of cookies.

"Let's not spoil the day by being cranky."

"This is serious, Mom. I'm not his guardian. There are laws surrounding this sort of situation."

She steps back and plants a hand on her hip. "Can you please settle down? We'll discuss this later. Or do you want to call the cops on your dear sweet mother right now?" She laughs uproariously.

I'm not about to let her squirm out of this conversation. I've made up my mind to have this discussion now, because otherwise I'm sure there will never be a right moment. She'll always find an excuse not to talk.

"Mom, can you be serious for a moment . . ."

"Go have some food, Jason."

"No. Stop being so selfish. Sheldon's moving to your apartment."

I notice Jan casually shuffle away toward the window. My mother takes me by the elbow and whispers in a measured, pointed tone. The conviviality has left her face.

"I don't have an apartment, Jason. But if you'd like to come over to Russell's and tell him that Sheldon's moving in, please be my guest. I'm sure he'll be delighted. What a thrill—a lifelong bachelor now responsible for a teenager. Then, when Russell decides he's had enough of both of us, Sheldon and I will move in with you, because I can't afford a place of my own."

She scampers off on her heels. I suppose she has a legitimate point, but still. I ball my fists and want to tornado through the floorboards like the Tasmanian Devil in Bugs Bunny cartoons.

I walk to the window, shaking my head. The garden has been covered in orange and white tarps.

"Well, that wasn't so bad," Janice says.

"She must be able to afford an apartment at her age. How can a person be that disorganized at fifty?"

"So what are you going to do?"

I watch a black bird pick at seeds scattered on the cold ground.

"Hire a lawyer, I guess. I don't know. Someone has to pay support for the kid. Where'd Sheldon go?"

"I don't know."

"It's not like him to miss a buffet."

I scan the room, which is now filled with at least thirty relatives in various shapes and sizes. We decide to look for him outside. The back door needs a good solid push from my shoulder to crack it open. Everything about this house feels nautical. The glass in the back door is round, like a porthole, and the paint is a thick glaze of waterproof white.

It's autumn, yet the lawn is still a shocking green. I wonder how much fertilizer Uncle Art pours on his small plot of land.

"He needs gnomes," I say.

We take a muddy path around the lake and decide to scan the area from the graveyard on the hill, where my relatives are buried. We walk through the gates and I instantly see it, at the far side of the great forest of stone. There, perched on a black mausoleum silhouetted against the bright sky, is the biggest, goofiest gargoyle I've ever seen.

"You don't think that's Sheldon . . ." Jan says.

"This ought to be interesting."

I think Shel sees us coming, because he wavers, like he's about to jump, then scampers to the far side.

"It's difficult being fifteen," Janice whispers as we move along the gravel road. "Fifteen is a different planet. Your body explodes and you get all gangly and awkward. People treat you like an adult one minute and a baby the next. I *hated* fifteen."

She hisses the last sentence. I'm curious to look at her high-school yearbook, wondering if she was a babe or a rebel or an oddity. My guess is she was a mix of all three.

"And your brother is under so much stress."

The grey stone building is partially hidden under the arching branches of two large trees.

"Shel," I say, craning my head upwards. He looks down at me but doesn't say anything.

"What ya up to?"

He continues to stare, then turns away. I take a look around the field of stones. There's a large black tombstone with the name Gap on it, and for a second I wonder if it's a macabre advertising ploy. There's another sign pointing mourners toward the Irish famine memorial.

"Shel," I begin, trying to keep my tone level, "is there a reason why you're up there? The building you're on . . . it has dead people in it, you know."

He looks down at the shingles in surprise. "Really?"

The building is limestone brick and looks like it was once a chapel. Its windows have been bricked up and three pipes jut out of the top, like small chimneys.

"Shel, the graveyard people probably don't want you up there."

"They're all dead," he says.

"Not them, dummy. I mean the caretaker and the guys with the backhoe. And probably the flower people."

"Shel," Janice says softly, stepping forward. "Why don't you come down. We can go back to the house and relax."

"There's food there," I add.

"Jay," Jan says, "take a walk for a few minutes, will you?"

I take a walk around the graveyard to where my grandparents are buried. Their stone is small and new compared with those around it, which are weather-beaten and worn down. My grandfather was killed in a car accident years before I was born. My memories of my grandmother are spotty at best, a collage of shuffling feet and homemade sausage rolls.

"Hey," I say to the stone. I look around and feel stupid. "Shel's on the roof of the mausoleum." I point. "Kids." I shake my head. "So how are you guys? I guess I could use some answers. I don't know. I don't pray, so this is the best I can do. If you guys know anything, feel free to send it somehow—lightning bolt, televangelist, horoscope. There's a reason for all of this, isn't there?"

The wind whistles between the stones and I feel the dead silence. So much for supernatural enlightenment. I read a few names and feel depressed, then see Janice waving to me from near the mausoleum. I head back and find Sheldon still sitting on the roof, wiping tears away from his eyes.

"Everything sorted out?" I ask.

"No," Sheldon answers.

"He thinks you're trying to get rid of him," Jan whispers. "Haven't you explained the situation to him?"

Her expression of mild indignation make me queasy, and

my throat tightens. I haven't discussed the situation with Sheldon, because there's no easy way to tell a kid his parents don't want him.

"I didn't want to upset him," I say.

"Nice one," Jan says. "God, Jay. He's your brother. You've got to communicate."

Sheldon is crying again. My stomach is cramping. How am I supposed to know how to deal with a teenager? I'm dealing with him the way I was taught growing up—ignore the problem until it works itself out.

"He thinks if he died no one would come to his funeral," Jan adds.

"Ah, Shel," I say, looking up and shading my eyes from the glare of the sun. "You've been gone from Art's for what, fifteen minutes, and we were worried enough to come look for you. People care. They just suck at showing it."

"I don't want to live with Mom," he says, sniffling.

"Why not?"

Before he can answer, the air is filled with a splintering crash and he disappears. The section of the roof where Sheldon was sitting has caved in like a gaping black mouth.

24

"So what happened again?" the doctor says, slowly pulling a stitch through the bloody gash on Shel's arm. He's OK except for one bad cut and a few scratches. Still, he looks pretty shaken.

"He fell through a mausoleum roof."

The doctor nods, staring intently as he makes another turn. "Oh yeah, right . . ."

This does not bode well for me winning brother of the year.

Later, I take Sheldon home and put him to bed on the floor of the living room. He is an orphan with two living, capable parents who have abandoned him. At times, I feel like they've abandoned both of us.

But then, family members always wound one another.

One of my clearest memories of the post-divorce period involved a Saturday afternoon with my mother when I was twelve and just coming into adolescent arrogance and cruelty. We were at her apartment, which she shared with her dumpy roommate, Marlene. I remember being so embarrassed that my mother had a roommate. Did she think she was in college? They were in the living room, smoking cigarettes, and I was in my mother's very small bedroom, listening to tapes on the floor. I could hear them talking about complete crap—men, jobs, drinking. I was listening to Bananarama, who I always got mixed up with the Go-Gos and the Bangles; but I knew I was listening to Bananarama because I had bought their tape that morning at Kmart from a discount bin.

It was almost time for me to go home. Marlene, with her tacky saddle pants and blood red nail polish, was going to drive me to Dad's. My mother came into the room and was speaking to me, but I was focused on the music, blocking her out, refusing to listen, refusing to be pawned off to a chain-smoking divorcée for delivery home. When she reached down and turned off the tape, I flipped. I yelled at her over and over again, telling her she was a moron, which was my father's favourite epithet for her. I suppose I expected anger, but she cried. I was shocked. Mothers were supposed to be caring and in control, but she was a wreck and a freak.

Of course, maybe I'm still a self-absorbed punk. I hadn't thought much about my mother being dependent on Russell, because she's never pointed it out to me. I suddenly realize she's always had to depend on someone—my father, Marlene, the lounge lizard.

I hear Sheldon snoring in the other room.

Jay Thompson hit for family cruelty: Bananarama, the Go-Gos, the Bangles, pick any song. I still can't tell the difference.

25

It's Friday and I'm home with Sheldon, who has settled into his usual introverted demeanour and is watching television while I think, write a couple of songs with clear and simple religious lyrics and generally mess around on my guitar.

I look at the sheet in front of me.

You are like salvation calling
When I see your brown hair falling
Makes me know I am a sinner
But with Christ I can be a winner

Turns out this type of writing is more difficult than I thought. I scribble out the verse with red pen and crumple the paper into a ball. My hook shot to the garbage can falls short. I wonder what Dr. Seuss would have written if he had found God with real zealot energy.

Green eggs and ham, saved I am.
Be redeemed in a tree, be redeemed with me.
Be redeemed on a boat, be redeemed with a goat.

I'm very tired.

By ten Sheldon and I are sharing the couch silently, watching repeats of *WKRP in Cincinnati* on the Comedy Network. At eleven, as I'm drifting into that semiconscious zone between watching TV and being asleep, the phone rings. I feel a cramp in my stomach and think how typical it would be for my mother to call and torment me while I'm in my weakest state. I close my eyes.

"Jay?"

Janice's voice is spilling into the answering machine.

"Jay? Jay, it's me . . ."

There's the unmistakable twang of country music blaring in the background, as well as male laughter. But Janice sounds upset.

"Jay? Pick up the phone."

"Hi. What's up?"

"Turn that down!" Janice yells. Then, to me, "Can you come over?"

"Yeah, sure. Are you OK?"

"Just come over."

Unsure of the situation, I decide to take someone with me. I don't feel the need to drag Sheldon out, so, of course, the only person I can find at this time of night is Tyler. He's cranky, but I bribe him with the promise of a free breakfast on Monday. He insists on driving and arrives semi-clad in loungewear and mismatched shoes, his eyes tired behind his specs.

We arrive at Janice's to a country bass booming from her

duplex onto the street. Male figures in plaid with beer bottles keep passing in front of the large plate-glass window. A pickup truck is in the driveway.

"I think we may have to call an exorcist," Tyler says as we approach the front door very slowly. A shrill "yee-hah!" cuts through the air, and we look at each other fearfully. "Or an exterminator."

Janice is standing in the hall, biting her fingernail and talking to a fat guy whose straw-like hair is cut in a bowl style. Janice runs her hand through her hair several times and Plaid pulls up his sagging jeans with a hefty tug.

I look at Tyler and he shrugs and taps on the glass. Janice looks over, flashes a relieved smile and waves us in. Plaid eyes us, tugs his pants once more, then slinks off to the kitchen.

"Thanks for coming. I'm sorry. I didn't know what else to do."

There are beer bottles everywhere and chip bags spilling their contents across the coffee table and onto the floor. The pillows have been tossed around and several CDs are littered in front of the entertainment unit. Two huge speakers are vibrating with every heave of the bass.

"I like the music," Tyler says. "What's going on?"

"My roommate, Tiffany, agreed to let these guys stay tonight. They're from our hometown. But they've been drinking all day and I can't really deal with it." She runs a hand through her hair.

"You want us to kick these guys out?" I ask.

"No. But I thought it would be easier for me to leave if someone came and got me. They're giving me a hard time."

The phone rings and she runs off to the kitchen. We sit on her yellow-white couch in silence. There's a Marilyn

Monroe print on the wall—the one where she's standing on the sidewalk grid and the wind blows up her skirt.

A tall, muscular guy—also dressed in plaid—stumbles into the living room and steadies himself against a bookcase. He's got short, cropped brown hair and an angular face. He leers at Tyler and me with a menacing intensity. He looks like a refrigerator come to life as he steps toward us, scrutinizing our faces. He turns his body to face Tyler, who slouches down in the couch.

"Hey, man," Tyler says. "How are you?"

"What's your name?" Plaid-2 slurs.

Tyler glances at me nervously. "Uh . . . Gordon Sumner," he replies.

Plaid-2 wavers and takes a step back to catch his balance. "You're not Billy?"

"No."

Right now I'm feeling sorry for Billy, whoever and wherever he might be. I wonder if rednecks have gangs that beat on one another for perceived indiscretions, such as hunting opossum on rival turf.

Because Tyler isn't Billy, Plaid-2 has no further interest in him. He shifts his body around to face me, and as he manoeuvres I expect to hear a high-pitched beep warning pedestrians behind him to look out. His eyes flicker. A new song with steel guitars and woo-hooing starts up.

"What's your name?"

"Declan," I say. "Declan McManus."

"You're not Billy?"

"No," I say slowly. "I don't know Billy. Maybe he's upstairs."

I point toward the stairs, and Plaid-2 rotates his entire body to look at them. After a few tense seconds, he puts his legs in gear and lumbers forward. Janice appears from the kitchen.

"Oh God, where's he going now?"

She goes after Plaid-2, whose feet have disappeared from the top stairs.

"Where are you going?" she shouts. "There's nothing up there. Now get back down here."

I hear him say something about Billy and can't help but laugh, now that he's out of punching distance.

"He's not here," Janice continues. "I told you. Todd, can you please come back down here?"

"I like your friend," I say. I'm now quite sure I'm not, in any way, trailer trash.

"Yeah," Jan says.

"Who is he?"

She runs her hand through her hair again. "My ex-boyfriend."

There's a moment of silence—to mourn, I think. The moment is punctuated nicely by a nifty fiddle solo. She explains slowly and awkwardly, as if revealing a secret.

"My dad worked in the city, but he commuted. I'm actually from a small town in the sticks. And when you live in a small town, you don't have a lot of choices growing up. This is a really long story."

"He wants you back, doesn't he?" Tyler says.

"Apparently."

"What is he, your high-school sweetheart?" I ask, still dazed. Jan has never mentioned living in the country. I had always assumed that she'd lived in the city, was pampered by her bureaucrat father and was sent off to private school or Montessori at the earliest age. I feel a bit misled.

"Yeah, well . . . We were engaged until I broke it off last year."

Torpedoed again. I'm stumped for the next question, which is obviously "Why?" I simply can't find any way of asking.

"Like I said," she continues, "it's a long story. See, we went away to different schools, but . . . we'd see each other in the summer, back home . . . I guess we'd just fall into the old routine. He *is* pretty good-looking."

She says the last line under her breath, as if justifying her poor judgment. At this point two more plaid boys come into the room. They shoot death-ray country-boy glares at Tyler and me, speak quietly to Janice and then stumble up the stairs like the Keystone Kops rescue brigade.

"Oh, for fuck's sake!" she exclaims after a few seconds of silence. She storms up the stairs. This country-and-western atmosphere doesn't suit the Janice I know at all.

"She's not staying here tonight," I say. "She can stay with me."

Tyler shrugs, and I go to the kitchen to cool off. I see a case of beer lying open by the back door, figure it belongs to the oafs and feel no guilt for swiping several bottles. One for now. One in my jacket. And a couple extra for being engaged to Janice. I wonder how well I really know her. Maybe my perception of our relationship has been purely delusional. As I reach for one more beer, to put in my pants, I feel a sharp stab, a smooth rush of pain and then a searing warmth. There's a broken bottle in the case. A spurt of blood surges in a stream from a small brown spike of glass in my hand. I've been crucified by a beer bottle. I'm squeezing a river of blood down my arm and onto the floor in large, lazy drops. I shake my hand violently as Janice and Tyler come into the kitchen. Apparently I've screeched.

"What did you do?" she asks, the question trailing off as she sees the drops of blood on the white linoleum. She grabs paper towels from the cluttered kitchen table. I pluck the brown fragment of glass out of my wound and squeeze again as a lick of pain shoots up my arm. I use a paper towel to soak up the blood. Not wipe it off, soak it up. There is an amazing amount for such a small cut.

"You're not staying here tonight," I gasp.

"Is it deep?"

"No."

"Do you think they'll destroy the house?" Tyler asks.

"Who cares."

"Apply pressure," Jan says.

"What?"

"No, soak it in cold water and then put sugar on it," Tyler says emphatically.

Jan frowns. "What?"

"You can stay at my place," I say.

"It's what my grandmother always used to do," Tyler says.

For a moment we all stand and look at one another. Finally, Jan takes me by the arm and drags me over to the kitchen table. She examines the wound under the fluorescent light.

"We need more light," she whispers. "Tyler, can you get the Polysporin from the bathroom cabinet?"

She drags me forward by the arm again, opens the refrigerator door and thrusts my hand inside, under the small bulb, directly above the orange juice.

"Maybe we can put some spinach on it?" I hiss.

"It doesn't look bad," she says, letting go. I think it looks like bloody hamburger.

"Why didn't you tell me?" I whisper, my voice a bit too shaky. The softness of her expression surprises me. There has to be something here, something more than friendship.

"I don't know," she says. "Because it's the past."

Tyler returns, and Janice washes my wound and douses it with an antibacterial spray. She wraps a bandage on it and smiles.

"I'll have to tell Todd."

"About his injury?" Tyler asks.

"In case I sue him for improper storage of a loaded case of beer?" I add. "Hey, maybe we'll all end up on *Springer*."

"I'll tell him I'm leaving."

"Why? Just leave him. He won't remember if you tell him anyway. The guy is blitzed. And who's Billy?"

She frowns. "Maybe I'll tell Don instead and he can explain it to Todd later."

I throw the blood-soaked paper towel into the garbage bin. I decide my injury entitles me to at least two more redneck beers and I fish very carefully into the case with my good hand.

Someone is messing with the stereo in the other room. For a second I think we're going to be hick-free, but then the Oak Ridge Boys begin blasting through my synapses.

When Tyler and I make it to the front door, we join the two support plaids and watch as Janice and Todd have an intense argument on the front lawn. From the sensitive look on his glazed face, I can tell that he wants to have a serious heart-to-heart conversation. He's touching his chest and raising his hands and keeps reaching out to touch her. Each time, she backs away. They move around the grass like two wrestlers feeling each other out before the match begins.

Fat plaid moves out of my way, heaving up his jeans as I pass. The other plaid stares at me, his thin face curled into a sneer. His eyes are bloodshot and his eyebrow is almost a connect-o. His forearms are lean and muscular. Fat plaid and Tyler are talking in the background. Ugly plaid takes a swallow from his beer and lets out a little laugh.

"You a big man?" he asks.

"We're leaving," I say, loud enough for Janice to hear.

Todd twists his big head around and looks over with a scowl. After a few seconds, he orients his huge body and steams toward the steps. Fear hits me like an elbow to the gut.

"Oh shit," Tyler murmurs.

"What's your name?" Todd asks, pointing at me.

I don't answer, so he turns to Tyler. "What's your name?"

"Declan McManus," he blurts.

Todd computes the name and turns his body back at me. His chest is like the grille of the pickup in the driveway. I can smell the remains of beer and cheap, heavy-duty cologne turning bad.

"What's your name?"

I feel moisture on my back. My mind is a blank. Tyler has stolen my name and, although I know he introduced himself using Sting's real name, I can't for the life of me recall it.

"You already asked me that," I reply.

"What's your name?" He takes a step forward.

"Sid Vicious?" I say weakly.

He's standing too close for comfort now, but I'm pinned between him and the door.

"You got a problem?" he asks, tilting his head. The skin on his face is lean and clings to the bone at sharp angles. I can see a small ball of muscle where his jawbone connects to the skull.

"No."

I look away to the street. A red car is pulling up to the red light. Its brake lights wink at me. I look back at Todd, who is staring at me, and think he's somehow grown larger in the last ten seconds.

"What's your name?"

My mouth is dry and my limbs are buzzing with a potent stream of adrenaline.

"It's Jay," Janice says, walking over to the steps. She takes my hand and holds it, turning back to Todd with defiance. Apparently she's trying to get me killed. But to my surprise, Todd glances down at our hands and takes a step back. He looks like he's about to cry.

We walk very slowly to Tyler's car and, once inside, I begin to breathe again.

"Well, that was close," Tyler remarks as we creep slowly through the tired suburbs.

"Thanks for your support," I say.

"His friend was right behind you. I thought he was going to grab you."

"He's not that bad," Janice says, staring out the window and drawing little happy faces in the condensation. "He was drunk, that's all. He'll be embarrassed tomorrow."

"Nice to know your ex-fiancé would be sorry for killing me tomorrow."

26

We end up at Pisa's, picking at poutine. I feel bloated, but after tonight's events the food is comforting and makes me feel whole again.

We sit quietly for a while. I order water and use the glass to smuggle the beer from my jacket onto the table.

"I really did think he was going to cream you," Tyler begins after a long silence, a small wad of cheese stuck between his front teeth. "I mean, you were really pushing it."

"Pushing it?"

"Didn't you see him?" Tyler continues emphatically, leaning across the table. "He was getting pretty tense. He's a big guy. You shouldn't have provoked him the way you did."

The gravy on my fries is beginning to congeal—white flecks of creamy fat are forming on the surface.

"Todd isn't like that."

We look at Janice, but she doesn't elaborate.

"Drunken country boys on a Saturday night are known to do some fairly vicious things," Tyler asserts.

Janice has a slightly lost expression on her face. I look around at the gratuitous beer posters, the fake wood panelling. The air is thick and buttery above the red booths and thin wooden tables.

"Well, it's not your usual night, anyway," Tyler says.

The restaurant is noisy and full of students. I'm divided between envying their exuberance and wanting to strangle them all. I don't remember being so loud and idiotically silly when I was their age. The sound of rattling steel forks on thick white ceramic plates echoes all around us. I look around to see mouths biting into white fries. What does this place mean in the grand scheme of life? Is this the sort of place where revelation can sneak in, where your focus can be jogged out of place just enough that you can see some fantastic sign in the western sandwich with home fries? In the drooping whipped cream on the runny pumpkin pie? Where do the modern saints congregate, if not in a gutter like this one?

I rub my face, think of Todd's face hovering above me, unaware and disconnected. Who are you? I look around at dozens of anonymous faces fighting against me and I don't know anymore. I want to find a newspaper and read my horoscope, want to stop at the noodle shop by my apartment and beg the hunched Asian woman for advice and ancient Chinese secrets of fulfillment and spiritual meaning. I want to raid the clear glass jar of golden fortune cookies waiting for me, waiting to enlighten me.

"Are you done with that?"

A stern-looking waitress with a rose tattoo floating under the pink of her diner uniform is picking up my plate. She's eyeing the shallow remains of amber in my glass.

"Go for it." I stretch back into the booth.

"Did you want another beer?"

"I didn't have beer."

"Uh-huh."

She shuffles painfully away on her swollen feet. She comes back, tears a small white bill off her thick, greasy pad. She drops it on the table and scoops up Janice's untouched plate.

"Thanks, Flo," Tyler murmurs.

She stops and looks as if she's going to say something, but she doesn't.

"Don't be an ass, Tyler," Jan says, staring out the window

into the muted darkness of the busy street. "For once, just be yourself."

We sit in silence for a few more seconds, strange lonely captives in the midnight anarchy of drunken bar-goers. Pretty young girls and lean young men swirl invincibly in and out of the revolving door, hysterical for cheap beer and greasy poutine.

We divvy up the bill. I drop an extra two quarters on the table and we slide out into the night.

"You guys want a ride or . . . ?"

Tyler is shivering on the edge of the grey concrete.

"We can walk."

My place is only a couple of blocks away. He nods and heads across the street. Janice and I huddle into our jackets and stride off under the blanched skies, crossing on the red, against the angry flow of taxis jumping into the main street, engines revving like cash registers. The night bleeds around us as we pass street people and buskers and university girls in tight, breast-hugging shirts who hold themselves as they laugh and talk and step over extended feet and coffee cups converted to begging dishes. East meets west as we kick blowing cardboard pizza plates out of our path and walk silently toward my apartment.

"Can I ask now?" I say softly, scooting by the noodle shop where my fortune lies. The shop is closed, but the counter is illuminated by the eerie light from a television set that no one has bothered to turn off.

"About?"

I look at Janice. I'm tired now, my brain beginning to flip through nonsensical tableaux of the day's images, losing the thread.

"Your life. Todd."

"Didn't I already go over that?" she says wearily.

"But why?"

She doesn't say anything. The sound of our footsteps rings in my ears.

"You know how you can be ten different people at the same time?"

"I suppose."

"Of course you do. Everyone acts differently in different settings, with different people. With your mother you're one way. With your friends another."

"I suppose."

"Well, Todd is—or was—a part of my personality. He was fun in a totally reckless and dumb sort of way. I don't always like to think about things, like how I'm doing philosophically. Most of my life has been one big mess that I've never been able to sort into neat component parts. Just like now. I don't know what I'm doing. I don't know why I was with Todd, except that he was fun. Then he was nothing."

The door to my apartment building is painted red, an iron red that crusts around the yellowing glass. The metal handle is black from so many hands leaving imprints on its surface. A mound of rotting junk mail festers year-round, and on some days you have to kick the door to get it past the pile. There are more pizza fliers in this building than mouths to stuff pizza into.

"My life makes no sense, so don't even try to figure it out. I don't know why I do anything."

And neither do I. I can't figure her out anymore, can't even think straight right now.

We trudge, drag, propel ourselves into the darkness of my apartment. The stale smell of leftover fish fingers and the sound of breathing remind me that my brother lives here.

He's asleep on a mattress in the corner of the living room.

"Want a drink?"

"No, I'm OK, I think."

I pop a glass down on the table, get the two-litre bottle of flat Coke that I've jammed into the vegetable crisper and unload the redneck beers from my pockets. I pour some rum into my glass and pop off my shoes. Janice is lingering and, for the first time, in this dim light, on this stupid night, she appears fragile.

"You can have my bed if you want. I'll take the couch."

She laughs and shakes her head slowly. "Couch is fine. I'm crashing, Jay. I'm not a houseguest."

"Of course you are."

We look at one another in the pale darkness, neither of us moving or glancing away. She is still and solemn.

"I'll get you some sheets. If I have any more. If not, you can have one of mine from my bed."

I put down my glass and slide my socked feet over the dirty linoleum toward the hall linen closet. I know I have a sleeping bag, maybe an extra sheet, and a couple of pillows tattooed with drool stains. That'll have to do.

I hear her flop down on the couch and I float off into a scene, imagine the soft drone of TV, the gradual movement closer to her on the couch as we watch late-night info-mercials for spray-on hair and Ginsu miracle knives, the warmth of her leg against mine, neither of us moving away, and another drink, maybe stroking her hair until we both decide silently to—

"Jay?"

"Yeah?"

My heart is racing from the shock of her voice and I feel like she has caught me out.

"I think I will have a drink."

"OK."

"Do you have anything besides rum?"

My mind flickers as I feel my cheeks flush slightly. Realizing this makes the flush worse. I break into a light sweat. This is ridiculous.

"Check the freezer for vodka. There's some orange juice in the fridge, but I'd smell it before you use it."

I gather up the linens and toss them on the couch, and then wonder when I'll have enough money to afford a couch that isn't so hideously ugly. I think the green fabric is made from some sort of flame-retardant synthetic material that was developed accidentally by NASA. I slump down and flick on the TV.

"Actually, Jay, do you mind if I go to bed? I just don't think I can handle being awake right now."

"Oh . . . sure." I flick off the TV. "I'm tired too."

I linger as she spreads the sheet, unfurls the sleeping bag.

"I had a sleeping bag once," she says with a smile, "but I left it on a bus in Scotland. It cost a lot of money, but I didn't realize it was gone until I was getting ready to fly home. Who knows, it may still be circling the country."

"Do you need anything else?"

"Actually, yeah . . . I don't suppose you have jogging pants or boxer shorts that I can wear to bed. I don't have anything to sleep in."

"Sure, no problem."

I feel a dull heat in my body. In my room I grab a pair of sweatshorts, walk back into the living room and toss them to her. I stand stupidly for a few seconds, then realize she's waiting for me to leave. Sheldon is breathing softly in the corner.

"OK, anyway, if you need anything . . . Goodnight."

I stumble off.

"Thanks, Jay."

"No problem."

The room is impossibly bright as I close my eyes in bed and then open them, try not to think but replay Janice's house, bad poutine, the way Tyler didn't want to drive us home, Flo the waitress. From my bed, I stare at the stars speckling the sky. I think about Janice and about the impossibilities and complexities of men and women.

I'm struggling against sleep and all of these things when a faint rapping echoes in the room. I wonder if I'm dreaming and wait until I hear it again.

"Yeah?" I whisper.

The door opens a crack and a thin flood of light pours in, followed by Janice's head.

"You awake?"

"Yeah. What's up?"

She slumps onto the end of the bed. The door swings open on its hinges, bumping lightly against the clothes-basket squeezed in behind it. Her head is hung.

"I don't know, Jay."

"Are you OK?"

"I don't know."

I realize she's crying, and I don't know what to do. I want to speak, want to say something, want to tell her that it's all going to be OK, but I can't seem to dislodge the confusion from my throat.

I don't even think to do it or consciously realize I'm reaching out, but I sit up and put my hand on the soft cotton of her shirt, feel the warmth that I knew was there, feel the impact of her bones, flesh, skin, and I begin to rub her shoulder. I feel like we're small and alone on an empty planet, far away in outer space, flailing off into deep, cold darkness. I know that this is what it means to hold on. I keep rubbing and she continues to cry.

After a few minutes she pulls herself together and wipes her face on the sheet.

"Relax, they're just tears," she says. "I'm not going to blow."

I tell her not to worry, and I pull back the covers for her to slide in. She tucks her legs to her body and lies on her side, away from me. I want to kiss her. I realize that if you care about someone and don't want her to end up engaged to a redneck, at some point you have to take that big, scary chance and make your move. If I never try with Jan, I'll always regret it. And this is the perfect moment, when she's seen that I'll do whatever I can for her safety and happiness.

She begins to snore.

I tuck her in tightly and drag my sorry ass to the living-room couch.

27

As I'm rooting through the cupboards for coffee, Janice emerges blurry-eyed from my bedroom.

"Morning, Princess," I say chirpily.

"Coffee," she whispers, looking embarrassed. "Sorry about last night."

"Not a problem. I only hope your house is still standing."

I feel a bit tense in a weird sexual way about having her in my home in the morning. I guess it's a matter of intimacy.

We did get a bit close last night. I scoop copious amounts of no-name coffee into a filter.

"Did you know that Tyler has a policy not to eat or drink no-name brands?" I say. "He says if they can't be bothered, he can't be bothered."

"Why am I not surprised?"

I've lost count of scoops, but throw in one more for good luck. She puts her head in her hands, her hair falling down to the table like a tapestry. I look out at the gloomy wet day, then open a window and breathe in a fresh earth smell.

"Style over substance," she continues, fumbling with my salt-and-pepper shakers and not looking at me. "Style over substance . . ."

We listen to the percolator gurgle in the still room. Obviously we both need to discuss what is happening between us, but my resolve has dissipated since last night and I'm no longer completely confident of Jan's feelings. I arrange mugs and spoons and the sugar bowl in a neat line on the counter, not sure what to say. Finally, the coffee is done. As I'm pouring our first no-names of the day, Sheldon stumbles in, rubbing his eyes.

"Morning, Princess," I say.

He looks startled to see Janice. I pour some milk into my cup and it instantly curdles.

"Oh, man," I say. "Milk's bad."

Sheldon pours himself a cup of coffee, then takes the milk carton from my hand. He pours some into his cup, and chunks of waxy white float to the surface; he gives it a stir and then spoons the chunks out into the sink.

"I don't think you should drink that."

"Haven't you ever heard of sour cream?" he says.

I should tell him it's not the same, but I don't want to

sound too parental. I need to strike that balance with Shel between being a friend and an authority figure. In a place as small as mine, we have to stay on good terms. And also, my authority runs only so far. If he doesn't want to do what I tell him, he doesn't have to. I don't even think he should be drinking coffee, but I can't tell him it'll stunt his growth; the kid is taller than me.

"Why don't they have no-name milk?" I wonder.

"No one would drink it," Jan says. "Even skinflints aren't going to blindly drink milk *of unknown origins.*"

"I would," Sheldon says.

"You've never met an *E. coli* bacteria," Janice replies.

"Who cares," Shel continues. "Expiry dates are a scam. Big companies put them on products to rip you off and make you buy more."

From my brother's mouth comes my father's voice. I've heard this spiel a hundred times and it's always recited with the same indignant expression that I see on Shel's face. I feel a bit creeped out and wonder how many of my father's traits and habits I've unknowingly inherited. At the same time, I'm glad that Shel is speaking at least a bit more since the graveyard debacle. And if I didn't know better, I'd think he had a bit of a crush on Jan.

"I'm going out for a double cappuccino and biscotti," Jan announces, standing up. She stretches her arms toward the ceiling and yawns. Seeing her body in a T-shirt and my shorts evokes an undeniable surge of pure, unabashed lust. "Anyone want to come?"

"Sure," I say. "I'll race you to the Italian coffee shop. Loser buys."

As we're leaving, we playfully body-check one another against the walls and act like a couple of kids. I decide there's no need to break the light mood with heavy conversations about feelings.

28

As we're swapping sections of the newspaper and drinking our coffees, it occurs to me that I've always wanted a rock chick. Love and music got intertwined in the very beginning.

My first guitar was given to me by my uncle Art when I was ten. He was a decade older than my mom, centuries old to me, and I always liked him because he gave me things. He bought me my first Bowie album, a secondhand copy of *Young Americans*, and the much-coveted Foreigner disk 4. And, of course, the guitar.

My mom paid for me to take lessons, handing me eight dollars every Wednesday before school, and insisted I practise at least twice a week. The first song I learned was "Country Roads," which was neither hip nor hard to play. After a few months and a few new chords, my fingers toughened up and I moved on to "Eight Days a Week," followed by "Jack and Diane," by John Mellencamp, who at that time was still known as John Cougar and hadn't yet written anything about little pink houses. Then came the bane of my youth, "The Rose."

My first teacher was a girl named Linda, a strawberry-blond university student who gave lessons in the nurses' room of my elementary school. She was soft-spoken and had delicate features, but admired strong females, like Deb Harry and Stevie Nicks, because I suppose they were the type of women she wanted to be. I loved her because she was beautiful and even more because she played in a real band. I thought she was the most courageous person on the planet. And she would talk to me like what I had to say about music really meant something. She might not have agreed that Taco's "Puttin' on the Ritz" was a seminal classic, but she respected my opinion, which was a nice change from my home life.

Linda was my regular Wednesday-night sanctuary. Her quiet voice and delicate hands were a perfect juxtaposition to my mother's throaty laugh and my father's thick sausage fingers. Surrounded by gauze and the faint odour of Lysol and vomit, Linda gave me my first taste of the underbelly of rock-and-roll, guided me through my first riffs and helped me write my first song. Unintentionally, she also introduced me to the beauty of cleavage while bending forward to turn music sheets. In retrospect, this seems truly fitting: sex, drugs and rock-and-roll.

Jay Thompson hit for the first stirrings of lust: Stevie Nicks, "Gold Dust Woman."

29

"Another night, another cigarette . . ."

Janice is wailing something unrecognizable and comically out of tune in the living room as I'm getting ready to go to Tyler's for practice. I'm feeling a bit guilty, because tonight is Natasha's birthday dinner and she's left several messages on my machine. But I can't compel myself to make any more excuses. Since I steam-cleaned the dog hair from my carpet, I've buffed my floor and Scotchgarded my couch. My place has never looked so clean in my imagination. All this lying is stressing me out, so now I'm ignoring her.

The phone is ringing.

"Eventually she'll realize you're not interested," Jan says, appearing at the door to my bedroom. "Besides, it's a bit early in your relationship to try to force you to meet her parents."

"We don't even have a relationship," I say.

"You don't feel anything for her?"

"Nothing more than voyeuristic curiosity."

She laughs. "God, that's flattering. That should be on a greeting card. I'm voyeuristically curious about you. Be my valentine."

She points to a bottle of cologne on my dresser. "Is this the stuff that makes my nose bleed?"

"It's Polo."

"So, do you develop a little horse and rider rash on your neck when you wear it? Now that would be corporate strategy."

She flops down on the bed and puts her hands behind her head. I wiggle my butt to the Beastie Boys and do a couple of catwalk spins. She's smiling, but I can tell from her expression that she's thinking about something else.

"Are you happy, Jay?" she asks suddenly.

"I'm dancing, aren't I?"

"No, but I mean really. Are you?"

I turn back to the mirror and continue to dance, swaying from side to side. I wet my hands with cologne, pat them together and slap my neck on both sides.

"I guess."

I think about my job, my brother, the band. I know my life isn't working out according to any Fortune 500 plan, but for some strange reason I'm starting to feel OK. I can sense changes in the energy around me, like my entire atmosphere is about to explode with new power and resolve.

"All I need is a bit more money so that I can take the next step and go back to school. I feel ready to get on with my real life now, which is a change. It's a good thing. Why?"

"No reason," she says, watching me. "Do you really want to go back to school next year?"

"Maybe. It depends on finding money. I don't know. I don't think Sheldon and I can live on tips."

I cap the bottle and wipe my hands on my jeans.

"They want me to do a Ph.D.," Janice begins.

"Who? The university?"

"No, *Rolling Stone*. They want me to write long, critical essays on the intricacies of Shane MacGowan's lyrics versus the poetry of Yeats. We're going to run a series . . . Maude Gonne, the 1916 uprising, touring with the Pogues . . . Yes, the university."

"Gonna do it?"

I check my teeth and do a last-minute floss, pulling the white ribbon between two molars. Janice pauses as I pull it out and inspect the results.

"Do you have to do that in front of me?" she asks, sitting up.

"You came in."

I continue to floss. She flops back on the bed and spreads her hands over her head, reaching lazily for the headboard. I watch her in the mirror, watch her stretch and move.

"I don't know if I'm going to do it," she says.

"Sounds like an opportunity," I say, still watching the rise and fall of her breathing.

"I don't think I want to do it, though. Not really. But it would mean I'd be staying here, in the city."

She sits up, and I look down at the top of the dresser and begin to sort through a pile of receipts. "Why would that be an incentive?" I force out a laugh.

She doesn't say anything, and when I look in the mirror again, she's watching me. I smile at her and do a final inspection. I'm not quite Brad Pitt, but I'm looking groovy enough to be hard to resist.

"You've put on a few pounds," Jan says.

I give her a look and tuck my T-shirt into my pants a bit tighter.

"Well, you have," she insists.

"Ready to go?" I say, turning to face her and putting my arms out to gauge her opinion on my look. She swings her legs around and stands up, straightens my shirt and dusts my shoulder. I pray my shirt isn't coated with dandruff. I try to inspect for dead skin flakes, but it's impossible to casually look down at your own shoulder.

"Where do you think you'll be next year?" she asks, yanking my shirt up. She turns me around and brushes something off the back of my pant leg, which makes every nerve ending in my body quiver. I exhale weakly and shrug my shoulders.

"I don't know. Ask me in a year."

She spins me around, holds me by the shoulders and inspects me one last time, nodding her head reluctantly. "That'll have to do. You're now ready to rock."

She kisses me lightly on the cheek and grabs her jacket from the bed. She stands with an innocent smile on her face, waiting for me to lead the way out. She's playing with me now. She must be. I know it.

"It's about time," Tyler sighs as we walk down the stairs. Everyone is huddled on the couch drinking beer and looking bored, Nicole especially.

"If you could have famous musician parents, who would they be?" Tyler asks.

"You've asked me before, Ty," I say wearily.

"I have not."

"You chose Al Green and Grace Slick."

"Oh, maybe I have. Bit testy today, Thompson? Someone leave a cigarette burn on one of your barstools?"

Nicole has put her arm around Tyler and rests her head against his shoulder. She smiles at him proudly and whispers in his ear. They laugh together and drift away to the planet Tycole right in front of our eyes.

"Well, I guess we should make some noise," Noel says.

Jan turns the stereo off on her way to the couch, cutting Neil Finn off in mid lyric. I haul out my guitar and sort through a few papers.

"So have we decided on a couple of songs?" I ask.

Tyler looks at me. "Snappy, snappy. I've been thinking. Given that your songs really need a lot of work to fit the guidelines of the competition, I thought our logical course of action would be to perform our most spiritual and soul-rendering performance piece . . ."

"You're not talking about *Space Oddity #2*," Noel says.

"Now I realize you all had some problems with it the first time."

"I believe Don Jenkins referred to it as confusing, cluttered and horribly self-indulgent," Noel responds.

"I blame that on background noise," Tyler murmurs.

"Tyler . . ." Jan whines.

"You have to take into account the atmosphere. *Space Oddity #2* is not really a bar piece."

Noel is holding up his hands trying to interrupt. Tyler pretends not to see him.

"Obviously we need something powerful that evokes emotion and grabs the audience's attention. We want to make a strong first impression, because we only have a few minutes to play."

Nicole begins to pass out sheets of typed paper. She holds one out to me, but I refuse to take it.

"We don't have time to polish new material," I say.

"That's exactly my point!" Tyler says. "It's not new. There are a few changes to the lyrics."

"We agreed to put all side projects on the back burner until after this competition," Noel says. "I realize you're eager—extremely eager—but we all agreed."

"But we want to win. And besides—"

I turn my dials and amp to ten for maximum interruption effect and shatter the conversation with an ear-splitting hard A.

"Do this and I'll quit," I say. "There are more pressing things in my life than arguments over songs for a stupid little garage band."

Everyone stands in silence—a silence deeper and more claustrophobic than usual. The energy in the room is pulsing.

"Let's start with 'Mona's Moaning,'" Noel says, placing his fingers on the proper frets. We all ease back from our predatorial poses. Noel has opened the safety valve, letting off enough steam to diffuse the situation, but some day soon he won't be quick enough to prevent a major blow out.

We find our marks and wait for Tyler. He's staring up at a small high window that blazes a shaft of light into the dim basement. After a few seconds his expression changes and he sighs. If I didn't know better I'd think his look was one of resignation. But I've never seen Tyler resigned to anything.

30

There are reams of psycho-babble television shows, infomercial self-help packages and Tony Robbins books to help a person deal with being a faulty professional, a bad lover or an inept parent. No one ever seems to consider that it's possible to feel inadequate as a brother.

I'm at the kitchen table noodling on my guitar, running through potential riffs and progressions, most of which quickly merge into a poorly disguised Travis song or a Beatles melody. The flickering light from the television dances against the wall like glimmers from a disco ball, distracting and hypnotizing me.

I put down my guitar and wander into the living room. Sheldon, as usual, is on the couch.

"I'm working on a song in the kitchen," I say as a shampoo commercial flashes on the screen.

Sheldon glances at me.

"It's called 'Get a Haircut, Sheldon.' I'm contemplating a B-52s-style wacky drum-machine rhythm."

"Really?" he says with unusual excitement. I feel a slight lurch in my stomach as my jest fails so pathetically.

"No." I look at the TV screen. "I'm kidding. It's my way of telling you I think you . . . well, might need a haircut."

I sit on the arm of the couch as he frowns and turns away.

"Dude, I can write a song about you if you like," I offer.

"Don't worry about it."

The commercials end and the screen is filled with an image of bloody flesh. I can see the white of bone as skin and muscle are folded open.

"Ow," I blurt. "What the hell is that?"

"It's called *The Operation*. They operate on people."

"Naturally."

The doctor is cutting the flesh with a scalpel.

"Oh, my God," I say. "But what are you doing watching it? Aren't there reruns of the *Simpsons* on somewhere? Or syndicated episodes of *Cheers*? Anything but this."

Sheldon shakes his head. "You're such a wuss," he says. "This is totally cool because it's so real. They're totally operating on this guy."

No one has called me a wuss since grade ten. I slide down onto the couch and watch the doctor suction a pool of blood from a mangled body cavity and poke a scalpel at a dark patch of flesh.

"That's the problem," Sheldon says, nodding. "Wait until they cut that puppy up."

I look at my brother, who is completely immersed in the gore. Despite my better judgment I watch them slice and dice around what I now realize is a kneecap. The doctor suctions again, then pats the area with gauze.

I've made a vow to try to communicate with my brother, to broach the subject of our family and let him know he's not alone. This sort of interaction looks easy in the movies. I decide to take the circuitous route.

"Shel, do you think Dad ever had a dream?"

"Yeah."

I wait for him to continue, but he watches TV. Getting Sheldon to talk is excruciatingly difficult, which might be why I don't really know him very well. He's never been eager to tell me about his life, his friends, what gets him excited. I wonder if I've been too hard on my mom, wonder if I was the same way growing up. Maybe she never knew anything about my life because I never shared any information with her. Even now, I'm not the best communicator. But after working in a bar, I want to come home, shut off my brain and relax, because most of my day is spent making small talk to strangers, asking them stupid questions about their lives—not because I really care about the answer, but because I have to fill that silence between sips. There's nowhere to hide when you're a bartender.

"What was Dad's dream, Shel?"

"He wanted to be a truck driver, dummy."

"He told you that?"

"No. But he has all those picture books on rigs."

"That doesn't mean he wanted to be a truck driver."

Sheldon points to the TV screen, implying I should shut up and watch the carnage.

"Why don't you ask him?" he says.

We continue to watch *The Operation* until a commercial for carpet cleaner comes on, at which point I chuckle heartily. I try to think of a way to continue our conversation, but I'm not sure how. I've never been a part of Sheldon's life. We've eaten meals together and interacted at family functions, but the age gap and the differences in our attitudes and personalities have made us more like business acquaintances than brothers. When we lived at home, I was a teenager and, aside from the nuisance of having to baby-sit occasionally, I never had any time or interest in a little kid. When I moved out, I guess that attitude never changed.

The Operation comes back on.

The sound of a car door being slammed in the city is not novel. But for some reason I notice the sound as I sit with my only brother and watch reconstructive knee surgery on a quiet Wednesday night. Something in the back of my mind gnaws at me.

After a few minutes the sound of heavy feet on wooden steps echoes up to the apartment. I hear the footsteps getting closer, and what's more, I honestly sense them approaching, like a storm growling over a summer lake.

The door erupts in a series of bangs. Sheldon looks at me as we hear the doorknob being twisted.

"Jason, open up the door."

I pause for a few seconds before getting off the couch. I've known this was coming, but I'm still not fully prepared. I walk to the door on wobbly legs as the pounding continues. I turn the lock and slide back the deadbolt, take a deep breath and open it for my father.

He nods and sloppily pushes past me into the front hall. He runs his hand through his short grey hair and looks around. It occurs to me that during the six years I've lived here, my father has never once been to my apartment.

"Can I help you?" I ask.

He glares at me and wags a finger in my face.

"Don't start. I've come to pick up your brother."

"I didn't know he called to be picked up."

My father frowns. He walks three steps into the kitchen,

then doubles back and stomps into the living room. Sheldon, to his credit, is still watching TV. He appears tense, but he's not showing any fear.

"You can't just barge in here," I say weakly, following behind. "This is my apartment."

"Get your things, Sheldon. You're coming home."

Sheldon continues to watch television.

"Did you hear me?"

"Dad," I say, putting my hand on his shoulder. He wheels around and pushes it off.

"Stay out of this, Jason," he warns. "I think you've done enough damage. I just got a fucking letter from your mother's lawyer."

He slurs damage so that it comes out *damash*, and my keen bartender senses pick up on the smell of stale alcohol. He's standing bowlegged, pointing at Sheldon, who isn't budging, who hasn't even moved or shown any sign of recognition. He's staring into the TV screen, burrowing into the sterile, well-ordered operating room.

"You can't do this," I say again, this time clearly and louder. My father turns to me. Even though he hasn't hit me since I was a kid I feel afraid. He's angled for a standoff.

"You think you and your mother can screw me? You should honour your father. Ever heard of the Ten Commandments? I am your father, and as your father I expect you to listen to me. When I tell one of my boys to move . . ." He's a mess, ugly sloppy. He turns back to Sheldon and yells. "I fucking expect him to move!"

I stare at him, watch his thin lips move, notice the blue vein bulging beneath the skin of his neck. His face is red and his eyes aren't focusing as well as they should. I notice the tension in his arms, how the muscle is wiry under his skin.

"Sheldon's staying here," I say. The words aren't strong or firm or certain, but emerge sounding formal and businesslike. "He doesn't want to go home. He's had enough."

My father turns to Sheldon. "Get your things," he says.

"He's not going."

"Don't disrespect your father. You don't know. None of you know what it's like to be me. All my life this family has taken from me. I'm tired of it. You two owe me something. We're going. Don't make me say it again, Sheldon."

Sheldon continues to stare at the television screen. My father sighs and runs his callused hand through his hair again.

"Get whatever you need and let's go," he begins in a more accommodating voice. "We'll pick up a bucket of Kentucky Fried Chicken, go home, and you can watch one of your movies."

Kentucky Fried Chicken. How many nights as a one-parent kid did I sit and eat Kentucky Fucking Fried Chicken. Fast food, empty houses, strange people filling that void of a missing parent. All my father's friends were bitter, divorced men who came over to recount stories of mistakes, alternating between self-condemnation and self-righteous anger. There was always booze, the raw fuel of emotion, driving the engines. People break. They don't always get over it, deal with it, move on. Sometimes they stall and sink and rust.

He takes a couple of steps toward the door, perhaps expecting Sheldon to get up and follow him. When Sheldon doesn't budge, he stops. I can hear his breath channelling through his thick nostrils.

"Come on, Sheldon. What are you going to do here?"

The three of us stand as points in a triangle. I sense that none of us is certain what to do next. We are in uncharted territory and the rules that have always been in place no longer apply.

"Come on, boy, show me some respect," he says again, with little certainty.

As I stand facing him, I realize that although I do love my father, I don't know if I respect him. I try to understand his point of view, but at the same time this is his job. When he gave life to my brother and me, he signed off on a certain amount of personal freedom. I'm only sorry that he's come to regret the choice.

"Come on, Sheldon," my father says, now wearily. He shakes his head and looks at me. "Jason, you can't take care of him. You can't even take care of yourself. I'm the one who makes him do his homework and makes sure he eats. You know it."

"You didn't even call," I say.

His face flushes, and I get a sense he's been waiting for this remark.

"Why didn't *you* call?" he asks. "How old are you? I figured you'd call when you needed . . ." He runs a hand across his face. I see him floundering in his own life like a drowning man. But he quickly gathers himself.

"I have a fucking job!" he yells. "I knew where he went. If he wants to wander off and not come back, that's his own business. I show him that respect."

He looks at Sheldon, then back at me and shakes his head bitterly.

"You're both a fucking disappointment to me," he says, pounding toward the door.

"That's ironic," I murmur.

He stops and glares at me. "What?"

"Nothing," I say.

He stares at me for a couple of seconds. "I don't care anymore," he says finally. "I wipe my hands of you. But don't think you can come begging to my door when you need money for his shoes and his . . . other things . . . Because that door will be locked. Someday you'll understand, Jason."

He's about to say something else, but I slam the door behind him and fasten the deadbolt. I stride into the kitchen, blood pumping wildly through my veins. I grit my teeth, flex my hands and try to calm down. I hear him lingering in the hall, so I pick up my favourite coffee mug and throw a perfect strike into the centre of the heavy wooden door. Fragments of glass ricochet in my direction, spinning and diving onto the rug. There's a large chunk of wood gouged from the door. I hear my father's footsteps pounding down the stairs.

I splash water on my face in the kitchen sink. My calves are shaking, as if the muscles were made of Jell-O, and I have to lean on the counter to stay upright. After a few seconds my head ceases to pound and my breathing slows to a manageable level. I hear Sheldon dialling the phone in the living room.

"Hello, I'd like to report a drunk driver in a blue Sierra near Prince and Lawrence. I believe he was driving toward Laurier Park. He nearly hit a kid. He's all over the road."

I listen to the rest of the conversation, listen to Sheldon calmly give a false name and number without a quiver in his voice. He politely thanks the dispatcher, hangs up the phone and drops his bulky, awkward body back onto the couch.

When I feel relatively sure that my father is gone, I grab my jacket from the closet, fumble with my shoes and slip out to the car. My mind is a jumble of thoughts and memories as I creep along the city roads to the highway. As I wind my way along the country curves and desolate bare stretches, I gun the engine and feel the car fighting centrifugal force, straining to slip loose. At every curve I think how easy it would be to let go, to let the wheel slip from my fingers and be pulled into open space; despite this, at every curve I grip the wheel a bit tighter and glide it around again and again and again.

I pull the car onto the side of a familiar dirt side road past two No Trespassing signs. There's a lake about a half-mile down this road and cottages and private homes and a marina, but I know a path through the bush to a diving rock, about twenty feet high, with a swim rope attached to a tree. We used to trek here from Uncle Gary's cottage. I step out into intense darkness, punctuated only by milky moonlight and the pinpoints of stars.

Shivering, I slowly make my way through the frosty wet leaves, pulling sharp branches out of my way and removing thorns and brambles from my clothing. Several times I stop and look into the darkness and feel the sheer stillness of the world. When I reach the diving rock I sit and watch the rippling water, watch shadows of birds drifting and diving, and hear the soft splash and trickle of the lake beating against the shore. The moon is calm and gentle, laying dull beams onto the water. I replay my confrontation with my father, and know I can't allow myself to feel regret.

As I look up into the stars I marvel at the imperfection of human beings, how we're all fumbling through our lives pretending we know where we're going. I've believed for so long that I don't deserve happiness because I didn't have a plan, didn't have my life in order like everyone else. How wrong.

I think of Janice.

Finally, I get up. My body is stiff and numb and feels like it's been nailed to the cold rock face with icicles.

It's two in the morning by the time I get back to the apartment. Shel is sprawled out on the couch, surrounded by a battlefield of chocolate bar wrappers and pop cans. His shoes are in the middle of the floor, and a trail of socks leads to the couch.

"Comfortable?" I groan, slamming down in a chair.

"You should buy one of these cookers," he says, pointing to a mini indoor grill on the Home Shopping Network. "Only ten left. They're going fast."

"Uh-huh."

"No, seriously, they're neat."

He flicks through a couple of channels, stops on a commercial for an air freshener, then turns to an arty film station. A group of peasants is cavorting by a stream.

"What's this?" I ask.

"I don't know," he says, "but there's a whole lot of nudity in it."

I join him on the couch and we watch some lame French film with bad dubbing, waiting for the actors to get it on. Instead, they do laundry in the river and talk about the nature of politics and love.

"I forgot I still have these channels," I say absently. "I should cancel them."

"Why?"

"Because they're like everything else—worthless crap that just clutters up your life. I don't watch them and I never really have. But they're there."

My stomach burns, like I might have an ulcer. After a few disappointing minutes, Shel gets bored and flicks around some more.

"You have to go to school sometime, Shel," I say. "I know it seems pointless, but you'll rot if you stay here all the time. You won't be happy."

"I'm not happy at school," he says.

"I know. But you're a smart kid."

He looks at me.

"You're not a genius, mind you," I say, smiling. "But you're good at things. You've got a good imagination. You always used to make up stories when you were a kid, really clever stories. And you created great excuses not to go to bed when I was baby-sitting. But you've got to work hard."

"Can I stay here?" he asks quietly, turning the channel again. I look around at my dilapidated apartment, look at Sheldon. His bulk and my small apartment will make for close quarters. Still, oddly enough, a part of me is happy for the company.

"Tell you what, bro. You can stay as long as you tell me whenever there's nudity on TV."

He looks at me, then back to the TV, and smiles. I close my tired eyes as he flips back to the Home Shopping Network. I hear eager voices, a ringing bell and a price being proclaimed at an incredible $99.99.

"We should get one of these, too."

31

The fateful day of the competition has arrived. It's Saturday
and I'm driving with Janice and Sheldon. Janice is bobbing
back and forth in the passenger seat, singing off-key lines
with Jewel on the stereo.

"Can't we just listen?"

Jan smirks and sings even louder. She seems to think it's
some sort of a cute game. I glance over at her as she stares
out the window. If I get a good chance today I'm going to
tell her exactly how I feel about her, consequences be
damned.

Maybe.

"Hey, Sheldon," she says, turning to my brother lounging
in the back seat. "You're so quiet. Are you in a good mood?"

Sheldon blushes and sort of mumbles an affirmative.
Being on a budget, he had to get his hair cut at the Hair-
dressing Academy by a short Asian woman studying to be a
stylist. He's now sporting the slightly uneven flattop look.

"Are you excited about today?"

He shrugs nervously, and the car falls silent, except for the
gentle hum of the tires rolling along the highway.

"Tell her about your candy bar scheme," I say.

Jan leans back expectantly. Sheldon shifts around in his
seat.

"OK, so, they have this contest to win a year's free movies
at Blockbuster. And all you have to do is send in a Mr. Big
chocolate bar wrapper or a hand-drawn fact-simile."

"Facsimile," Jan corrects. "Uh-huh."

"So I drew a hundred and eleven fact-similes. We're
totally gonna win."

I smile. My brother has taken my remarks on his creativity to heart and is now drawing chocolate bar wrappers. Not high academia, but it shows some initiative. Two huge black battered and smelly Converse running shoes drape over my shoulder.

"Get your feet off, Sheldon. And make sure your seat belt's on."

A cop car cruises by us like a shark cutting water. I check the speedometer. I squirm in the seat and once again try to get comfortable. There's a transport that's been closing in on us for the past few minutes and it's now spreading into the passing lane.

"Can we stop here?"

Sheldon's big head is leaning forward and he's motioning toward a service station with a coffee shop.

"We're eating as soon as we get there, Sheldon," I say, watching the mirror as the big rig finally gears up and pulls by us. The hubcaps are spinning wildly, like crazed roulette wheels, and the grumble of the engine shakes my chest.

"I have to go pee," he whines.

Jan giggles softly. Sheldon turns red and sits back in his seat.

I pull the car into the off ramp at the last second, darting in front of a minivan full of men in turbans. I glance in the mirror and give a short wave of apology. As we glide into the parking lot, I let them pass, then park as far away from them as possible out of embarrassment. We get out of the car, stretch and mill around aimlessly like car-drunk commuters do, and Sheldon hobbles off stiffly toward the restaurant. I look around at the people coming and going, the mad desire for coffee, the mutual stiffness and our everlasting need to be travelling somewhere else. I can sense Janice beside me. I'm about to speak.

"I'm going to get a drink," she says, punching my shoulder lightly. "Do you want anything?"

"Yeah."

She waits for me to continue, but that's it. I want something, but now isn't the right moment. I know it absolutely.

"What do you want?"

I laugh. "I want to find the meaning of life and I'm pretty sure it's hiding in a greasy truck stop. Maybe among the naked-woman mudflaps or the pine-scented air fresheners."

The drone of the highway enters my mind as something more than background noise. She licks her lips and looks at the asphalt.

"I was thinking about getting an iced tea."

I nod and she wanders off. I squint at the clear blue sky and try to imagine life before cars and highways and drive-through restaurants, try to imagine a world without TV or satellites homing in on us from the heavens. I can't do it, can't even fathom the possibility. I watch the cars buzzing by like intent wasps.

A few minutes later, a relieved-looking Sheldon squirms through the double glass doors with a coffee and a bag of doughnuts. The minivan I cut off honks as it slides past, and I wave.

"Maybe I'll get a coffee," I sigh as Shel lumbers up to me.

"Not if you're driving," he says, biting into an icing-sugar-coated jelly-filled. The jam squirts onto his cheek, and he sticks his grey tongue out to lick it back into his mouth.

"What are you talking about, Shel?"

"You shouldn't drink coffee and drive. Or talk on

cellphones. I saw it on TV. They had a guy who was driving on the highway with hot coffee and the lid came off and he scalded himself and it caused him to lose control of his car and crash."

"Really."

"Yup. They figure a bunch of fatal accidents happen that way, 'cause they find spilled coffee."

"In the wreckage?"

"Yeah."

"Gee, that *is* strange. Coffee being spilled in a high-speed crash. I'll be right back." I start toward the coffee shop.

"Get something cold," he yells.

32

"What took you guys so long?" Noel asks. One uncomfortable trip in my car has helped him overcome his wear-and-tear phobia.

"We were bonding," I say.

We're parked in front of a converted old-style movie theatre. The marquee juts out over the sidewalk like a strict teacher leaning over the shoulder of a naughty student. Where the list and times of current movies should be are a couple of nifty religious slogans ("Fear equals Faith" and "Christ was born, Christ is risen, Christ will come again") and an announcement that the Martin Luther King Jr. Youth Choir is coming to town for a performance in January. In the backlit windows reserved for coming attractions are the words "Jesus Saves."

"I wonder if they still sell popcorn," Noel says.

Sheldon immediately perks up.

"Not exactly what I expected," I say.

"It's better than what I expected," Jan murmurs. "You know what would be a really clever slogan for their marquee? 'Apocalypse Now.' Think about it. Wouldn't that be ironic?"

A car horn blasts behind us, and Tyler pulls his mother's minivan into a parking spot across the street. Nicole is next to him, checking her large, wavy hair in the sun visor mirror. Behind her I see a third party.

Tyler skips across the street. He's wearing jeans and a beige shirt. His hair is truly shocking. It's his natural brown.

"Man, rough edges are getting filed as we speak," Noel says.

"Greetings all," Tyler says. "I trust that your excursion was as stimulating as ours. Bad night, Jay? You look a bit worse for wear. I made sure I stopped last night after two brandy Alexanders."

"Zip it, Tyler," Jan says.

Tyler appears unfazed. He doesn't look at her. "Quite the place," he says.

Nicole wanders across the street. Behind her I see two tall, gangly guys opening the rear hatch to the minivan.

"Dude, you brought roadies," Noel says. "I'm impressed."

I feel an inkling of dread in my stomach. Nicole comes up behind Tyler, puts her arm around his waist and whispers into his ear. He nods. She doesn't look at us.

"There's been a minor change in plan," Tyler says, a bit unsteadily. "Preston is our new keyboard player and William plays guitar. He was trained as a classical guitarist but has adapted exceptionally well to my experimental music."

I look at him, but he avoids my eyes. Even by Tyler's standards, this is a new low. He's often stubborn and pig-headed and comically pretentious, but he's never been outright devious. Jan glances at me and Noel, but seems too tired to continue her long-standing fight with Tyler. She rolls her eyes and paces off a few steps leaving me to get an explanation.

"I'm feeling a disturbance in the force, Ty," Noel says softly. "I think you're out of line to try and force us to accept new people into the band."

Tyler clears his throat. Nicole looks at us.

"Clearly his talent is being stifled by Jay's lightweight pop sensibilities," she announces.

"Personally, I'm not upset by playing Jay's songs," Tyler adds quickly, "but there does come a time when a serious artist has to move to the next level. I can't afford to waste this opportunity."

I'm staring at him, but he refuses to look me in the eye.

"What are you saying, Ty?" I ask.

He looks off into the distant action of the busy street. I see his Adam's apple bob in his throat.

"Well, I'll play with Trailer, but we've also entered the competition separately, under the name Elastic Soul Band. Nicole will be playing the tambourine for us."

"So you want two chances to win the competition?"

"Jay, honestly, you can't be serious."

"Why can't I be serious, Ty?" I say bitterly. "Not that I care, really, but there is a certain principle. You compete in two bands, you have two chances to win. Do you know if you're allowed to play twice?"

"I am," he assures me. "I asked in advance."

"You're a real Burt Bacharach," Noel says.

"If I wasn't allowed to be in two bands I would have arranged for a substitute drummer for Trailer. Don't get so uptight."

"You're incredible, Ty." Noel kicks at the pavement, his head down.

"Come on," I say. "This is getting out of hand. I know we could all use the prize money and the recording contract would be a dream, but after what I've seen with these fundamentalists, we're really only here for a laugh. I mean, look at this place."

Nicole whispers something to him. He squeezes her hand and looks at me with an expression of cool defiance.

"Perhaps that attitude is part of the reason why I feel I've evolved beyond this band. Personally, I want to move on to the next phase of my creative development. I had hoped to elevate you people, but instead of taking a chance on my ideas you fought and attacked me. Get Tyler. Isn't that always the way? But what am I expected to do, dispense with all my hard work because you've decided to take the easy way out? You're my friend, Thompson, but you obviously cannot understand that this is my vocation. You can't understand the depth of my commitment. Now, we're quite willing to share the equipment—"

"That's great, because half of it's mine."

Tyler holds up his hand. "Let me finish. We'll share the equipment and I'll play the drums for your songs, but we're also going to be entered and judged on our own merits."

"We don't need a drummer," I say. "You're out of rhythm half the time anyway."

I sit down on a bench and seethe. Jan sits beside me and Noel stands looking pensive. We watch Preston and William as they cart equipment across the road and into the church.

"The only sensible thing to do is have a drink," Noel says, gazing down the street.

"Do you think it's a good idea," I ask, "to show up to a right-wing religious gathering stinking of booze?"

"Sounds like the only sensible thing to do."

"Maybe this was a mistake from the start and we should just chill out," Jan says. "Maybe we've tainted our karma and the good Lord is smiting us."

"What's smiting mean?" Sheldon asks.

Noel glances at him. "It's something God did to the huddled masses in the Old Testament. I believe plagues of locusts were one of his favourite ways to smite."

"Just think of an episode of *Jerry Springer*," Jan offers. "At the end when everyone goes ballistic."

"Cool."

"Well, I'll tell you what," Jan says to Noel, rising from the bench. "You get us registered with the high priest of whoever is running this show and I'll take gimpy and the Beav down to the nearest pub."

Noel nods and we go our separate ways. We find a seedy-looking pub a block away and huddle into a corner booth. The seats are worn, but soft and velvety. Sheldon and Jan order hamburger platters and I pick at stray fries. As they finish their meals, Noel finally arrives, looking unnerved.

"It was a zoo in there," he says, dropping his jacket on a chair and turning to the bar. "We're scheduled to go on at two-thirty, so we've got a couple of hours to kill. Apparently they've got forty or fifty acts auditioning."

Over the next hour we sit and wait and drink. I add a couple of shots of vodka in between pints. These help a bit to ease my nerves. My anger at Tyler and apprehension about playing music in front of a couple hundred faithful churchgoers has the strange effect of offsetting the sleepiness of intoxication. I feel generally sober, even though I know I'm not.

At one-thirty we put on our jackets and head back to the church to check out the competition and watch the premiere performance of the Elastic Soul Band. The booze has softened my malice and has made me irritated and maudlin at the same time. Part of me wants to see Tyler do well, because he's my friend, but most of me wants him and his stupid ragtag ensemble to fail miserably.

Noel is right. The auditorium is packed with an assortment of hopefuls. There are kids in costumes, teenagers, old men and women—the whole societal gamut is here, eager to impress. The seats sloping down to the stage are nearly full. Behind the modest-sized stage is a big white movie screen. On stage a group of teenage girls move in synchronized dance steps while singing a song about being lost and then found set to a tune that is an obvious knock-off of the Spice Girls. Surprisingly and disturbingly, they are pretty good.

I look around for Natasha and her reggae band. I don't see her, but near the stage a pensive-looking Tyler is pacing slowly. Nicole is sitting in the front row, looking bored as usual.

"This is Bethlehem," Noel says, reading a typed program and indicating the girls on stage. "Tyler's band is due up next."

"Are you entered in the competition?"

A short girl with a clipboard steps up beside me. She looks dangerously perky.

"Um, yeah. We're Trailer."

She looks at her clipboard.

"Welcome to the Pashel Street Fundamentalist Christian Annual Talent Competition." She hands us each a pin identifying us as entrants. "In the past we've sent such glorious bands as Praise Him, Search Your Soul and Failing the Cross to the regional competition in Chicago. Last year's winner, Wretched Sinner, made it all the way to the finals in Oklahoma."

"There's a final?" Noel says.

Our perky friend beams. "Absolutely! The winner from today goes to the regional competition to compete against state chapters. That winner then goes on to compete for the grand prize of five thousand dollars and a recording contract with Church on the Rock Records in Oklahoma."

Noel closes his eyes. We both start to laugh drunkenly.

"But there are lovely parting gifts for participants today, right?" Jan interrupts.

Perky smiles widely. "Oh yes, we have a number of donated prizes—prayer books, cds, T-shirts . . ."

"Coffeemakers?" Jan asks.

"I don't know. I'd have to check."

"That'd be great."

"Would you be interested in donating an offering to help fund the competition?" Perky continues. "Half of each dollar goes to aid missionaries doing the Lord's work abroad and half goes to paying for this event."

She hands me a prayer card and an envelope.

"We'll get back to you," Noel says.

"OK. Sure. I understand. God bless you anyway and good luck."

She looks around for the next person to harass and beelines for a doughy woman in her mid-forties. I hand the prayer card to Jan.

"All yours," I tell her. "I need both hands to wring Noel's neck."

Noel puts his hands up and floats around like Mohammed Ali. The absurdity of this entire scheme has been cemented.

"I wonder if anyone has informed Tyler," I say.

Jan's laughing fit is so intense I'm afraid she might cause an embolism.

Bethlehem has finished and is bowing to the audience. I entertain a few mildly impure thoughts about the well-endowed red-haired girl on the end as she bounds off stage.

We find seats in the middle of the theatre and wait as Tyler and the Elastic Soul Band get set up. I rest my head on the upholstered red seat back and begin to feel warm and sleepy. I close my eyes and begin to drift away when suddenly I hear the faint sound of David Bowie.

"What a surprise," I say, opening my eyes.

At the key moment I see Tyler lean over and pretend to accidentally knock a bowl off a table beside his drum kit. The sound of breaking glass echoes through the microphones on stage.

"That's clever," Noel says, sitting back in his chair. "I suppose they can't disqualify him for clumsiness."

Tyler begins to sing.

In her eyes I see his stiff corpse
in her hands I feel my childhood
Oh Mary, mother of God
Oh Mary, with your sweet virgin bod . . .

I feel a communal cringe run through the audience. Tyler's opus sounds even worse as a member of the audience than it does on stage. Tyler finishes the first verse, then Nicole comes to the microphone and begins to wail.

"Oh, man," Noel says, leaning forward and putting his chin in his hands. "This is too much."

I sit back and soak up the performance, feeling both embarrassed for Tyler and vindicated. I glance around at a sea of bewildered, God-fearing faces. A few people are smiling incredulously. The woman behind me comments to her husband that the song sounds like homosexual music. I'd like to turn around and ask her what exactly that genre encompasses.

Despite a few hostile shouts to repent and get off stage, Tyler continues, and the band plays abbreviated segments of scenes one and two. The lyrics for the bridge, like much of the rest of the song, have been modified for the occasion. Nicole steps up to the mike and screeches.

Mary, intervene!
Mary, you're supreme!
Women are so strong!
The Pope is never wrong!

A gasp echoes around us and the place erupts. Some people are standing and shouting, others are stupefied. I can feel anger welling up like the wrath of God as the Elastic Soul Band continues on through the bridge.

A woman and a tall, bald man are pounding on the stage and screaming. Preston looks bewildered and the band— except for Tyler—seems to realize that something has gone drastically wrong.

Finally, as papers and magazines begin to cascade from the audience, the speakers cut out and the stage area goes dark. People are pounding their feet and shouting abuse. The audience surges forward as a single body.

"This is wicked," Sheldon says, his mouth dropping open.

We sit mesmerized as two men in dark suits bound onto the stage and stride toward Tyler, who has finally stopped playing and is looking around in confusion. They're gesturing wildly.

Our perky friend sprints up the aisle, still clutching her clipboard, but no longer smiling.

"It's gotta be that bad karma," Noel says. "We've cursed ourselves by faking it."

The pandemonium continues. One of the suited men grabs Tyler's collar and pushes him toward the side of the stage. Tyler holds his ground and appears to be shouting back at the two men. Some of the faces are genuinely fanatical.

"I'm getting a pretty dangerous vibe here," I say to Noel, who nods in stunned silence.

"If he'd just get off," Jan says.

Members of the audience are climbing onto the stage. Nicole and the two new stooges are lurking nervously near the exit, waiting for Tyler. Finally, when I think the fever is reaching a pitch and he might get swarmed and lynched, Tyler strides off. In the middle of the stage he pauses for a second, shouts something at the audience and vigorously gives us all the finger.

"He certainly is an entertainer," Jan says.

Tyler and the Elastic Soul Band scurry off the stage, leaving their equipment behind. We sit back down in our seats and huddle together.

"So what course of action would be prudent now?" I ask.

"I'm for staying," Noel says. "I didn't come all this way

and work on these songs just to turn around and slink out because of Tyler. I say we go on as long as the crowd doesn't start burning all non-believers or agnostics or whatever we are."

"Jan?"

"We're here, aren't we? We might as well do it. It'd feel like a waste if we didn't. And besides, this is probably the last time we play together as a band."

No matter how many times I hear that comment, it always hurts.

33

I'm more nervous than usual as we're setting up and for a few seconds I truly panic. I'm worried about two things: first, getting attacked; second, sounding terrible. There's a good reason why bands have drummers. Jan is confident her bass playing can drive the beat, but I'm not so sure.

"We can't do this," I say to Noel as he casually tunes his guitar. He holds it close to his ear and hits strings. He nods to me without any true concern.

"Don't you ever get nervous?" I snap, resenting that I stand to suffer the most humiliation because I'm the lead singer. This could be "The Rose" all over again.

"You'll be fine," Noel says with a shrug. "And if not, well, most of these people are needy geeks anyway. No offence to the church . . ."

Jan chooses this moment to pinch my behind, which really freaks me out. For a second I teeter on the edge of throwing a tantrum, my nerves are so jangled. Then I see

Natasha lingering in the corner of the auditorium. She's watching us intently and talking to a guy with dreads.

"OK." Jan smiles as we get the thumbs-up from one of the co-ordinators. "This one's for Tyler." She winks at me.

"Hello, radical fundamentalists!" Noel yells into his mike, pumping his fist in a very un-Noel sort of way. "Who here loves Jesus?"

This gets a good reaction from the crowd, who until this point impressed me as highly intent on remaining skeptical and judgmental.

"Of course you do!" Noel yells. "Because you're freaks!"

This one doesn't get the same response and I feel a total-body nervous spasm. For a split paranoid second I realize that I can't remember the words to start the first song. My hands are cold and heavy and my bladder tightens up.

"Because you're Jesus freaks!" Noel yells.

This one gets a rousing cheer.

"And you're proud!"

I look over at Noel, who is smirking.

"We know that we're all searching for something, that we're all scared that we live in a world where bad things can happen to good people. That's what this song is all about. This is called 'No, Not the Highway.'"

This is not according to plan, nor is it even vaguely religious. This song is about my dog. But I have no option, other than to launch in and go along.

Eighteen wheels pounding down the highway
Don't go near that road today
Stay, stay, stay away from the big trucks
Isn't there a better way?

And they love it. By the third verse people are up from their seats surrounding the stage, swaying and swinging their arms over their heads. There may even be a person or two gyrating, but it's really not our fault.

Noel works his way through the killer solo, digging deep and pressing on hard. As the guitar screams through the speakers we hit the heights of Christian rock. A young girl directly in front of us begins to quiver and spasm, flailing wildly, her mouth forming intense divinity-driven words—indecipherable to all but those who speak in tongues. I feel alive with inspiration.

Which is why I'm surprised when the song collapses and I see Noel jumping off the stage into the crowd. The speakers drone out feedback as the sound of electrically amplified strings slowly fades out. Noel is pushing people away from the girl and yelling, "Give her some space!"

Jan and I put down our guitars and climb down to the scene below.

"WWJD?" a university-aged guy yells at Noel.

Noel is holding the girl's head steady and putting a belt in her mouth.

"What would Jesus do?" the guy yells.

"He'd keep her from swallowing her tongue!" Noel shouts back. He looks desperately to us. "Get these people away, she needs air."

We obey, asking people to move back and directing traffic. Everyone is panicked and anxious, including me. I don't have much experience in emergencies. Noel turns to a girl nearby.

"What's your name?"

She looks around nervously, then looks back at Noel. "Me?"

"Yes, you. What's your name?"

"Heidi."

"OK, Heidi, I need you to go call an ambulance. Tell them there's a girl having a seizure and she's having trouble breathing."

Heidi strides off purposefully. I squat down beside Noel, who is still holding the girl's head and talking to her.

"Noel," I murmur. "Are you sure that girl wasn't speaking in tongues?"

Noel keeps talking to the girl. After a second he turns to me.

"Jay, get these people to give her some air. People speaking in tongues don't turn blue."

I stand back up. I suppose he has a point. I'm glad someone is in control. After about ten surreal and frayed minutes an ambulance comes. They strap the girl to a stretcher and take her out of the auditorium.

A man in a blue suit wanders over to us. "Sorry about that," he says, looking at a clipboard.

Jan and I shrug, not sure what to say.

"The organizers think it's best if we reschedule. It's been a really bad day. Maybe God wants us to resume another day. First those saboteurs blaspheming and now this unfortunate affair . . . Can you come back next week?"

"We'll pray on it and get back to you," Jan says.

Blue Suit nods solemnly. "That'd be great."

Noel talks to a few more people. The woman in the floral dress hugs him and kisses him on the cheek. He shakes a few hands, then finally rejoins us.

"So they want us to come back next week," he says as if nothing has happened.

"Noel, you're a freaking hero," Jan says, shaking him by the shoulders.

Noel smiles shyly. "Oh, that. Well, the girl needed help. I've seen it before. Anyone else would have done the same thing."

"Stop being modest."

He pulls us into a huddle. "So we coming back next week?" he asks.

"Not on your life," Jan retorts without a pause.

"I was hoping you'd say that," he says. "These people pay more attention to us than our regular fans, but this definitely is not where we belong."

34

I pull the bomber out to pass a minivan. My foot feels slightly numb on the pedal. I'd like to find a rest stop and pull over to stretch and have a coffee, but there don't seem to be any restaurants on this strip of highway. I haven't seen the comforting warm glow of a fast-food franchise for miles.

Jan tosses a kernel of sugarcoated popcorn into her mouth and chews on it vigorously. I'm going to tell her tonight. No, really, this time I'm super-serious. I've made a vow to myself. She pulls a cassette out of her pocket, takes out my mix and pops in her tape.

"I do believe it's time for some chick music," she says.

"Three songs, then put my tape back in."

She shakes her head. "I'm expanding your taste in music, Jay. Have you noticed that your music is mostly male-oriented? You've obviously been single way too long. You need a woman's influence."

A No Doubt song blasts from the speakers. The grey horizon flows by us, a monotonous quilt of autumn fields. I try not to think about the implications of Jan taking it upon herself to expand my mind. I think about the day, and it all seems quite funny and strange, a story we'll tell years from now. Probably no one will believe us.

"I need to take a break," I say, putting on the turn signal.

"We're almost home," Jan says.

We drive down a sleepy, winding street. I pull the car over in front of a dilapidated mom-and-pop store. The windows are a dirty yellow and cluttered with sun-faded signs advertising milk, cigarettes and RC cola. I just hope their coffee is hot and fresh.

"Everybody out, and don't get lost."

The car doors opening sound like triggers being cocked. I see Noel pulling his car in behind us.

"I was wondering when you were going to take a break," he says out his window. "My bladder's been breakdancing for the last half-hour."

Noel and Sheldon go into the store. I stretch my arms above my head and feel a pinch in my lower back, as though I'm being prodded with a blunt nail. I bend forward to touch my shoes.

"Hey, nice butt," Jan says, wandering around to my side of the car. "You shouldn't tease a girl like that."

"Me teasing?" I mutter incredulously.

She brushes a wisp of hair from her eyes. I can feel the cold of dusk seeping into my body. Jan claps her hands together and looks around.

"Yeah, well, I've been thinking," she says. "And I'm going to get straight to the point. I'm wondering if you've ever wanted to kiss me. I know I'm no kewpie-doll airhead supermodel, and I know I'm not a cute blond fundamentalist, but you can't always get what you want."

Her voice is shaky near the end. I smile, unsure of what to say. And then, probably unwisely, I start laughing.

"Hey," she says, punching me hard on the arm. "You can't laugh. This was really difficult for me, you little rat."

I laugh harder and she joins in.

She says, "We're not going to be a band much longer, so you can't cop a conflict of interest plea or anything stupid like that. And you'd be lucky to have me."

"I know," I say. "I'm not questioning that fact."

And then we lean in and kiss. Her lips are warm and soft and comforting—comforting more than anything else. And I suddenly realize how tired I am and how I'm no longer sure if I can deal with my life alone.

"Wasn't so hard, now, was it?" she says, smirking and punching me on the arm again, this time affectionately.

"No," I say, looking over at the store window and wondering if Noel saw us. "Not too difficult."

She kisses me again softly, then squeezes my hand. We go inside. Sheldon is at the cash register with three chocolate bars, a pepperoni stick and a litre bottle of Coke. He smiles sheepishly when he sees me.

"It's been a long day," he says.

Noel is at the far end of the last aisle looking at a jar of mayonnaise. He's reading the label.

"Is this a snack for yourself, or are you buying for the entire group?" I ask.

Noel puts the jar back on the shelf. "Just checking out the competition," he says. "As part of my new promotion, I'm being moved from coffee to the meals and condiments division. I'll be in mayonnaise."

"Sounds kinky," Jan murmurs.

"The excitement never stops, dude," he says. "But I'm pretty happy. I was getting a bit bored with coffee."

"Don't be dissin' java," I say, looking toward the counter. "I hope they have some brewing."

I buy a small coffee and a dusty bottle of aspirin for my stiff back. I swallow three aspirin, add copious amounts of milk to the coffee and gulp it down. We get back out on the road with Jan driving and me in the back seat trying to stretch out and get comfortable. Sheldon watches me from the front seat as he takes bite after bite of his Coffee Crisp. We hit a deep pothole and I yelp. Sheldon shakes his head.

"You're such a wuss. What if you need a back operation? What if they have to cut you open and remove one of your vertebrae? I saw them do it on *The Operation*. They had to fuse two disks together. It was way cool."

I close my eyes. Apparently the day has worn me out because I instantly fall into a shallow sleep. I wake up when the car engine cuts out. We drop Sheldon off at my apartment, then Janice drives in silence until we're almost to her place.

"So, what do you figure happens now?" she asks, turning off the engine.

"I don't know," I say. "I guess we just keep going. I'll keep looking for a new job, you'll concentrate on school, we'll rent movies on Friday nights and when we're really tired we'll get take-out. You'll come to realize that I'm basically a boring guy who loves music and movies and spends most of his time doing very little."

She raises her eyebrows. "Très romantic, as Tyler would say."

"I'm sorry, I thought you should know. That's about as good as it gets with me."

We go inside and she scrambles around her tiny apartment. I'm looking at ceramic knickknacks on the shelves—Alice in Wonderland, the rabbit, the Queen, a couple of large mushrooms—littered among candles of various colours, shapes and sizes. The place is warm: used furniture disguised with batik covers, throw rugs, and black-and-white prints on the walls.

She walks in and I take my hand off the rabbit.

"Oh yeah, those," she says with a shy smile. "You haven't been here yet, have you?"

I had to work the day she moved in last week, so Noel and a few university friends helped her.

"No."

I sit down. The place strikes me as a home, Jan's home, a comfortable sanctuary with a unique feel that reflects her personality and spirit. She has a rack filled with magazines, a stack of coasters, a table with matching chairs—all the little elements that I've never been able to collect. With every breath, I smell the faint scent of her perfume, her hair, her skin.

"It's different than the old place," I say.

"That's for sure."

"I miss the country music. And where's the TV?"

"I don't have one." She begins to straighten the throw on the couch underneath me.

"I can't stand a messy couch," she says, her body bent, her face close to mine, looking at me. I can feel her breath.

She stops and we stare at one another, neither moving nor looking away. For seconds we're suspended in front of each other, feeling the faint pulse of heartbeats and warmth. Her eyes are lagoon green, her skin smooth and powdery. The hair that falls gently over her forehead brushes against my cheek.

"I'm not waiting for you anymore," she says, grabbing my face and pulling me into a kiss.

35

The apartment is empty the next day. Janice has gone off to class. I look around the immaculate room as the bright autumn sun filters in through the bay window. With the addition of some stained glass and organ music, the beatific atmosphere would be complete.

I move slowly and calmly, drink a large glass of orange juice—the premium kind—and then brush my teeth using her toothbrush, which is exciting and mildly arousing. I phone Shel, but he's not home—or at any rate he doesn't answer—and I hope he's gone to class. Then I sit on the couch and stare at the place on the wall where the TV would be if there were one.

I feel good, beyond fine, enraptured. There aren't enough words in the English language to express how I feel. I turn on the stereo and boogie, dancing with the sunbeams, singing and giving in to celebration.

"Thou art late," Chad says as I stream peacefully through the door. I nod gently and mentally send impulses of unity toward his hostile soul.

"I know," I say. "But have I missed anything? Does it matter? I mean, in the grand scheme of the universe."

He takes a slow sip of his coffee and stares at me like I'm insane.

"Are you feeling OK?"

"Yeah. I'm good. I think we all need to relax more, find out what's really important."

"Cold beer for our customers is what's really important," he says, lifting a case onto the counter. "Put that in the cooler, will you?"

I get my cash drawer, unlock the cage and put glasses on the bar. A retired plumber named Lou, who comes in almost every morning, strolls over and puts a bill down in front of me.

"The usual, my good man," he says. I want to ask him why he's here every day, want to point out that his drinking isn't charming, it's sad. But I make him his usual.

"I love Thanksgiving," he says heartily. "Gives me an excuse to get drunk."

He laughs and I force a smile, ring up his drink and hear the hard metallic tinkle of coins hitting an empty tip jar. Somehow things have changed. Somehow none of this matters to me as much as it did a week ago.

Lou shuffles to a corner and sits by himself. As I'm filling up my second sink with ice, John slides onto a barstool with a coffee in one hand and a cigarette in the other. He gives me a nod.

Chad stops at the bar and glares at John and his two vices. John notices, but doesn't seem to care.

"Special casino party, this Friday."

Chad hands us each a photocopied sheet of paper with a graphic of a smiling slot machine and a description of the event. Across the top it says, "Come Shake Your Money-maker."

"I've rented extra tables. Invite whoever you want. No skanks. And there won't be any live music this time."

John leans back casually. "Fuck you."

"Sorry, man," Chad says with smile. "Nothing personal—"

"It's just business," I say.

Chad walks away, and John sits and sucks on his cigarette for a few minutes, staring aimlessly at the back of the bar. Finally, as I'm polishing the wood, he snaps back to reality.

"Oh, hey, man, didn't you have some sort of a gig yesterday? Some contest?"

"Yeah." I place the rag on the bar.

"Did you win?"

"No, the day was a complete farce. We lost Tyler, and the band will probably never play together again."

John thinks about this for a few minutes, then nods philosophically, getting off the stool and looking at his watch. He finishes his coffee and throws the Styrofoam cup over the bar toward a garbage can. He misses.

"Ah well, what can you do, eh?" he says. "Don't quit your day job. You can always find another hobby."

He winks and wanders off toward the kitchen like he does every day. I fight the urge to follow and knock him around with a bag of frozen french fries.

That evening as I'm walking home I see a familiar figure shivering on the sidewalk out front.

"Evening, Judas," I say, putting my key into the decrepit lock and swinging the door open.

"So you're still upset about that minor misunderstanding," Tyler says, shaking his head and turning to follow me up the stairs. I stop.

"Tyler, you piked on the band."

"I said I'd play with Trailer too," he protests.

"Good thing you didn't. The crowd would have killed us. I'm glad you're happy with Nicole, but if there's one thing I've learned through experience, it's that you don't forsake your friends just because you're in a relationship."

He frowns. "Interesting," he says. "I refuse to admit any negligence in concern to my actions—I did offer to play. However, from a certain perspective I can see how some might think I got a bit caught up in events."

"So what happened?" I ask, taking my small assortment of groceries out of their plastic bags.

"With what?" Tyler asks. "Oh, yes, that . . . Nicole made a few last-minute additions vocally. She uh . . ." He shifts on his feet. "Well, she didn't know there was a difference between Catholicism and other Christian faiths."

I start to laugh, and to my surprise Tyler smiles with slight embarrassment.

"I'm still surprised that we didn't win," he says as we open a couple of beers and sit at my kitchen table. I've put a TV dinner in the microwave and a Poe CD, lent to me by Jan, on the stereo. "We were spiritually powerful."

"Shocker," I say. "I thought you had it clinched. Did you hear about Noel?"

He gives a thumbs-up. "Nice work. I always said he was conscientious."

We sit in silence for a few minutes, drinking our beer and listening to Poe croon about her desire to kill Johnny.

"Well," he says, "I wanted to say sorry that things didn't work out. But I've got some really great ideas for a new direction in which we can take the band."

"What band?"

"I admit that it's a bit commercial, but I think we can play with the nuances of the form and really do something different—hybrid, something that has never been attempted before that will blow people away." He drops a piece of yellow memo paper onto the table.

"Radio jingles?" I say.

"My uncle works at a radio station in Toronto. We can compose a few jingles for some local companies, gain exposure in the greater market and then use our leverage to get airtime for our real music. Très excellent, don't you think? Using pop culture against itself. I love it."

I look at the sheet of paper. "Stunning idea, Ty," I say quietly.

He smiles.

"It's nouveau riche . . . You've got to trust me."

36

I've got to find a way to get thrown out of Trailer, because no one will let the band die quietly. We are the Rasputin of rock. To my great surprise, Noel has once again shown up at the bar with a look of manic expectation and the urge to pitch Tyler's asinine scheme. There must be some sort of medication for this type of obsession.

"Remember how you felt when Tyler ditched us?" I say.

Noel waves me away. "I've forgiven the man. He had a weak moment. You've got to understand his motivation. He passed us over for a girl, which as a guy is reasonable. In some cultures his selfishness would be noble. I think he's realized his mistake and won't repeat it."

I look at him warily. "I thought you got a promotion," I say. "Aren't you supposed to be swamped with work?"

"I got bumped out of mayonnaise. They gave the job to this dweeb from the pudding division. My manager said he got the job because of one of those internal seniority issues, but I think they're yanking my chain. Know what I mean?"

"Crystal clear."

"He does have more seniority than I do, but in a big company there should be more to a decision than how long you've been stuck in your cubicle doing your job by rote. I'm all for fair play, but I've laid down a lot more sweat and overtime than Adam and I'd like a Darwinian cage match based on the quality of our work."

Noel has been watching too much wrestling again.

"So you don't like this guy," I say.

"He's a Van Halen fan."

I feel the sting of Noel's pride. Being passed over for a metal fan does nothing for your ego. In grade nine I was absolutely in love with a semi-cute, sinewy volleyball player named Shelley Rusedski. She lived in one of those nondescript rural farming villages outside town, the kind too small to have its own high school, so she was bused in every day. I learned how to flirt from Shelley. I'd prepare jokes at home and execute my whimsy every day at ten-forty in science class. She sat in front of me. I was good. I was on. I was the man.

Except I wasn't the man. The man was a complete doofus named Mark Wallace, who had big, goofy sprayed hair and a denim jacket covered in iron-on patches for Poison and RATT and Warrant. Being young and naïve, I had assumed that everyone *normal* had pretty similar musical tastes to me. I mean, the Jam and the Smiths were objectively the

best bands on earth. Subjectivity didn't come into the equa-
tion. People who liked country and Robert Palmer and the
other useless detritus of the musical world were odd,
stunted creatures—like the slinking goth types who gath-
ered across from my English literature portable to smoke
and kick dirt around with those freakishly sadomasochistic
knee-high Doc Martens boots. I couldn't understand how
Shelley could laugh at my jokes and like the hammering
guitar work of AC/DC. I couldn't see how the two could be
in any way compatible. To tell the truth, I still don't.

Jay Thompson hit for disillusionment: The Smiths, "Half
a Person."

"So you're going back to the coffee division?"

"No," Noel says. "They filled my position. For the next
couple months I'm on exclusive loan to flavour enhancers."

"Which means . . ."

"Cheese flavouring, powdered onion flavouring, assorted
chemical compounds that simulate the real taste of foods
but are laced with sodium and designed to stay fresh and
edible for the next thousand or so years."

A customer wanders up to the bar. He's young, rough
looking and is wearing painter's scrubs. He orders a double
dark rum and cola and motions to the stereo as I'm fishing
out his change.

"Can't you put on some decent music?" he says. "This
whiny shit is making my head ache."

I have to get a new job.

"So, you see," Noel continues, "with my career on hold, I
have a bit more time to play. And besides, that competition
really stoked me. All I want to do is rock. You know, sometimes I think you're really lucky not to have a career weigh-
ing you down."

I nearly choke. Noel owns a new car and has investments. He takes vacations and has sick days. The sweater he's wearing probably costs as much as my entire wardrobe. Staff at the local secondhand clothes shops know me by name.

"How do you figure?" I ask.

"The whole deal comes down to happiness. My job is fine, but it demands so much of my time. You have no distractions from the dream."

"So why don't you quit?"

"Are you kidding? My stock options haven't even vested. And once you jump off the corporate ladder, you've got to fight to get back on. But I'm willing to put in the time and effort to try and slip in the back door to success."

"Great song title."

Noel is forced to concur. I have little doubt that he's done things the right way. He has a mix of security and passionate musical ambition that I envy. And he gets along with his father. They play golf together.

"Tyler's idea is pretty good," he continues. "Television commercials are flash and hip. They're not really that different from music videos, except they're shorter and more focused."

"I thought we were doing radio jingles."

"Yeah, we'll start with radio, but if we work on commercials, we'll have access to people who can help us shoot our own music video. Truly successful artists need TV exposure. If Andy Warhol were alive today, he'd be doing television commercials."

"There were commercials in the seventies."

"Well, they weren't the same. We've gone beyond the age of the talking head. Don't worry, this will be good for the band. And after all that religious whoring, dictating the next wave of consumer desire will seem downright virtuous."

Though I tell Noel that I'll think about it, I'm not feeling the dynamic vibe. As I drive home, I look at the advertisements on billboards and bus stops. I see one of a man on a beach with his arms spread wide, rejoicing in the fact that a local clinic has helped him with his impotence. The world has lost its sense of shame.

Later that night I tell Janice about my doubts.

"So we write a few tunes," she says. "Maybe we'll have a few laughs, gain some insight into studio recording and make a few bucks in the process. It doesn't mean we're part of a worldwide conglomerate conspiracy. We're not investing in a sweatshop."

"What do I know about advertising? Image and style weren't part of my upbringing. My father wears shoes with Velcro instead of laces. He has a push lawn mower, the kind with rotating steel blades and no motor."

"Yeah, well, your family is a throwback to feudal times," Jan says. "Maybe we'll regret this later, but I want to continue playing with the band. Let's just see what Tyler has to say."

37

Against every instinct for self-preservation and self-respect, I pick up the phone the next morning and call Tyler.

"I'm not saying I'm interested," I explain. "But I'm curious."

Tyler chuckles softly. He gets another call and puts me on hold. He loves to put people on hold.

I hum along to the music designed to keep me from hanging up. About a year ago Tyler recorded his own hold music, another scheme that he claimed would elevate his status in the music business. He came up with a plan to compile CDs for every business to suit the musical tastes of their customers. Help lines dealing with irate customers would get the mellow mix, sales lines would get upbeat, energetic music, suicide hotlines would get hymns. Needless to say, everyone he approached with the idea reacted with amusement or irritation, and the scheme died on the vine.

Burt Bacharach's "This Guy's in Love With You," the Muzak version, is playing in my ear. This must be one of the mellow mixes.

"Thompson, I can pencil you in at eleven, but you have to come to me."

At eleven-thirty I'm alone and annoyed in the university food court. I'm about to leave when I see Tyler, head down, steaming toward me through waves of students dragging themselves to class on stiff, cadaverous legs. He marches to my table and drops his bag on a chair.

"Wait," he says, holding up a finger. "I need coffee."

He turns back toward the concessions, then darts and weaves and cuts in front of two girls moving toward the coffee carafes. They begin to protest but he ignores them. He finds the shortest line at a cash register, pays and comes back to the table. The whole operation has taken less than a minute.

"You will not believe the morning I've been having," he says. "How these troglodyte professors get tenure in the music department is beyond me. I'm not inspired."

My gaze wanders as Tyler complains about his faculty. I'd

be more interested if his complaints were in some way relevant to the outside world, but student life is inherently insular. I really didn't appreciate the simplicity of my life when I started university—tumbling out of bed, throwing on a pair of dirty jeans and arriving late for class with a danish and large coffee. I laugh to think my greatest worries were meeting the minimum word count for a psychology essay and showing up at the right time for a midterm exam. Then again, I suppose I had cause to worry, because my essays were late and poorly done and my exams showed a spotty knowledge of the finer points of Pavlov and conditioned responses. In some respects, I regret leaving university so early, because I feel there's a gap in my experience, a great secret all my friends know to which I'm not privy. I suddenly realize Tyler has stopped talking and is staring at me. He isn't impressed.

"So, jingles," I say.

He pulls out a binder from his bag, undoes the rings and spreads three stacks of paper across the table.

"Jay, forget jingles for the moment. I think we should pitch complete *advertising campaigns* for radio, print and television. We'll outline themes, do storyboards, compose the music—everything. We're more likely to succeed if they see we're serious about the whole process—"

"Of convincing people their lives aren't complete without a super juicer and tighter abs."

He pauses and purses his lips. Despite his outward eagerness, this descent into consumerism has to be hard on such a staunch and proud nonconformist as Tyler.

"We have to remember this is a means to an end," he says, lacking some of his usual zeal. "We're seeking exposure for the band. Let me show you what I've come up with."

I reach for one of the piles of papers on the table. He points at my pop can.

"Don't drip. I've put a lot of work into this."

I debate doing a runner. His storyboards are a mix of sketches and pieces of pictures cut out of magazines and catalogues.

"These are ads for investment aimed at senior citizens."

In the first ad, a miserable-looking elderly man is working behind the counter of a fast-food restaurant. He's wearing a brown pin-stripe uniform and humiliating paper hat. The caption says: "Have you invested wisely?" The next ad features elderly people eating cat food.

"Too dark?" Tyler asks, sensing my revulsion.

"They're evil," I say.

He sighs and begins to crumple the pages into a ball.

"I wasn't sure. I thought they might be borderline . . . Still, I bet they'd sell."

He stops crumpling. I refuse to say anything, because speaking will only give Tyler a forum for debate. If I argue, he'll argue back and could, conceivably, convince himself that there are merits to exploiting the elderly.

"OK, we'll stick to writing a few jingles," he says finally, coming to his own moral conclusion. "It was just an idea."

38

Janice rolls over on her side. I can't sleep, so I've turned on the small reading light by the bed and am looking through an assortment of school course outlines I ordered over the Internet.

"Jay, it's after midnight."

"Sorry, I'll only be a few more minutes."

She grumpily slams her head into her pillow. I pause to admire the shape of her bare back, the way the muscles run and intersect beneath the skin. I'm amazed that she's here with me, and I move between feelings of elation and fear that I'm going to find some way to screw this up. Or she could lose interest in me. I've decided that I'm going to make a serious effort to finally get my priorities sorted out. For the first time ever, I'm focusing on a career. I know that Jan is willing to hang with a slacker for a while, living the simple life, but eventually she's going to decide that she wants more than a dingy one-bedroom apartment with a bartender. I think I can be satisfied with a life not completely dependent on music because now, with her, I've got something to keep me going that doesn't involve the fantasy of jamming at Madison Square Garden.

Tonight, I presented her with her own toothbrush and let her slip it into the yellow rinsing cup beside mine. The nice thing is, it's a deluxe, grooved head with soft bristles, not a cheap semi-disposable. I feel we've reached a milestone in our burgeoning relationship.

She remains silent for a few minutes, and I underline key course details in red. But slowly she slides into me, her flesh replacing blanket against my leg, her head finding the crevice between my shoulder and chest. I attempt to write, but my hand can't twist around her and the pen makes an inky swirl on the page.

"Jan, I can't write like this."

She opens one eye mischievously, a faint smile curling up along the base of her lips.

"Can you write like this?"

She slides her leg over mine, then an arm, pinning me in place against the bed. I laugh as she pulls herself on top of me like a conquering giant. Her smile is wide and mocking, because she knows I can't resist her. I am beaten.

"Don't let me disturb you. What are you looking at, anyway?"

I show her the pamphlet.

"Is that for Sheldon?"

"No, it's for me. I thought maybe I'd study computers. The pay is good and this school offers a co-op program."

She stares at me. She looks disappointed.

"You can make good money," I say.

"But you're a musician."

"Oh, get serious."

She slides off me. I want her back on top of me, want to feel the weight of her body pressing me into the bed.

"God, you're a misery sometimes, Thompson."

"I am not. I'm a realist."

"You're a pessimist and a worrier. You have a passion for music. More passion than most people have for anything, including their families. And you want to throw away everything to be a computer guy."

"I.T. professional."

"Doing programming?"

"I'm not exactly sure. The course outline is a bit vague. Apparently I have to learn something called Java. But trust me, it's a good job."

"For some people. But I'm sure most of them have at least a passing interest in computers. No doubt they're into new software, radical mouse designs and whatever else is involved. You'll hate it."

"I have to get serious about something."

"Why?"

"Because I'm a bartender."

"So what?"

"So look around at the splendour . . ."

Her gaze follows mine as I take stock of the room.

"You're pursuing your dreams," she says. "Think of the experiences you're gaining."

"Like cleaning ashtrays at two o'clock in the morning or running lipstick-stained glasses through the dishwasher for a third time?"

"Exactly. Or taking a chance, living big, showing some initiative and desire. Those are the qualities I admire in you."

I knew she liked me and felt some strange passion for my muscle-free body, but I never considered that she would admire me. Love must be blind—if not deaf and mute on occasion. I sort through my pamphlets, then pass another one to her.

"What about going back to university?" I say.

In one deft ninja movement, Jan flips over on top of me again, gently wraps her hands around my neck and begins to strangle me.

"Say 'I'm going to be a rock star.'"

"Stop chok—," I gurgle.

"Say it!"

She strangles a bit harder. Her expression is comical and taunting, but I detect a sense of seriousness as well. All I can think about as she crushes my windpipe is how soft and warm her hands are.

"I'll be a rock star," I say. She grunts and falls off me. "But until our big break, we might have to live in this apartment for a couple decades."

She rolls her eyes and begins kissing around my shoulders. Her hair obscures her face and, for a brief second, I get the sensation of a small woodland animal nibbling my neck.

"I don't care," she says.

"We might have to eat discounted pasta and pudding donated to us by Noel. And we might start buying lotto tickets and going to bingo."

She sits up, brushing the hair from her eyes.

"Don't stop," I say.

"Do you really think our lives could come to that? I'm doing a master's degree and you're smart enough to get a job in the music industry."

"You don't have to stop," I say, turning my head to give her easier access to my neck. "What would I do in the music industry?"

"I don't know—promotion, marketing? And who's to say you won't make it as a musician and songwriter? Would I be here if I didn't believe in you? Give me some credit."

"You did date the drummer from Rabid Angels."

She begins to choke me again.

39

And so, as always, I find myself in the Dwyer basement on yet another Thursday night.

"Nice to see you, Thompson," Tyler says as I descend the stairs. "I thought you might have gone AWOL."

"I promised Jan I'd come."

Noel is hunched over the coffee table, scribbling notes on a series of papers. I flop onto the couch, close my eyes and meditate quietly. The bar was hopping today but the tips were absurdly low. A few minutes later, I'm jolted by a loud bang, followed by a series of muted expletives, as Jan accidentally rams her guitar case into the wall while coming down the stairs.

"Sorry about that," she says, holding her hand over the impact point, as if her palm might heal the gouge in the plaster. Her cheeks are flushed and her movements are jerky and jangled. Her eyes are red and puffy.

"Not sleeping much?" Tyler asks.

I feel a surge of puritanical guilt, as though we've been caught. There's absolutely nothing wrong with having regular sex when you're in your mid-twenties—in fact, I don't fully trust people who pass through their university years still holding on to the idea of celibacy as virtue—but some residual anxiety still exists. I blame it on too many farcical sex comedies from the late 1970s. After all, I learned most of my attitudes to sex from episodes of *Three's Company*.

"I'm having a bad day," Jan says quietly.

"Feminist criticism overload?" Tyler asks. "Or are pesky students dropping in after office hours? My policy is not to entertain fools or late-coming slackers."

She puts her case down on the couch and flexes her hands. "My students are fine. My computer started acting up in the middle of my Beckett paper, which was due last Friday. Then my cat projectile-vomited all over my new throw rug. Do you know how difficult fish-flavoured ash byproduct is to get out of fabric?"

"We have a cleaning service that comes in every Friday," Tyler says.

Jan takes a deep breath and exhales slowly. She rotates her

shoulders and bounces up and down as she tries to relax her muscles. Finally, she looks to me for the first time.

"Hi," she says.

"Hey—" I catch myself before calling her pumpkin.

We look at each other awkwardly for a minute. Am I supposed to get up and kiss her or just act normal? I smile stupidly and remain seated. Her expression wavers toward confusion and I feel a surge of panic, keenly aware I've made the wrong choice.

As we set up, Noel mills around anxiously and hums to himself. Apparently the jingle idea has truly inspired him.

"So, I've polished my two best pieces," he says, handing us lyric sheets. "I've got the rhythm and riffs worked out and know what kind of progression I want from the bass."

He plays and sings the first song for us, a short, snappy tune with one repeating chorus, written for a cellphone company.

Let the people sing
Let them speak aloud
When the world gets connected
We can all stand proud

As he starts through the piece again, I watch his chord progressions and play along. Tyler picks up the beat, and Jan comes in on bass with a perfect run. I've heard that the best songs come easily and can't help but smile as we loop the tune and Noel riffs. From everyone's expressions, I can tell that we all know we're on to something amazing, that perhaps we've produced radio's next snazzy jingle from our first session. I imagine office workers across the nation humming our song as they step into elevators. I see music executives eagerly asking us to record a demo, impressed that we're the band that wrote that phone song.

After a few more loops we break, and I give Noel an enthusiastic high-five. I feel silly that I didn't see the potential in this idea.

"So you like it, dude?" he says.

"I love it. It's perfect. This is the one."

"The music is tight and punchy," Tyler adds. "Complex enough not to be generic, but pithy enough to be catchy. You could learn something from this, Thompson."

I ignore him. Noel turns to Jan, who is tuning her top string and looking distracted.

"You played that exactly like I wanted," he says. "I'm amazed that you understood what I was vying for so quickly."

Jan looks up uneasily. "Yeah. Well . . ." She clears her throat. "You know the gum commercial from a few years back, the one where the couple are kissing on the beach until the sun sets and the tide comes in?"

"I'm not sure I know it," Noel says.

"The one where the shark fin circles around them in the darkness, but they keep chewing and kissing?"

"OK. I know the one."

"Yeah. It's the same song."

I try to think of the tune in question, but my internal jukebox can't pinpoint the selection.

"The songs might be similar," Noel says slowly. "But I really don't think they're the same."

She points to Noel's guitar and motions for him to play. She picks up the bass run and sings:

Let the world turn
Let the seas rise up
When you chew on Mintleaf
It's never enough

The songs are exactly the same. Noel looks at us sheepishly.

"No wonder it was so easy to write. I can't believe I ripped off Mintleaf. You guys know I wouldn't do it on purpose, right? The song was just in my head."

"The subconscious is a powerful force," Tyler says. "You've got to be very vigilant when writing, which you learn over time."

Noel sets up his second song, but with less enthusiasm. He issues several disclaimers in case he has unwittingly churned up a Water Pik tune or Lysol melody. This jingle is for a fast-food chicken shop.

Cluck, cluck
There are wings in the bucket
Cluck, cluck
And fries on the side
Cluck, cluck
Food so tasty
Cluck, cluck
You'll be satisfied

He notices that we're not joining in, wavers and finally stops. The last chord slowly fades from the amp.

"You don't like it?" he says. "Does it need another cluck? What if we change the lyrics to 'Cluck, cluck, cluck, there's wings in the bucket?'"

Noel looks to Jan and me for support. I stare into the corner, avoiding eye contact. I don't want to discourage him, because I know how difficult composing a song can be.

"Ah, come on," Noel says. "We can work with it."

"Cluck, cluck, cluck, your song sorta sucks," Tyler says, rooting through a file folder by his drum kit. He hands out sheet music, and I feel like a slacker for having done nothing except show up. But my heart isn't into these schemes anymore. I haven't told anyone, not even Jan, but I've been asking around at a few of the music stores about rock bands looking for guitar players. Ironically, quick lunges for fame aren't nearly as interesting or satisfying as playing two covers and one original song for forty drunken, mostly uninterested audience members.

Tyler explains the transcendental nature of his pieces, both of which are for one of his uncle's biggest clients, a financial company.

"I want the music to reflect a progression from despera-tion to the promise of good returns," Tyler explains. "I want the listener to feel moved instinctively to seek out security."

I'm staring at him, wondering when his grip on reality fully slipped. We play the first song a few times, each of us feeling for our proper place in the mix. The piece begins down tempo and sombre, then kicks up in a flourish of enthusiasm halfway through. I struggle with the transition from funeral dirge to elation.

"We need a bridge," I say as we cut out in a well of feed-back. "Otherwise the rise feels artificial and chaotic."

Tyler stares at me wryly. "Is that right?"

"Yeah. I feel like we're playing two entirely different songs."

"Do I tell you how to pour beer?"

He looks mildly repentant after the words leave his mouth, but quickly covers up his self-consciousness by picking at his thumbnail and ignoring me. I feel the rise of heat in my chest and tension in my temples from a headache. I'm trying to make his insignificant song better. I'm tired of always letting Tyler be the bully.

"Tyler," I say evenly, "I bet you took two old songs and stuck them together. I bet you had two radically different, mediocre songs and decided you'd combine them without considering that you're going from one musical extreme to the other. You're asking your audience to jump from sombreness to joy. All I'm saying is moods can't swing that far without some sort of rising transition."

Jan smiles. My assertiveness makes me feel strangely masculine—not quite Tarzan beating his chest and howling in the jungle, but strong and confident nonetheless. Tyler is shaking his head, still ignoring me.

"I'm not saying they're bad songs," I continue. "I'm just saying they don't jell without a bridge."

Tyler gently taps his cymbal with his knuckle. I get the sense I've caught him off guard. I try to think of other grievances I can raise while he's off balance, but my window of opportunity quickly shuts.

"They are good songs," he says. "I suppose their energies do compete, but the advertising medium requires a certain amount of abrasiveness. You have to understand that . . ."

He rambles on, but I can tell he's making up his theory as he goes, saving face in the usual Dwyer manner. When he finishes, he stands before us with an expression of expectation. Jan clears her throat.

"I don't think the song works," she says.

"Maybe we'll work on it after we fix up Noel's song," I offer.

"Well," Tyler murmurs, "let's try the second piece."

We play the second piece, which is uniform and pretty nifty in a foot-tapping way. After the third run-through, Jan holds up her hands, we break, and she asks Noel not to play for the next go. As we rise in tempo, she steps to the mike and begins to sing. After a few seconds, Noel leans toward his mike.

"Congratulations, Ty," he says. "You've written a Neil Diamond song."

I expect Tyler to freak out and orate on his strategy or the finer points in which his song is different and unique. Instead, he listens to the tune for a few seconds, leans forward and joins in singing the chorus to "Sweet Caroline."

We jam through a poorly executed Neil Diamond medley, followed by some of our favourite songs from the Rose and Crown gigs. This is what I've missed. As we play, I remember why I picked up a guitar in the first place—the absolute freedom, that sheer ability to completely lose myself in music. Everyone is having a laugh, even Tyler. He really can be a lot of fun when he lets his guard down and stops trying to prove he's intelligent and creative; because Tyler loves music, loves it as much as I do, breathes facts and opinions about songs from morning to night, knows obscure bands and yearns for new sounds. I feel the energy surging through my body—waves and vibrations rocking my chest cavity. We play hard and long, the four of us ensnared in our love affair with music, obsessed and dazed and crazy.

Finally, we're all exhausted and covered with sweat. Tyler throws his drumsticks playfully and dramatically into the corner and collapses on the floor. We put down our instruments and sprawl out beside him with our feet up on couches and chairs, all of us heaving in deep breaths. I nudge Tyler with one of the cold beers Noel retrieves from the fridge. He cracks it open, takes a couple deep swallows, then wipes his mouth.

"Nicole broke up with me today," he says.

40

I wake up with a harsh hangover. My stomach is acidic, my skin icy cold and my sinuses congested, as if filled with grey lead. Jan is lying beside me, snoring lightly, her long limbs tangled up in the sheets. The bed looks ransacked. After Tyler's news we packed up our equipment and went to the Rose and Crown for several hours of commiseration. Apparently Nicole has become infatuated with a graduate student in the fine arts department who specializes in graffiti murals. Tyler's taking the breakup hard.

Jan's hair is sprayed out across the pillow. Her duvet is thick and soft, and she clutches at it like a child holding on to a favourite teddy bear. She's beautiful. I catch a glimpse of myself in the mirror. I look like I've slept in a laundry basket all night.

"I want to die," Jan moans, her eyes still closed. "Why did you make me drink so much tequila?"

"You were drinking gin."

One eye pops open.

"That's worrying. My mouth tastes like it spent the night in Tijuana, in a gutter, and I think my body was used as a piñata."

After several aborted attempts, she manages to get up and trudge to the shower. I make coffee, slump in a chair and look at the world through the living-room window. I'm shocked how quickly the leaves have turned from bold green to autumn orange and red.

Jan pokes her head around the corner. Her hair is dripping wet and hangs off her scalp like a wilted spider plant.

"Did I say anything stupid?" she asks.

"You told Tyler he had cockroach resiliency. You said you never liked Nicole and he'd get over her in no time."

"Really?"

"Don't worry, he took the cockroach remark as a compliment."

Jan has nothing in her fridge, and we both feel too weak to shop, so we decide to go out for breakfast. We end up at Pisa's, because cheap, greasy breakfasts are their specialty. Jan sits and looks over the menu rather aimlessly. She flips it over, frowns and pushes it into the centre of the table.

"I'm sorry, but this just won't do anymore. You can't take me out for breakfast to a diner."

I didn't realize I was taking her out. I look around the room, from the red vinyl booths to the Bud mirror to the jar of bright green mints near the cash register marked "one per customer." I like this place. I'm comfortable here. And besides, no other place offers three eggs, bacon, sausage, toast and waffles for $4.99.

"What's wrong with it?"

"Nothing . . . No, everything. It's time for a change, Jay. I don't mind coming here once in a while, but not today. This place is gross."

She suggests a midscale Italian restaurant downtown, and I reluctantly agree. Despite sucking down three aspirin, I still have a pulsing headache. Jan's restaurant turns out to be clean and nice and flooded with morning light from a wall of windows fronting the street, but it lacks Pisa's character and gritty charm. The waiters wear tuxedo shirts and dress pants, smile and give prompt service, all of which spells a big tip on an already overpriced meal.

I feel like the jagged edge of a newly opened tin can. I should be lying in bed, by myself, coping with this hangover in solitude, because my social skills tend to suffer when I'm consumed with nagging pain.

"The food won't be any better here," I mutter.

Jan makes a face that clearly expresses the sentiment: *please spare me your idiotic remarks*. But I don't care. I take the opportunity to act just as grumpy as she did at Pisa's. And I have justification, because the menu is disappointing, to say the least. There's no waffle-and-egg combination plate, and all the specials have stupid, cute little names:

THE HUNTSMAN—two eggs, any style, bacon, toast, fried mushrooms and/or tomato. $6.99

THE WAYFARER—two poached eggs, fresh tomato salsa, mild sausage. $7.99

Oddly enough, I don't see any rugged mariners or men with guns occupying the tables. The meals don't even include bottomless cups of java. I shake my head bitterly.

"Do you remember when coffee was just coffee?" I say. "When did it mutate into lattes and cappuccinos?"

"I don't know, Jay," Jan says tersely. "Those damn Europeans. Next they'll be pressuring us to eat baguettes."

"Saffron eggs? What is a saffron egg? My father would

love this place. He'd be in the kitchen right now rewriting the menu."

I watch Jan's jaw rotating in tiny circles. That can't be good for her dental work. The people beside us are having bacon and pancakes covered in maple syrup. The smell is driving me crazy with hunger. Jan is still searching the menu. If we had stayed at Pisa's we would have been finished eating by now. I pick up my fork. The cutlery is oversized—heavy forks and knives that make me feel Lilliputian.

"This is a bit much, isn't it?" I say, holding up a spoon. "What are they trying to prove?"

She puts down her menu and glares at me. I decide to shut up. Usually, with Jan, I can get away with a mildly bad mood, but her fuse is short today. I'm already looking ahead to the afternoon. She has to catch up on work, most of which is overdue, so I fully intend to utilize my day off by napping and flipping through useless television channels. We've been spending a lot of time together, which has been great, but I'm starting to feel uninteresting and a bit burnt out. There's nothing new in my life to tell her about, because she's with me constantly, and I'm tired of sharing stories from my childhood. I don't feel like working for conversation today.

"I can't decide between waffles and eggs Benedict," she says.

"So get them both. Oh wait, this isn't Pisa's."

"Nothing like change to make Jay Thompson grumpy."

Our sniping is interrupted by our waitress, whose positive energy clashes badly with my mood and the vile toxicity of my body. I order an omelette, breathe deeply and try to relax. We sit in awkward silence. I don't want to talk, but realize I can't cope with complete quiet either. Dead conversation is a killer. I remember sitting next to an unhappy couple at a Chinese restaurant a few years ago. They spent most of their meal struggling for small talk, and I got the feeling they were on a first date. As they waited for the bill, the woman gave up altogether, took a book from her bag and started reading. The guy stared out the window while anxiously thumbing his gold card.

"I have to say hello to someone," Jan says.

She puts her napkin on the table, gets up and winds her way through the tables toward a tall, dark and obnoxiously handsome guy standing near the door of the kitchen. He has thick, full hair slicked back in a *GQ* style and is wearing a tuxedo monkey outfit like the rest of the staff. When he sees Jan, his face lights up, and he holds out his hands for a big hug. I count the seconds until he lets her go. They talk for a few minutes. Jan's body language is energetic and borderline flirtatious. She smiles and motions with her hands. I wonder if she's doing this to teach me a lesson, to demonstrate that there are lots of men in line to take my place. Our meals arrive, but I've got a lump in my stomach so big that I can barely swallow. I imagine it's a malignant tumour, eating away my stomach lining cell by cell, growing bigger and bigger until there's no room left for eggs.

Jan gives her friend another big hug, his large hands lingering a bit too long near her waist, and makes her way back to the table, never looking up to make eye contact with me.

"Who's your friend?" I ask, attempting to sound indifferent and accommodating, but not quite pulling it off.

"This looks great," she says. "I would have introduced you, but you're a bit too snappy."

"But who is he?"

She looks up. Her eyes are tired and tinged with a vague annoyance.

"That's Billy," she says. "We shared an office for the first few weeks of the semester until they found me a new one. He works here part-time as a host."

Billy? I look at Mr. GQ lingering near the kitchen and dismiss him as country-boy Todd's intended victim on our fateful night not long ago. However, the more I think about things, the more I think maybe Todd wasn't angry with a fellow hick but rather jealous of an interloper into Jan's life. Something close to panic grips me.

"That's the Billy your ex-fiancé wanted to decimate with his huge, beefy fists?"

"Maybe," Jan says. "He's a great guy and really funny. You'd like him."

"So why did Todd want to mangle him?"

"Because Todd's immature and stuck in the past."

She hoes into her food. My omelette tastes metallic. I wonder if she brought me here to start some sort of rivalry, to make Billy jealous or sorry for dumping her.

"Did you date him?"

"No."

"Did you want to date him?"

"Nope."

"Even though he looks like a Calvin Klein underwear model?"

She glances toward the kitchen. "Do you think so?"

The sugar packet in my hand tears open, sending waves of granules onto the table. Jan snorts in laughter. I watch her cut her food and wonder how serious she is about me. I've seen her date and discard men before. Why should I be any different?

"Jan, no offence, but I don't believe you. Todd came to your house looking for Billy, so something must have been going on."

Her eyes narrow and she puts down her fork. At this moment, I wouldn't be surprised to see wisps of steam rising from her ears. It occurs to me that the intensity of my hangover has caused the important link between my brain and mouth to sever, because I've given life to a line of questioning that can bring nothing but disaster. If only I could stab my stupid comments with a fork and chew them down again.

"Jason, don't ever call me a liar," she says quietly. "And don't get jealous on me, because it is so unattractive. I had enough of that with Todd, who I don't talk to anymore because he can't accept we're no longer a couple. But that's none of your business."

"None of my business?"

And now it's Jan's turn to look uncomfortable.

"If your boyfriends aren't my business, maybe I shouldn't be with you," I say.

"Boyfriends? Since when do I have boyfriends?"

"Todd, Billy, there sure seems to be a lot of guys milling around."

"Would you listen to yourself? I don't need this."

"*You* don't need this?"

For a split second I begin to get up. My hand is on the table, my chair angled, I'm ready to shift my weight, push myself up and storm off. And I almost say more stupid things. I almost ruin everything good that has happened lately in my otherwise miserable and pathetic life.

But I don't.

Because of my father, his misery, the thought of one split-second decision that wrecked his life. And because some-how, even in the heat of argument, I know I've never been happier in my life.

"I'm sorry," I say, easing back into my chair. "I was being stupid."

Finally, her expression thaws.

"Me too," she whispers. "I'm sorry. I should have intro-duced you to Billy and realized you might feel jealous. I'm not used to thinking as a couple again."

"*You* aren't? I'm the perpetually single one."

We dig into our now room-temperature breakfasts. We talk about communication and letting each other know how we feel and all the other negotiating points of relation-ships. I hadn't really thought of relationship skills as some-thing you had to learn. I thought when you met the right person everything just came naturally. But maybe people who seem to know what they're doing are just patient enough and humble enough to learn. As we wait for the bill, Jan unscrews the ketchup bottle and sticks her finger into the cap. She dabs ketchup in the centre of both hands, then shows me her palms.

"Look, I've got stigmata."

We giggle as people around us turn and stare. I'm glad she didn't pull out a book.

41

Today is yet another monumental day in the life of the band, and I'm preparing in the manner I feel is appropriate: I'm drinking syrupy strawberry daiquiris, made from a mix that has been in the back of my fridge since early summer. I can't taste rum, so I tip the rest of the bottle into the blender and swish it around with my finger. I've got an hour before Tyler picks me up. He has arranged a meeting with some advertising people in Toronto and we're going en masse in his mom's minivan.

"New cologne?" Tyler asks when I open the door. "Eau de rum, I presume."

Noel and Jan are sitting in the minivan. When we get in, Tyler starts the engine and Michael Bolton erupts from the stereo. Noel and Jan crack up in spasmodic laughter.

"That tape belongs to my mother," Tyler says defensively, jerking the cassette out of the stereo like it's radioactive. He roots around in a case on the floor.

"I always knew you were a closet fan," Jan says.

"OK, where did you put my tape?"

"I refuse to listen to techno music all the way to Toronto," Jan says. "This isn't Electric Circus. I can't cope with repetitive beats at the moment. I'm pre-migraine."

"Those tracks were specially chosen to infuse us with the proper energy," Tyler says. "Studies have shown that electronic music stimulates normally dormant parts of the brain."

"Hasn't worked for you," Jan says.

"Ooo, such serrated wit," Tyler replies.

Tyler can't find his cassette, so he digs out a mix tape he deems acceptable and puts the van into gear. We lunge forward on another pilgrimage. I'm in the back, trying to locate the source of a vile, yeasty smell that I suspect is old beer. There's a number of competing smells: fresh pine air freshener; lingering perfume; baked goods, likely cookies, perhaps oatmeal; and decomposing beer molecules. If I lean to my left, I also get Noel's cologne into the mix.

"Did you know Michael Bolton used to be a heavy-metal guy?" I say. "I'm pretty sure he wrote a song that was recorded by Kiss or AC/DC."

"No way," Jan says, looking dubious.

"I heard that too," Noel says. "I think it was AC/DC. And now look at him. But I guess you have to do what works for you."

"He's a whore," Jan replies.

I would tend to agree, except that we're on our way to the big city to beg and bargain to record senseless jingles for pizza parlours and disposable razors. The irony seems to be lost on everyone else.

We make good time and slowly wind our way through Toronto congestion to the downtown core. Tyler directs the van down a dark ramp, and we come to a stop in a concrete parking lot bunker.

"This is where we'll be living after the holocaust," I say. "Cockroaches, rats and humans wearing designer labels waiting out the nuclear winter."

"Good to see you're keeping the mood light, Thompson," Tyler says. "I've put a lot of hard work into getting this meeting set up. The least you can do is behave like a normal, ambitious young ad executive."

"Your uncle set up the meeting."

"Trust me, I had to badger. He wasn't keen to help."

I decide to be good, not for Tyler but for Jan and Noel, who are still eager to explore the machinations of corporate brainwashing. Realistically, I don't even know why we're here. We haven't got anything to pitch, because we haven't composed any decent jingles.

We take an elevator up to ground level and wander

around a huge glass and stainless steel foyer, like microbes in a petri dish, while Tyler speaks with a couple of security guys behind a large granite desk. Behind them is a wall of monitors, keeping a watchful eye on men in sport coats and women in business suits scurrying around the labyrinth of corridors and cubicles. The security guys listen to Tyler with blank expressions. They must get so bored sitting there, watching people go through the same routines day in and day out, popping outside the revolving doors for a fifteen-minute smoke break, rushing back to the gulag with their Styrofoam cups of corporately produced coffee, holding their sore backs from ergonomically improper workstations.

"They're on the forty-fourth floor," Tyler says exuberantly. "The better the company, the higher their offices. We're really on to something this time. I can't believe we wasted our time with those Christians."

"I thought it was a good idea," Noel mumbles.

The reception area of Len Burton Advertising Co. Inc. is lush and luxurious, filled with ultra-green exotic-looking potted plants that surround deep leather sofas and creep up matte grey walls. The room is accentuated by rows of elaborately framed paintings spaced equidistance apart precisely at eye level, and by marble in an abundance that would make Italy envious. I feel like I've arrived in a strange new world, one designed by faceless denizen gods to make me feel small, ant-like and aware of the astounding power of money. We pad along the thick, moss-like carpet, and every footfall seems to whisper *want this, want this, want this . . .*

Behind a wide desk are two women wearing thin wire headsets. They manage the flow of traffic like air traffic controllers, seamlessly moving from phone call to computer screen to couriers delivering manila envelopes from important offices in the city. They act with co-ordinated efficiency, chatting easily and happily.

"We're the band Pure Energy," Tyler says. "We've got a one-o'clock appointment with Rick Weller."

Our latest name doesn't surprise me. Being friends with Tyler necessitates building an immunity to these sorts of asinine but tolerable revelations. The receptionist punches us into her keyboard.

"Of course. Please take a seat. Can I get any of you a coffee, tea, pop?"

"I'd love a coffee," Tyler says.

"Are those unionized beans?" I murmur. If he hears, he doesn't let on. We settle into the leather couch and flip through magazines. The people who come and go through the lobby seem friendly and generally pleasant. I had always thought any office job would involve nothing but misery. I imagine coming here to work every morning with a muffin and briefcase in hand, wearing a suit and richly shined shoes, saying hello to these two friendly receptionists and settling down into a cozy cubicle. Perhaps it wouldn't be the worst thing in the world.

Noel is looking at one of the large canvases beside the desk.

"That was painted by Winston Churchill," the second receptionist says.

"You're joking." Noel stands back. The painting is of Venetian canals, done in the Impressionist style. A large gold coin in the corner of the frame, featuring the late prime minister's bulbous head, testifies to its authenticity. I'd say Winston was a better orator than artist.

"You all right?" Jan asks. She rubs my leg affectionately. Tyler stirs from his thoughts. His brow crumples.

"You people don't tell me anything, do you?" he says. "How long has this been going on? I hope this won't affect your work."

"What work?" I ask.

"We'll try not to paw one another too much during rehearsal," Jan says.

Tyler frowns as he considers the concept of Jan and me.

"You should have told me," he says finally. "But I suppose you didn't tell me because of Nicole. I appreciate that."

"Right," I say. I didn't tell him because I didn't need the scrutiny.

After twenty minutes, we get ushered into a large meeting room. The entire outer wall is glass, from floor to ceiling, providing a stunning panorama of the city. We can see straight down Yonge Street to Lake Ontario. To the east are smokestacks and shipyards.

A man maybe in his mid-thirties strides through the door. His suit is crisp and new, his hair recently styled with professional precision. He smiles comfortably, in a way that makes me feel at ease, maybe even important to his day. This would be Rick Weller. The energy of the room has become instantly charged with his charisma.

"Yum yum," Jan murmurs. I know she's being funny, but seeing her so taken by a person I can't begin to emulate is disconcerting, humbling even, like when I flipped through her women's magazines and read an article entitled "Ten Ways He Drives You Wild" and realized I hadn't even considered seven of them.

"So, who's Tyler?" Rick asks. Tyler waves. They shake hands vigorously. "I can't say enough about the job your uncle does at CRTT. He's one of the best in the business."

He motions for us to sit down and reclines comfortably in

the plush leather chair at the head of the table. He puts his hands together in a this-is-the-church/this-is-the-steeple manner and looks at us earnestly.

"Welcome to Len Burton Advertising."

He gives us the gist about the company, how successful they are, the fact that they hold accounts for some of my favourite chocolate bar brands, the challenges of the industry and a lot of really dull information. Finally he sits back and opens the floor.

"I assume you received our package," Tyler says. "The tape of our music?"

This rouses Noel and Jan. Obviously no one was consulted about strategy or knew about a tape being sent ahead.

"I certainly did," Rick says. "I thought the songs were great, absolutely hilarious. And that send-up of David Bowie was priceless. I can't say enough about how important a good sense of humour is if you're looking to get into this business."

Tyler leans back and mimics Rick's hand gesturing in sheer mockery.

"Right," he says. "Well, Rick, why don't we leave all matters of artistic interpretation aside for now. We're here because we want to write radio jingles for CRTT. My uncle says your company produces quite a few."

Rick takes great care to look truly pained. He bites his lip ever so gently and searches for just the right words. If I didn't know better, I'd think he and Tyler were related, cousins schooled in the fine art of feigning sincerity.

"Well, we don't actually write songs, Tyler. We produce campaigns—all the way up. We pitch ideas, concepts, create storyboards, shoot commercials. We commission the music from studios, most of which have their own stable of full-time, very well-established musicians and songwriters."

"So you don't accept groundbreaking freelance work?" Tyler asks.

Rick shows even more angst. "I'm afraid not. But I liked your work. And I'm always happy to speak to the next generation of advertising people. I think you guys are great. The industry needs young people such as yourselves. And let me tell you, the payoff can be huge."

He rambles jovially while playing with his cuff links and adjusting his silk tie. Apparently he thinks we're marketing students. Unfortunately, his enthusiasm doesn't radiate back to him. I'm not annoyed so much as I am bored.

"As for music, I can get you a list of studios if you want. But agencies do tend to stay with a few proven composers."

Rick shakes his gold watch, apologizes for having to leave for a conference call, and departs. Tyler is immersed in thought, and I hope he is accepting this current stunning failure as a life lesson. After a few minutes, he taps his finger on the table.

"What about cruise ships?" he says. "They always have bands onboard. The clientele would be upscale."

"Quite possibly nouveau riche," Jan adds.

Tyler turns to Noel. "Do you think you could take a sabbatical?"

42

Thankfully, Noel's company won't give him a sabbatical unless he's studying for an M.B.A. Still, I wouldn't be surprised if the idea popped up again in a year or so, when his stock options vest. Once again, the band is back to square one, searching for a gig and some exposure. On the personal side, to my surprise, my mother shows up at my door a few days later with a box of cookies.

"Did you bake these yourself?" I ask.

We laugh in unison as she shoves the box into my chest. I usher her into the living room, glad that Sheldon isn't home. My mother has the advantage on me, because she has caught me completely by surprise and I've had no time to dwell on her recent behaviour and get a good bitter stew brewing. But this doesn't stop me from being instinctively suspicious.

"So why are you here?"

"Oh, Jason, can't a mother check up on how her boys are doing? I've been meaning to come to the city since you and Sheldon and Becky fled from that party at Art's house."

"We were at the hospital."

"You know what I mean. How is Sheldon's arm?"

"He's fine."

"Good. Aren't you going to offer me cookies and coffee? A good host always serves coffee."

Apparently she's started reading *Good Housekeeping*. I leave her to peruse *Guitar Magazine*, trot to the kitchen and put on some java. I run through potential arguments and grievances so they'll be handy if I need them. I'm not happy about the way she's handling my dad, Sheldon and the house, but I figure she's made an effort to come over, so maybe she just wants to talk. I give her the benefit of the doubt.

"You and Russell should get together to play a few songs," she says.

"I don't think so."

"Well, why not, Jason? You two would get along famously if you gave him a chance. You should visit more. You never make an effort to see us."

Russell is a sweaty little troll who likes to tell me ad nauseam about his time in Las Vegas working at Circus Circus. My mother likes to promote the idea of us as peers, both working toward our musical dreams. But his dream is so lame. He went to Vegas to break into the lounge-lizard business but ended up cashing chips like a chump.

"When your band gets famous, maybe Russell can be your opening act on the road?"

"Yeah, well," I say, flagging the comment for later recounting to Jan, Noel and Tyler, "I don't think we have to worry about touring. The band is essentially kaput."

"Oh, don't give up. Look at Russell, he's forty-eight and still looking for his big break. Even now, he makes a living. You're every bit as talented as him."

I think I have every right to laugh uproariously and point out that her boyfriend is a caricature from Billy Joel's "Piano Man." But she cares about him and he makes her happy, so I keep my mouth shut.

"Mom, did Dad ever want to do something other than work at the university?"

"I should certainly hope so," she says. "Not many people grow up wanting to be a janitor."

My father hates the word *janitor*. He's almost come to blows over the word. He is a custodial engineer.

"Seriously, did he have a dream?"

"Most of your father's dreams involved a six-pack."

"What about being a truck driver?"

"Well, yes, you must remember when he wanted to be a

driver . . . You know, he took that course for a while, but then his back problem flared up . . ."

She waits expectantly for me to pick up the thread, but the story is news to me.

"I can't believe you don't remember, Jason. He went to a number of doctors and they told him his back was too messed up to drive full time. He hurt it in high school playing hockey. It was his lumbar something or other. He could have had an operation, but you know how your father is with pain."

She thinks for a few seconds, half smiling.

"I remember for a while he decided he was going to fix his back himself." She breaks into giggles. "He started doing three hundred sit-ups every night before bed to strengthen his muscles. I was impressed by his drive, but he'd come to bed all sweaty and it drove me crazy. Your father's armpits can be quite offensive . . ."

She laughs. Spotty memories of being on my father's lap behind a huge steering wheel swirl in my mind, but I'm not sure if they happened to me or on an old episode of *Happy Days*.

"So what happened?" I ask.

"Oh, nothing. His back still hurt, so he gave up. He didn't want to risk losing his benefits from the university. What about me? Don't you think I had dreams?"

"Did you?"

"No, but you could have asked. All I wanted was a comfortable life in the suburbs and a man who liked to play cards."

"So why did you marry Dad?"

"Oh, because I loved him."

"What about Sheldon?" I ask.

"I love him too," she says. "I love all of you. I've talked to Russell about the situation, but Jason, honestly, there's really no space, and our money ... We don't do very well for people our age. We don't even have investments or a house."

She says this almost as a plea. I refuse to pity my mother, because she's made her choices. But I've been drained enough by the situation lately that I don't feel like starting another argument.

"I'll take care of Sheldon," I say.

"Thank goodness. You know, he'll have much more fun here with you. He doesn't want to live in a small apartment with two old people."

"Yeah, well, as far as fun goes, neither of us is exactly sucking the marrow out of life at the moment. We need some money too. You know, support."

"Your father," she says bluntly. "He's the one we need to talk to. I can't help."

Unable to offer any more advice or financial assistance, she shifts into a discussion about Russell and her faceless friends at the bar. I drink my coffee and grunt every now and again. This is often how our visits go, with her making conversation about people I don't know. I drift sporadically into daydreams. The cookies are pretty good.

"Well, I should get back," she says, looking at her watch. "What a nice visit we've had, Jason. You and your girlfriend should come to the hotel one night and we'll all play euchre."

"Yeah, maybe," I say.

She's halfway to the door when she stops and fishes into her purse. She puts an envelope on the telephone table.

"I know you don't approve, but try and see the situation from my perspective."

She leaves and I can feel the numbness seeping through my body, down into my joints. From the window, I watch my mother get into her car, a rusty 1982 Honda Civic. She waves, and I wave back.

As expected, my mother has provided me with a copy of her lawsuit against my father.

43

"Just come outside."

Sheldon is looking at me from the couch. He's watching *Hollywood Squares*, which is reason enough to disturb him. I've been prodding him for the last two commercial breaks.

"Why?"

"I can't tell you. You have to come and see for yourself."

Finally, after I bribe him with the promise of a pepperoni and onion pizza with extra cheese, he trudges after me. You'd think the kid would want some family interaction, but all he wants to do after school is sleep, eat and either watch TV or play my PlayStation.

We walk down to the parking lot and stop on the gravel next to the sidewalk. I open my knapsack and pull out an assortment of objects: the envelope my mother left; a troll doll; a Yankees cap; and a plain white envelope with a letter inside. I put them in a small pile and douse them thoroughly with Brut aftershave.

"Hey, that's mine," Sheldon says.

"Trust me, you'll thank me in a few years. And get rid of that Old Spice too. OK, last night I broke down and bought a self-help book that was pretty poorly written but had one redeeming idea in its appendix section. They suggest a cleansing bonfire to get rid of all the suppressed feelings of anger and resentment a person might have toward their parents."

"Man, you're whacked."

"Maybe, but just listen. I think you should do this too. The book said to collect stuff from the person or people you want to start anew with. Mom gave me that stupid purple troll doll one year for my birthday. I think she probably won it at bingo or something. Dad gave me the hat in a misguided attempt to get me interested in sports. The book also said you should write a letter that expresses every reason you can think of why you're angry."

"Are you going to light that puppy up?" Sheldon asks.

"Yes. But there's a spiritual logic behind the process."

"Who cares? Go pyro. This is cool."

The prospect of being encouraged to publicly burn things is probably enough to entice Shel to collect his own emotional kindling and cleanse his angry, confused adolescent soul. The means might not suit the end, but maybe this will help him get motivated about his own life, so that he doesn't have to go through my process of self-evaluation years too late. I had considered contacting my father, meeting him on neutral ground and maturely discussing the situation about Sheldon and the house. But for now, I'm accepting that real life doesn't follow the agreeable pattern of book, movie and TV plots. There isn't always resolution. But there is usually hope.

Sheldon takes the aftershave from my hand. The smell is overpowering and sickly sweet.

"You need more on that troll hair."

He slicks the pink material until it's completely matted. I

light a match and drop it on the pile. A sharp whoosh of air is followed by a blue-green flame, which rises and falls. The troll is enveloped in fire, its skin contorting from purple plastic into charred black goo. The fire licks onto the legal envelope. The Yankees cap is resilient, so Sheldon douses it with the rest of the cologne. Flames lick up the stream toward his hand.

"Whoa. This is definitely cooler than *Hollywood Squares*."

After my bonfire begins to die, Sheldon and I retreat back to the apartment. He doesn't have much stuff from home with him, but he manages to scrape together the required ingredients: shoelaces from the runners my father bought him and a Nike key chain from my mother. He quickly dashes off a letter of protest and we head back outside and coat his items, as well as a fair amount of newspaper he's brought down, with his entire bottle of Old Spice.

Thank God for small mercies.

"Shel, you do know that cologne's not an alternative to showering, right? Because if you just use cologne people can still smell what's underneath."

He squints at me bitterly and turns back to his pile of memories. I bite my lip. I'm trying to talk to him like an adult, not condescend like he's a little kid or an idiot. And I know we'd both like to avoid these types of conversation altogether, but being a teenager requires a bit of help, I seem to recall.

"We should get some gasoline."

"Just light the pile, Shel."

44

Life proceeds at its mundane pace. As usual, I've made no significant changes. But I'm thinking about it. Jan has been pestering me to send my songs to producers and music companies, and I've slowly been compiling a tape of recordings, just me and my acoustic guitar. She's getting her overdue work done and we're edging into a routine better suited to her schedule. We seem to be a happy, contented couple, which in a way is bizarre, because I've gone from years of solitude to instant partnership. The transition has been easy and natural and so amazingly cool. This morning before leaving for school she made me French toast and coffee and brought it to bed. How great is that? Small gestures really do make trudging to the bar every day a lot easier.

"I got followed home by the cops last night," John says.

He stubs the end of his cigarette into the ashtray. We're sitting at a table, drinking coffee and enjoying the lull before the noon rush. Trina from the kitchen is sitting with us. She pulls a cigarette from her pack and lights it up, apparently to keep the thick smoke haze hanging over our table.

"Oh yeah?"

"He must have seen me pull out of the parking lot when Stu and I left. He followed us for at least a mile, watching us, waiting for me to make a mistake. Finally, when I'm sweating and think he's got to back off soon, he flashes the lights and pulls us over."

"He nail you?" Trina asks.

"Almost," John says. "He made us empty our pockets and went through the glove compartment and everything. He actually opened an old cigarette pack where I had a joint hidden, but he didn't see it and tossed it back on the floor. I thought Stu was going to lose it, but he was OK."

"So the cop just let you go?"

"What could he do?"

Trina sucks the cigarette so the end glows deep orange, then tilts her head back and exhales toward the ceiling. The only two customers in the bar are sitting in front of our new big-screen TV watching sports highlights. Chad has decided to start a betting pool for horse races and felt we needed the largest screen possible to be legitimate.

"Intense."

"It's no big deal. The cop was OK about it. He knew he was beat, so he let us go. It doesn't even faze me anymore."

Despite his musical deficiencies, I've begun to like John. At least he's not dull. The door opens, spreading a flash of light through the room, and Chad walks in. He looks annoyed and heads directly for the office. Trina looks at her watch.

"I guess we better get ready for the rush."

John gulps down the rest of his coffee and we all get up and go our separate ways. Lunch is the same as always. The same faces walk through the door, making the same jokes and eating the same fried food. As the rush subsides Chad slips behind the bar. He pours himself a soda and looks edgy.

"So, your band," he says.

"Yes?"

I can tell whatever he has to say is killing him.

"My uncle feels that we should have a music night. He sees it as good business for some reason, despite the fact that I'm making us a killing with casino nights. But he's getting old and a bit fucking senile, I guess. There's no way

I'm letting John back on stage, so I was thinking you can have Sunday nights again if you want."

"You're kidding."

"I wish. But who cares, eh? I'm moving casino night to Friday. Knock yourselves out."

He pauses by the door.

"Oh, wait, what's your band's name again? I have to make some posters."

"Archangel. No matter what you hear from Noel or Tyler, our name is Archangel."

He looks perplexed, but isn't interested enough to inquire further.

"Just don't play any of that experimental shit. If you're going to play, I want to hear Top 40 songs. You know, rock-and-roll. If I hear one glass break I'm putting Stoned Quarry up there for good."

I smile. "You've got my word. We'll rock. And we'll play lots of Jay Thompson originals. I've got some great new stuff."